Dick Donovan: The Glasgow Detective

The Editor

BRUCE DURIE has been a paper-bag salesman, bus conductor, research scientist, journalist, broadcaster, Director of the Edinburgh Science Festival, museum director, senior academic and manager at various universities and best-selling author.

His books (fiction and non-fiction), plays and screenplays include a number of best-sellers on Internet and e-business subjects, popular local history and Victorian detective novels, including *The Murder of Young Tom Morris* (2003).

He lives in Glasgow with his son.

The Glasgow Detective

DICK DONOVAN

J. E. PRESTON MUDDOCK

EDITED AND INTRODUCED BY BRUCE DURIE

Mercat Press
EDINBURGH

First published in 2005 by Mercat Press Ltd
10 Coates Crescent, Edinburgh EH3 7AL
www.mercatpress.com

ISBN 184183 0887

Set in ITC Fenice and Bodoni at Mercat Press
Printed and bound in Great Britain by Bell & Bain Ltd

Contents

FROM A PAINTING BY EDWIN A. WARD.

Foreword:
The Man Who Was Dick Donovan

◈

Ask almost anyone with an interest in Victorian crime, or detective fiction in general, whether they have heard of Dick Donovan—the answer will almost certainly be: *Yes, but I've never managed to read any of his works.*

And right there we have the paradox of Dick Donovan—famous, but unread; as popular in his time as Sherlock Holmes, and predating his popularity, but now virtually unknown; prolific, but these days uncollected. Well, this volume and its follow-ons seek to redress this lamentable state of affairs. So who was this great Glasgow Detective, one of the truly influential literary characters in the closing years of Victoria's century?

DONOVAN AND MUDDOCK

'Dick Donovan' was the pseudonym used by Joyce Emmerson Preston Muddock (1842–1934) for almost 250 detective stories and nearly 50 books written between 1889 and 1914. Muddock not only created Dick Donovan and other characters, but largely invented himself as well, and he was as colourful as any of his creations.

Born James Edward Preston Muddock near Southampton, he came from a relatively well-off background, but his father lost his job and savings and had to stay abroad to recoup. Muddock gives the impression he was a sea-captain, but he was more of a shipping clerk and latterly ran a boarding-house and billiard-hall in Calcutta. The family moved to Manchester, but young James later joined his father in India while not yet 14. He saw the Indian Mutiny at first-hand, joined the East India Company's gun foundry at Cossipore (where he was involved in the manufacture and delivery of the notorious Dum Dum bullets) and had a variety of adventures. When his father died, Muddock was briefly in England. An early marriage in 1861 to an American 'Theatrical' called Emily Jane Varley at Manchester Cathedral involved them both lying about their ages. They were 17, and Emily appears to have died soon after. Possibly as a result of this, Muddock took off for Australia, where he had a spell in journalism with an *unsympatico* relative and then tried gold mining. The theft of his profits (£150) and an illness led to his taking a position on a ship for China, and he spent some months in Shanghai. For some reason he decided to join the rebels at Amoy, who were defeated by 'Chinese' Gordon, who broke the Taiping Rebellion in May, 1864, and died in the defence of Khartoum against the Mahdi, 26 January, 1885, as later portrayed by Mr. C. Heston in the well-known moving picture.

Further adventures around New Guinea and the Solomons, including dinner with cannibals, but on the fortunate side of the table, culminated in a return to 'that awful hole', Shanghai, trips to Hong Kong and Singapore and then passage back to England. He was engaged by his eldest sister's husband, a Lancashire cotton baron, to visit America and find blockade-runners to help get cotton out at the height of the Civil War. He neglected to see Lincoln's corpse lying in state, he says, because of the queues.

After another trip to America in 1867 and a short sojourn back in Manchester, Muddock went to stay with relatives in London, some of whom had newspaper connections. By 1868 the ever-restless Muddock was again in Melbourne, where he almost talked a cousin into walking across Australia with him, a brave feat considering Dysart's very own John McDouall Stuart had accomplished it only five years previously. Instead, Muddock returned to London. He never saw Australia again, but his last published book (as Dick Donovan) was *Out There: A Romance of Australia* (1922).

Claiming to have been inspired by hearing Dickens read at the Manchester Free Trade Hall in 1861, and by winning schoolboy prizes for writing, Muddock turned to the pen. He bought a weekly newspaper, and also started a monthly magazine called *The Coronet*, which folded thanks to a copyright action brought by Sir Isaac Pitman, inventor of shorthand. Muddock was running a highly popular series of articles on Pitman's system, and Sir Isaac felt he had the rights to the character diagrams. So Pitman sued, and the court agreed.

Around this time Muddock came up with the idea—he says he discussed it with Wilkie Collins—of providing the many small and circulation-hungry local newspapers around Britain with stirring tales of derring-do, on a syndication basis. Taking advantage of the excitement engendered by the supposed capture of Nana Sahib, instigator of the Cawnpore Massacre, Muddock dashed off *The Great White Hand* and offered it around. This not only made him, he claims, £1,500 (equivalent to almost 100 times that in 2005) it also led to invitations to write more fiction. Muddock contracted with Tillotson's Newspaper Fiction Bureau of Bolton and, when that agreement expired, he had enough willing clients to take his works direct.

From 1870 to 1874 Muddock continued editing his paper and writing short fiction, but also published his first novels, including the successful *Wingless Angel* (1875). At this point, he was married to a Mary Lucy Hann, and had a daughter christened Evangeline Hope Muddock. Eva Muddocci, as she styled herself, was later a celebrated concert violinist throughout Europe, and was famously a subject for her lover, the depressive Norwegian Edvard Munch, and for Matisse. One of Munch's drawings of Eva is the basis of a well-known Andy Warhol print.

After his own periodical stopped, Muddock sub-edited *The Mirror* (a high-class but short-lived weekly) and contributed to *The Young Folk's Budget* and the incredibly successful boys' paper, *The Weekly Budget*—then selling 500,000 copies a week and including *Funny Folks* (1874–1894), originally a pull-out supplement, but the first publication which could properly be called a 'comic'.

When *The Mirror* was cancelled, Muddock took a post with of a new, ultra-Protestant Conservative-leaning paper *The Hour*, where his earlier experiences made him a natural as their 'special Asia/ Pacific correspondent' and co-edited *The London Scottish Journal*. When *The Hour* crashed in 1876 amid high regard (Disraeli said he 'heard with a pang that *The Hour* was no more') but low readership figures and a financial scandal, Muddock took to the freelance life, visiting France, Portugal and elsewhere. On his return he edited another boys' paper, but was enticed to Scotland to help revitalise the moribund *Greenock Advertiser*. Living in Rothesay on the Isle of Bute, Muddock continued to produce serialisations, short fiction and other works, as well as his regular *Rothesay Recluse* columns for the *Advertiser*. The experience of living on and by the Clyde shines through in *A River Mystery* and also in his later horror and gothic stories.

In 1879, however, Muddock inherited a small but welcome inheritance from his father's brother, Henry Gregson Muddock, who had been so infuriated by his nephew's conduct when staying with him in Southampton prior to his leaving for India 22 years previously, that he had disinherited him. Fortunately, when Uncle Henry went down with 900 other souls on the pleasure steamer *Princess Alice* after a collision on the Thames, the old man was fortuitously intestate, and Muddock inherited after all. This allowed Our Hero the time and finances to tour the Continent again, taking in Alsace, Germany and Russia.

After a brief return home in 1879 to collect his legacy, Muddock headed off again, this time to Davos-Platz, Switzerland. This marked a turning point in Muddock's career as a writer. He decided to take on the growing resort as a project, and published at his own expense a phenomenally successful guide book to the area, as well as a more general guide to Switzerland. He also persuaded Phillip Holland, a noted analytical chemist, to visit and test the air, water and local milk—with all of which Muddock found fault as well as criticising the drainage, food, transport and practically every other aspect of the place. By Muddock's account, this was instrumental in convincing the villagers to develop the place properly as a health spa, although he was nearly lynched.

The still restless Muddock then headed for Villefranche in the south of France in order to write up his Swiss notes, pausing only to get married in Paris in 1880 to a lady from Brough, Westmoreland, called Eleanor Rudd, presumably after divorcing Lucy Hann and abandoning Evangeline. He lived there for over two years and might have stayed, except for the fact that, he tells us, his neighbour, the Russian Prince d'Oldenburg, had requested that Muddock vacate his villa in order to accommodate two guests who had been badly injured in a carriage accident. Apparently, they were unable to stay *chez Le Prince* because the excitement of a Russian Christmas would have delayed their convalescence!

Muddock then headed for Geneva, 'in the interests of my guide-books' and served as Swiss correspondent for *The Daily News* for six years until 1887. Mrs Muddock was equally busy, producing four daughters and twin sons, one of whom died before his first birthday. His time abroad was curtailed by poor health (he blamed the bad drainage around his house in Geneva) and he took a house in Deal, Kent. However, the new owners of the *Dundee Weekly News* and the *Courier*, W & D C Thomson, enticed Muddock to the city of jute, jam and journalism. Muddock signed on for three years and arrived in 1887, where his wife, Eleanor, promptly had a further set of twin boys. It was while in the Thomsons' employ that Muddock started writing the Dick Donovan stories, and from that point on Muddock was better known by this name than by his own.

After his three-year stint plus one more, Muddock says he wearied of Dundee and headed for Canada. What a wife and seven young children, including two sets of twins, thought of it is not told: only 10-year-old Ruth went with him. A bankruptcy may have concentrated their minds. An eighth surviving child, Eleanor, was born at Shortlands, near Bromley, Kent in 1893, and a further girl was born and died.

Back in London, Muddock met Galloway Fraser, a journalist he had known in Scotland and now an editor of the successful weekly news digest *Tit Bits*, started in 1881 by George Newnes, a former vegetarian restaurant owner. Fraser introduced Muddock to Newnes, who asked for a topical piece and was offered a story on the persecution of the Jews in Russia. Asked for a title, Muddock proposed *For God and the Czar*, and was persuaded to churn it out in two weeks flat. Muddock claims it 'sent the publication of the paper up like a rocket', and certainly when it was published in book form under the same title in 1895 it was a worldwide best-seller, particularly amongst Jewish readers, but unsurprisingly was banned in Russia. Muddock also wrote *The Life of Vidocq* for Newnes (published in book form by Hutchinson as *Eugene Vidocq: Soldier, Thief, Spy, Detective* in 1895, but authored by 'Dick Donovan'), and started his run of Dick Donovan stories in the other magazine from the same stable, *Strand*.

Overall, Muddock had a successful career as a journalist and wrote thrillers, historical novels, his wildly popular guide books to Davos-Platz and a rather self-aggrandising autobiography *Pages from an Adventurous Life*, which dealt mainly with his Bohemian cronies of the Savage Club and did not mention his wives and eleven or more children even once. His total output included over 180 detective stories, involving or written as if by Dick Donovan, collected as fourteen books, but he also used the same pen name for other, unrelated works. Presumably he realised that the name 'Dick Donovan' had greater recognition and commercial cachet than his own. Examples are *The Chronicles of Michael Danevitch of the Russian Secret Service* (1897), *Tales of Terror* (1899), *The Adventures of Tyler Tatlock, Private Detective* (1900) and 'true crime' collections including *Startling Crimes and Notorious Criminals* (1908). He regarded these as well-paid hack work separate from and inferior to his 'real' writing, mostly historical romances.

But in the late 1880s crime and detection were in the air. Everyone was cashing in on the earlier publishing success of the real-life James M'Levy, the Edinburgh Detective, and the many sleuth stories appearing from France. In the 1870s, soon after M'Levy's hit, a series of books appeared by one James McGovan, ostensibly the autobiographical casebook of an Edinburgh policeman. The author was

Edinburgh violinist and editor William Crawford Honeyman, whose wryly humorous detective tales were almost certainly as great an influence on the young Conan Doyle as M'Levy's 'true' stories.

So Muddock did not start the tradition of using a pen name the same as that of the detective, but may well have embedded it as a technique for the genre. It was later adopted by his American counterparts such as Ellery Queen and Hank Jansen. What prompted him about this time to change his own first names from James Edward to Joyce Emmerson is not clear, but is wholly in keeping with his romantic literary tendencies.

Muddock was also keen to show off his learning with quotes from Shakespeare and the classics, but often got them wrong. The poem on page 146 is not from Horace at all, but Stephen Harvey (*ca* 1627) translating from Juvenal's *Satire IX*.

DONOVAN AND *THE STRAND MAGAZINE*

Dick Donovan and Sherlock Holmes are exact contemporaries. But Donovan is not merely another one of the horde of penny dreadful Holmes take-offs which sprang up in the 1890s. Far from being an imitator of Conan Doyle and Holmes, the popularity of Muddock's Glasgow detective predated and exceeded that of the Baker Street sleuth. Contrary to popular mythology, the first Sherlock Holmes short story in *Strand* was not Conan Doyle's first piece for the magazine—that distinction belongs to an anonymous and strangely anti-feminist piece entitled *The Voice of Science*—nor was Holmes in the first issue of *Strand* in January 1891. Moreover, the first *Strand* Sherlock Holmes story, *A Scandal in Bohemia*, was printed in July 1891, but Conan Doyle had already published two earlier, longer adventures—*A Study in Scarlet* in *Beeton's 1887 Christmas Annual*, and *The Sign of the Four* in *Lippincott's Monthly Magazine* of February 1890. By this time *Strand* had already published some detective fiction, starting with Grant Allen's short story *Jerry Stokes* in the third issue. But the earliest Dick Donovan stories were published early in 1888 during Muddock's stint with

Thomson in Dundee, before being collected in *The Man-Hunter* in 1888 and subsequent compilations. The *Dundee Weekly News* of 25 Feb 1888 boasted a certified circulation of 121,000, which means that upwards of 250,000 people may have been reading the weekly *Stories of Criminals and Crime by An Ex-Detective*, as Muddock's yarns were bylined. In contrast, hardly anyone had noticed *A Study in Scarlet* a couple of months before in Beeton's, and it would be another two years before Holmes and Watson had another outing. In the meantime, two Dick Donovan collections had already reached a mass market in Britain and America.

In a real sense, then, Dick Donovan predates Sherlock Holmes. Furthermore, his reader-drawing power was well recognised. The owner of *Strand*, George Newnes, and its editor Herbert Greenhough-Smith recognised the value of a good detective yarn in circulation terms. (Greenhough-Smith became part of the family in 1900 when he married Muddock's second daughter, Dorothy, a noted figure-skater and tennis player, although fully 26 years her senior and consistently unfaithful.) The idea of a series of related, short detective stories—a form Conan Doyle is also often erroneously credited with originating—had been common in detective fiction since the 1860s but truly caught the public imagination in the 1880s. The publication of *The Man-Hunter* in book form in 1888 was undeniably popular, and it also appeared the following year in America, though what the readers there made of the Glasgow and London settings is a mystery in itself. Clearly, the craze for short detective fiction was well established by the time Holmes first appeared, and Bleiler's observation* that Donovan 'was as well-known on the lower reading levels as Sherlock Holmes later became on the higher levels' is not far short of the mark.

Holmes undoubtedly made Conan Doyle one of the best-read authors of the age in any genre, and the readership of *Strand* escalated whenever he appeared. But there could not be a Holmes story every issue, so in the months when Doyle was busy writing a new batch of stories Newnes and Smith turned to—who else?—Dick Donovan to fill the gap.

* E F Bleiler in John M Reilly (ed): *Twentieth Century Crime and Mystery Writers* (Macmillan, 1980)

Strand used Muddock's detective stories after the first series of Holmes stories had appeared in 1891–92. Dick Donovan appeared in the July, August, September and November 1892 issues of the magazine. (The October detective story was Grant Allen's *The Great Ruby Robbery*). Three of these are rather different from the regular Donovan casebook-type tales of a working policeman and mainly involve exotic Eastern artefacts, mysterious secret societies, opium-taking, valuable jewels and the like. The fourth *Strand* story, *The Chamber of Shadows*, concerns a more mundane business fraud, albeit with sensational elements such as love unrequited, gambling debts, obsession and a macabre exhumation.

In the earlier and more day-to-day 'notebook of a detective' type of stories, such as those collected in this volume, Donovan is usually the protagonist, but sometimes acts, Hitchcock-like, as the narrator, to tell us of crime and criminals. The variety of unlawful acts and their perpetrators is wide and varied, and the stories range in tone from realistic policeman-on-the-beat procedurals and case-book accounts to out-and-out melodramas involving black magic, mysterious Eastern villains of a Fu Manchu cast, menacing secret societies (again!), sinister master criminals and suchlike.

In the beginning, Donovan's work is street-level and prosaic, just a Glasgow detective. His quarry was much the same as those of other crime story policemen: petty thieves, murderers on the run, child exploiters, sharpers and resetters (fences), con-artists, for-eign counterfeiters, mail-train robbers, forgers, pitiless murderesses, Fagin-like characters and their criminal gangs, long-lost heirs to fortunes, swindlers and so forth. But even in the first stories and collections there is an occasional hint at the more far-fetched as-pects of the later Donovan yarns—ghostly goings-on; a thief called 'The Knave of Spades'; the notorious real-life villain Charles Peace etc.

Muddock openly declared that he regarded his Glasgow detec-tive as a flash in the pan, maintained by economic realities: 'When I began these stories I had no intention of continuing them beyond a certain number which I had determined beforehand; but their success was beyond anything that had been anticipated… I could not turn back; I was lured on by the cheque book. I freely confess my weakness, and hope I may be forgiven.'

On the other hand, he tells of meeting people on trains who claimed to have a friend of a friend or 'a man at my club' who knew Dick Donovan well, policemen who pretended his acquaintance and those who firmly believed he, Donovan, had been or still was an agent of the Tsar (confusing Donovan with the Michael Danevitch book, written by 'Dick Donovan', as amanuensis to the great Russian master-spy and detective). All great fun.

WHO WAS DICK DONOVAN?

Strangely, we know little of Donovan the man from the stories and books. Muddock took the name from that of an eighteenth century Bow Street Runner. Frankly, Donovan appears a touch nondescript, but this could be put down to Muddock's interest, and the point of the tales, being in the plot and the cleverness of the detection rather than in the lead character. Dick Donovan was an apparatus to tell a parable in the first person, rather than the reason for it, as was more the case with Holmes, Raffles or Batman. On the other hand, we do know that Donovan started working as a policeman in London, beginning in the East End Division, but spent the most important part of his career in Glasgow; that he was fluent in at least four languages; was (like many another fictional crime-buster) a master of disguise and a skilled undercover worker; not shy of taking on private detective work for a fee; physically strong and well up to a fight; and a good swimmer, but unable to dance. However, he dearly loves dressing up, often as a Jew. He carefully makes the point that his face and complexion are perfect for the role but hastens to assure his readers that 'I have not a trace of the Israelite strain in my composition', although he plays the part well enough to hoodwink his quarry, complete with mock-Yiddish accent ('Goot-evening, shentlemens', as in *The Pearl Necklace*). He even claims to own the beard used by Lecocq, the creation of French writer Émile Gaboriau but firmly based on Eugene Vidocq, the crook-turned-policeman who had invented the Sûreté in 1811 by way of evading a prison sentence.

There are contradictory clues as to whether Donovan is English, Scots or Irish, as he adopts any of these origins, and others besides, with ease. He was brought up partly in France, according to *The Devil's Dozen* (not in this selection). Of course, these are all plot devices, introduced by Muddock without back-up or explanation, to further a particular storyline. If Muddock had required Dick Donovan to be an expert in fifth-century Cephalonian erotic pottery and adept at playing the bouzouki for the purposes of a yarn, rest assured he would had worked it into the story somehow, without much by way of explanation beyond 'I once spent some time in Greece…'. Mind you, much the same could be said of James Bond, of whom Muddock's handiwork *Michael Danevitch of the Russian Secret Service* (1897) is in some sense the *fons et origo*.

Muddock, like Doyle, gave his detective an ability for logical reasoning. But as a detective, Donovan is painstaking rather than inspired, and draws conclusions based on the evidence at crime scenes or from interrogation, rather than great leaps of imagination. All too often, though, Donovan has made up his mind who the culprit is early on and proceeds to vindicate his judgement, usually to the embarrassment of his superiors, other policemen, the victims of the crime and so on. This 'I told you so' attitude would have made him something of a boastful prig to deal with, the reader often feels. But this may have been Muddock knowing his market—lower-class and lower-brow readers than Doyle's, who would revel in Authority Upset and Stuffed Shirts Confounded. Donovan is not shy of telling the directors of the railway or bank officials or even senior police officers that he knows better than they do, but usually lets them think what they like at first, keeping his powder dry until vindication in the *dénouement*, at which point it's Collapse of Stout Party. A later century might consider Dick Donovan, like Holmes, borderline autistic.

Use of deductive logic and gritty persistence are Donovan's method —dedicating a whole week to working undercover in a department store to discover the theft of some trifling items (*All For Love's*

Sake) or taking a boat to Ireland (*The Lady In The Sealskin Cloak*), or putting himself, Simon Templar-style, into prison (*How I Snared The Coiners*)—although the author does throw him the occasional coincidence or piece of sheer luck.

While the stories, and Donovan himself, are steady rather than brilliant, they did set a number of trends for later police-procedurals. Donovan makes intelligent use of what evidence Muddock has him find; and keeps up with the latest methods in forensic criminology. In *The Tuft Of Red Hair* he compares the hair clutched in a murder victim's hand to that of a suspect's beard. Muddock later worked this taste for forensics into a set of stories collected as *The Triumphs of Fabian Field: Criminologist* (1912).

Those familiar with the works of Rankin, James and Jardine may find the Donovan stories lacking in character information and light on scene-setting, and Donovan seems lightly-drawn compared with Dalgliesh, Rebus, Morse, Skinner and their like. The stories also contrast sharply in tone with the wealth of locational detail in the (real but romanticised) M'Levy and (fictional) James McGovan tales, where Edinburgh emerges almost as a character in its own right. Donovan's Glasgow setting is most colourful in the early tales; later, the locale is less specific and largely irrelevant. Possibly, Muddock realised he was restricting his market, especially with the sophisticated *Strand* readers and with international sales looming, and invented a London 'past' and private detective 'future' for Donovan, in order to tell stories of the capital plus adventurings abroad. In fact, Donovan is not named at all until *The Robbery of the London Mail*, Muddock's twelfth detective tale in the *Weekly News*.

Dick Donovan, like Sherlock Holmes, Paul Temple and Dick Tracy, was often thought to be real, and Muddock claims to have received many letters soliciting his detective skills, including one from a Brighton woman who asked him to follow her husband. This clearly bamboozled even *The Scotsman*, which great organ was completely taken in. Reviewing *The Man-Hunter* in 1888, it said 'The stories are not the less enthralling in their interest because they are the record of actual experience, and not, like so many of the detective stories of the moment, the creation of ingenuity and imagination working in fiction... The stories are narrated with a forcible simplicity which makes them more effective than would any subtleties of style.' And of *Caught At Last!* (1889)—'Mr. Donovan's stories are true. They are genuine leaves from the note-book of a detective... The book shows a clever detective at his work, and it throws much real light on the ways of criminals and the lives they lead in the haunts of vice.'

How true, if erroneous.

A LASTING LEGACY

Muddock's remarkable output dwindled after 1907, as befits a man who is approaching 65. But during the First World War he joined the police as a Special Constable, as did another detective writer of the time, Arthur Morrison, as well as many men who were too old for military service overseas but wished to serve their country. Muddock would have been over 70. Was it losing his three surviving sons between 1914 and 1917 which prompted this? Or was it his interest in crime? Interestingly, Muddock stopped writing detective fiction about the same time. Perhaps the reality was at odds with the romance. But ever keen to turn an experience into a profit, in 1920 Muddock published a book about the work of the Special Constables, *All Clear*, as 'J E Preston Muddock (Dick Donovan)'; clearly he or his publisher recognised the continuing value of using the detective alias to popularise it.

Muddock lived out his last days in virtual penury and supported by his daughters. The implication is that, while his books were bestsellers and he made—and spent—a considerable amount of money, he died, if not in poverty, at least not well-heeled. There had been two more brushes with bankruptcy, in 1900 and 1906, and most of his books had been sold for lump sums rather than royalties. He left estate and effects worth a total of £74, a figure more like £8,000 today, but by no means a fortune. The Old Man (as his family called him) was consigned mostly to his study, even for meals, so that his outbursts would not disturb everyone else. In 1931 the Wandsworth house was sold and Eleanor, his wife of 54 years, went to live with the youngest daughter, also Eleanor, and her school-chum and lesbian lover 'Goo' (Grace Martin). However, he is remembered fondly by his only grandson as a kindly old man who smelt of stale porridge and tobacco, who would write fairy stories for him and could race him to the shops even in his late 80s.

Muddock died on 23 January 1934 at 5 Crockerton Road, Upper Tooting, London, living in a small flat with Rose, the only daughter who could be persuaded to have him. He died of a stroke in a hot bath, having just recently told an interfering doctor that he had taken hot baths all his life and they had never done him any harm. His work was mostly out of print other than in cheap editions, and he was all but forgotten as an author. However, there was small posthumous fame of a sort in reprints of his true crime stories in the Mellifont Celebrated Crimes series of 1936.

Like Conan Doyle, Muddock wanted to be remembered chiefly for his historical fiction, such as *Sweet 'Doll' of Haddon Hall* (1903), *Basile the Jester* (1896) and *Young Lochinvar* (1896). This last was made into a silent movie in 1924 starring Gladys Jennings and matinée idol Owen Nares, who, coincidentally, had earlier appeared as 'Danny Donovan, the Gentleman Cracksman' in a 1914 silent movie of that title, alongside Gladys Cooper. *Young Lochinvar* is wrongly credited in most movie databases as taken from a 'novel' by Sir Walter Scott (which in any case was a poem). Muddock received the princely sum of £50 in consideration of the rights, and complained about it long and loud in various tetchy but polite letters to his publisher, who promptly died, presumably of either apoplexy or boredom. But it is Muddock's detective creation which has lasted in the popular memory. Dick Donovan was very much of his time, and that time has passed. Nonetheless, the vast canon of Muddock's work influenced detective and mystery fiction more than almost any other writer of his day. Ellery Queen puts him high in the 'most influential' list, right up there with Edgar Allen Poe.

Muddock's greatest legacy is that the name of his signal creation has entered into common parlance as a result of his fame and status across the Atlantic—ever since 1908 Americans have referred to a police detective as a 'Dick'. He even crops up, as does every other historical and fictional luminary of the period, as 'Inspector Donovan' in Alan Moore's glorious amalgam of Victorian sensational fiction, The *League of Extraordinary Gentlemen*, right alongside Mr Hyde and Mrs Dracula.

There is also a mining town on the Saskatchewan-Manitoba border named Flin Flon, in honour of Josiah Flintabbatey Flonatin, hero of *Sunless City*, Muddock's 1905 science-fantasy about an underground civilization. Even Jules Verne and H G Wells have no such memorial.

As to literary merit: Dick Donovan stories always entertain, and if they seem vaguely dated now, this may be the familiarity of the once-original. Marx Brothers movies, Tarzan books and Dennis the Menace seem corny today because they were primary, and everyone else copied them slavishly. They are also firmly of their time.

So here are a dozen-and-a-half of the best Dick Donovan stories set in, or when Donovan was working in, the Second City of Empire. They start with *The Saltmarket Murder Case*, a locked-room mystery written four decades after Poe's *The Murders in the Rue Morgue*, but four years before *The Speckled Band* and long before John Dickson Carr or Jonathan Creek came on the scene.

There are many other long-uncollected Dick Donovan stories out there, and be assured, Gentle Reader, they will be brought to your attention, provided you keep them away from your children, your servants and the excitable elderly.

But for now, put on your tarboosh, smoking-jacket and Turkish slippers, light your pipe at the gas-lamp and revel in the first, the greatest, the Glasgow Detective, Dick Donovan.

Bruce Durie 2005

Notes to this Edition

◈

The stories collected in this book are a selection of those specifically set in Glasgow, or when Dick Donovan was working from 'The Central'. The text is taken from the original printings, but has been amended in places to reflect modern punctuation, hyphenation, foreign spellings, accents and other usages, and with corrections to sundry typographical glitches and spelling mistakes perpetrated by publishers who were, after all, pushing them out at 3s. 6d. a go or 2s. Limp.

The order presented here is that in which the tales originally saw light in the *Dundee Weekly News*, not in the collections, and the Appendix (p.224) shows the order of publication in periodical form with dates and thereafter in *The Man-Hunter*, 1888, *Caught At Last!*, 1889 and *Tracked & Taken*, 1890.

Not every story from the original 1888–1889 *Dundee Weekly News* run is included (examples would be *The Tinker's Wedding*, 21 April 1888 and *The Tragedy of Law's Building*, 28 July 1888).

Acknowledgements

Dave and Frances were always only encouraging; Jamie gave me the space to do it; Adrienne let me rant on about Muddock; Tom and Seán had vision and patience. Everything else is the editor's fault, as usual.

The Saltmarket
Murder Case

It may be doubted if the annals of crime can furnish any more mysterious and romantic murder than that which a good many years ago startled Glasgow, and kept it on tenter hooks for many weeks, and which came to be known in local parlance as 'The Saltmarket Murder Case'. Not only was the double murder one of great barbarity, but the mystery which surrounded it baffled for many a long day all the skill and ingenuity that was brought to bear in order to try and unravel it. Apart from this, one of the victims had gained something more than local notoriety, as he was known pretty well all over Glasgow as 'Lord John, the Saltmarket Lawyer'. Not that he really was a lord or a lawyer, but he was conspicuous amidst the squalid neighbourhood in which he lived for an air of refinement, a polished manner, some amount of dandyism, and considerable learning, and so his neighbours, with that ironical humour peculiar to the lower classes, came to refer to him as 'My Lord'. His legal appellation had been bestowed upon him owing to his exactness in his bargains and his invariable custom of having the smallest detail of any transaction in which he was engaged committed to writing with a great deal of legal jargon. His name was John Micklethorpe, or rather that was the name he was known by for upwards of twenty years, but, as was subsequently proved, the surname was not his at all. Nothing whatever had been gleaned about his antecedents, and he himself never referred to his past history, or alluded to any of his friends or relatives. These things, added to his very strong personality and marked characteristics, drew upon him a good deal of attention, and he became one of the most noted personages in that part of the town. He had occupied for about twenty years, and still occupied at the time of the murder, a small shop and house at the south end of the Saltmarket, not far from Steel Street. His shop was rather of a nondescript character, but he dealt principally in old curiosities, old prints, china, paintings—in fact, *bric-à-brac* of all kinds. Such a repository for old rubbish seemed somewhat out of place in such a neighbourhood, but then so did Lord John himself. His reputation, however, as a collector of antiquities spread far and wide, and customers or orders came to him from all parts.

I have often wondered, who the people are who buy the lumber which is classified under the head of 'antiquities'. But that such people exist in very large numbers is self-evident, otherwise there would not be so many speculators in the trade. Lord John's curiosity business, however, was quite a secondary matter, and it was principally as a money lender that be had accumulated the large fortune which rumour said he possessed. He was known to be very exacting with his debtors, and would have his pound of flesh to the uttermost grain, but he bore the character of being scrupulously honest, and would owe no man a farthing.

In his personal habits he was very eccentric. At the time of the murder he was about seventy years of age, but looked younger, although his hair was white. He was somewhat below the medium height, with a sparse, light frame, and was noted for his remarkably neat hands and feet. His usual costume was knee breeches, silk stockings, and buckle shoes, and a dressing-gown instead of a coat. During all the years he had been in the Saltmarket he had never been known to go away even for a day at a time, with one exception; that was about three months before he was murdered. He was then absent, much to the astonishment of the neighbourhood, for three days. And it was this fact which subsequently afforded an important clue in bringing the ghastly crime home to the guilty parties. For many years, almost without exception, he had been in the habit of walking up and down the Saltmarket from seven to eight; spring, summer, autumn, and winter, no matter what the weather was. He took this matutinal promenade for the sake of exercise, and as soon as eight struck he retired to his shop. His household affairs were looked after by a housekeeper, an old woman about sixty-five, who was known in the neighbourhood as Jessie M'Laughlin, though there is reason to believe that was not her real name. Jessie was as close and reserved as her master, and the person who could have got any information from her about the mysterious old man might have hoped to be successful in finding the Philosopher's Stone. In a word, Jessie knew how to keep her own counsel, and though she was always ready to take a snuff or a half-mutchkin with anyone who would offer them, she never allowed her tongue to betray her thoughts. Lord John's premises occupied the basement of a very old building, the upper part of the tenement being reached by a common stair, though Lord John was independent of this stair, as he had a separate entrance.

His shop, which was very much crowded with lumber, was entered from the street by two steps and a rather narrow doorway. The door was half glazed, but the glass was always screened by an old faded, dingy green curtain. The shop was a mouldy, dusty, cobwebby receptacle at the best, and the odour of it was always suggestive of decaying bones. At the back of the shop was a room where Lord John transacted his money-lending business. It was lighted by a barred window that looked into a dismal little yard or court about as big as a dining table. The room was no less dusty, cobwebby, and mouldy than the shop. It contained an old desk with many pigeon-holes, an iron safe of a very old-fashioned type, a table, two or three chairs, and some book-shelves.

From this room a flight of wooden stairs led to an upper storey, consisting of four rooms—namely, a kitchen, a sort of sitting-room, and two bedrooms. The furniture in all these rooms was very anti-quated, and the general aspect of the house was that of sombreness and decay. Nevertheless, for a period verging on to a quarter of a century, Lord John and his housekeeper had dwelt here in their seclusion; and as he had never been known to be laid up for a single day with illness during that time, the place, in spite of its gloom and seeming insanitary condition, could not have been so bad after all. Of course, during the long years that the man dwelt there, the question was often asked, 'Who is Lord John?' but no satisfactory answer was ever forthcoming. He knew how to keep his secrets, and whatever skeletons he had he never paraded them for the gratification of idle curiosity. Nor did he visit or receive visitors. His only visitors were those who came to borrow money or pay it back, and this business was always transacted in the room already described. His existence, in short, was exceedingly like that of a hermit, although it would appear he did not altogether exist on hermit diet, but indulged in plenty of the good things of life.

As may readily be imagined, the neighbourhood took great interest in this eccentric character, and so one dark November morning folk were surprised that his shop remained closed, although nine o'clock had been proclaimed by the Tron Church. The people remembered that he had not taken his usual morning promenade. And when ten o'clock came, and the shop still remained closed, suspicion took the place of curiosity, and little groups of neighbours collected on the pavement and began to indulge in all sorts of speculations, until it was suggested that the police should be communicated with. In the course of ten minutes a constable was found, and, on being informed of the strange fact that Lord John's shop remained closed in spite of the late hour, he could not help sharing the general belief that something was wrong, for be was well acquainted with the methodical habits of the old man. Still it was no part of the constable's duty to break into a person's house on the bare suspicion that something was wrong. He, therefore, contented himself with knocking at the door, repeating the knocks with increased vigour, but he failed to get a response. It now became evident that either the old man and his housekeeper were absent, or something was very decidedly wrong. The theory of their absence was dismissed as being utterly improbable, and as the large crowd which had now gathered began to get excited, the constable sent a message to the station asking what he was to do. In the

Acknowledgements

Dave and Frances were always only encouraging; Jamie gave me the space to do it; Adrienne let me rant on about Muddock; Tom and Seán had vision and patience. Everything else is the editor's fault, as usual.

course of a short time a sergeant arrived, and an inspection of the back part of the premises was made. No door opened into the yard already referred to, and the heavily barred window, which was screened inside by a blind, precluded all attempts at entry that way. It was therefore decided to burst open the shop door, and this was soon done. The sergeant and a blacksmith, whose services had been engaged to break the door open, then entered, while the constable remained at the doorway to keep back the crowd, which now numbered many hundreds, while the suspense and excitement were intense.

The sergeant called 'Lord John' three or four times, but the silence was unbroken save by his own voice. The two men then groped their way through the dark shop, and gained the back room. The blacksmith was proceeding towards the window to draw the blind up and let in some light, when he slipped on what seemed to be some greasy substance, and fell heavily to the floor. The sergeant immediately struck a light, as he had a box of matches in his pocket, and reaching the window he drew the blind up. The light revealed that the greasy substance on the floor was a great pool of congealed blood, and glancing upward, the man saw to his horror that blood was still oozing through the old, cracked, and broken ceiling. There was no longer any doubt that a tragedy had occurred. The sergeant helped the blacksmith to rise, and the two mounted up the rickety wooden stair, and when they gained the upper room a ghastly sight was revealed. The room was the kitchen, but a press bed stood in a recess; and lying half on and half off the bed, and clothed only in her night-dress, was the body of the old housekeeper, and a great wound in her forehead showed that she had been shot. On the floor and close to the bed was the body of Lord John, with a ghastly, gaping wound in the throat, which had been cut from ear to ear. From this wound, as well as from that of the old woman, an enormous quantity of blood had flowed, and had made its way through the decayed floor to the apartment below.

As may be imagined, the two men were horrified at the dreadful discovery, and, leaving everything exactly as they found it, they proceeded at once to the station to give information, leaving the constable to guard the house.

As soon as the news of the tragedy spread throughout the city the excitement was intense, and thousands of people flocked to the Saltmarket. Of course the question instantly arose, Was it a case of suicide and murder, or a double murder? Examination soon proved it to be the latter. The woman had been shot, and the bullet had entered by the left temple, traversed the crown of the skull, and had come out at the base, and was found on the floor. No pistol of any kind, however, could be discovered. Lord John's throat was cut in such a manner that the doctors stated positively that he could not have done it himself. Besides, there were deep cuts on the back of the neck, right in the nape, as well as many gashes on the hands and fingers, showing thereby that he had struggled for his life. Now came the query, Who was the murderer? and where were the weapons with which the fearful deed had been done? The most exhaustive search failed to find them. Then, again, how did the murderer enter the premises, and how did he leave them? The shop door was properly secured, and entrance by the back seemed impossible.

The authorities felt from the first that the case was a difficult one, and shrouded in mystery, and it was placed in my hands. I must confess I took it up with a great deal of reluctance, for although I had had the good fortune to unravel a good many tangled skeins in my time, this promised to baffle me, and I did not like to have to own to failure.

My first step was to make a very careful survey of the premises, and I came to the conclusion that the criminal had not entered nor made his exit by the shop door, because, apart from its fastening with a strong lock, there was a large bolt at the bottom and one at the top. The door had not only been locked but bolted as well, as was evidenced by the sockets of the bolts being forced off when the door was burst open. Now, a person might have locked the door from the outside, but unless he had been endowed with superhuman powers he *could not have bolted it.* The murderer, therefore, could not have escaped by the doorway. The window of the back room, which was practically Lord John's office, I have already spoken of as being heavily barred. These bars were four in number, and were placed vertically, each bar being firmly let into the stonework. The space between them was too narrow to admit of a fair sized cat, and as they were quite intact the murderer did not enter or escape that way.

At the very outset, therefore, I found myself in the face of an unusual difficulty. Firstly, I could discover no trace of the weapons which had inflicted the terrible wounds. Secondly, it seemed impossible to form any theory as to how the criminal had entered and left the premises. Then, as to the motive of the crime? Robbery was suspected naturally; but the safe in the office was intact, and a sum of money—I think about 12 *l.* in notes and gold—was lying loose on the shelf over the fireplace in Lord John's bedroom. An antique but very massive and valuable gold repeater watch was hung on a hook at his bed head, and in such a conspicuous place that the most careless observer could hardly have failed to notice it. There was also a few pounds in gold and silver in the old man's breeches pocket, and in other parts of the house there were many valuables, such as real silver spoons and forks, old-fashioned rings, and other jewellery. *Robbery,* therefore, had not been the motive. An examination of the contents of the safe showed that the old man had several thousand pounds deposited in a Glasgow bank. There was also nearly a hundred pounds in cash in the safe, as well as bonds, share certificates, and other valuable documents.

As all these details were made known to the public through the medium of the press the excitement in the city increased. And, as is usually the case, there was a good deal of wild talk about the police being at fault, &c. But, as a matter of fact, there wasn't the shadow of a shade of a clue. No particular person was suspected, therefore no description could be given; and as nothing seemed to have been stolen, what is often an important thread in such cases was entirely wanting. The public soon began to see themselves that it was no ordinary case in which vulgar motives of robbery had been the incentive, but that it was a very cold-blooded murder, of a very perplexing and mysterious character, and one of the leading organs of the press was good enough to say, in speaking of the crime, 'That a terrible murder has been committed seems to be beyond doubt, but it is also equally certain that the crime is shrouded in a great deal of mystery, and the most astute detective might be pardoned for feeling himself baffled. We are in a position, however, to assure the public that the most extraordinary exertions are being used to trace the criminal or criminals; and from our knowledge of the person who is conducting the inquiry we feel sure that the mystery will not long remain unsolved'.

This of course was very flattering to my *amour propre*, but nevertheless I had to own to myself that for once in my life I was beaten. I was aware that it was no use attempting to track down the criminal until I had some clue to begin with, and I was perfectly sure that clue was only to be sought for on the scene of the murder, and yet the more I examined the place the more I felt puzzled, and when a fortnight had passed I was almost hopeless. But at last, when I was beginning to despair of ever being able to throw light on the mystery, I discovered the very clue I wanted.

The kitchen, which was over the office, was lighted by a window, which was at least thirty feet from the ground, and I felt sure that unless by means of a ladder the human being was not born who could have reached that window from the yard. The kitchen, as is usual in such places, had a sink for washing-up purposes, and this was placed close to the window. It might be described as simply a wooden trough lined with lead. I took it into my head one day to examine that sink, over which was the water-tap, while the drainage pipe ran through the outer wall and connected with the pipe common to the whole tenement. By my examination I discovered two things. First, traces of blood on the inside of the sink, and I said to myself the murderer washed his hands here after the deed. Second, on the end nearest the window were some almost imperceptible nail-marks in the lead, that is, marks made by the nails of a boot. The window was old, and the brass sneck had long ago been broken off, and I found by actual experiment that the sash could be very easily lifted or lowered from the outside, and that with little or no noise. As the window sill was rather an unusual distance from the floor, a person coming in or going out that way would be almost certain to stand on the end of the sink. Having made this discovery, I said the murderer came in and went out by that window. But, as he couldn't have carried a thirty foot ladder with him, he didn't come up from nor go down into the yard. How, then, did he reach the window? I wasn't long in answering that, to my own satisfaction; *he came from above.*

I was confident now that I had made an important discovery, but I was by no means elated. It was after all only a slender thread, and might lead to nothing. But I was determined to follow it up. The house above that of Lord John had been untenanted since the last term. My next step was to make some inquiries of the landlord, and from him I learnt that a few days before the murder a middle-aged lady had come to look at the house with a view to renting it. The key was given to her, and she went over the place by herself, subsequently returning the key with the remark that the house would not suit. I asked to be allowed to have the key in order that I might visit the house myself. The landlord offered to accompany me, but I expressed a wish to go alone. As soon as I got the key I took it to my own residence first of all, and put it under the microscope, and I confess that my heart beat faster as I discovered traces of wax between the wards. This revealed to me that a wax impression of the key had been taken, and another one made, and by the duplicate key the murderer had gained admission on the night of the murder. This theory was strengthened by what the landlord told me—that no one had visited the house since the lady referred to. In going to the place my first step was to examine the window of the kitchen, which was exactly over the window of Lord John's kitchen, and the sill of it was exactly fourteen feet from the sill of the other. Now, it was a simple feat for anyone with a certain amount of nerve to lower himself from the one window to the other by means of a cord; and, on examining the edge of the stonework of the sill, I found distinct traces of a rope having been used. But I reasoned with myself, although it is comparatively easy for a person without any training to go down fourteen feet by a rope swinging against a wall, it wants trained muscles for anyone to come up again. And so I said the man who did the murder belongs to some profession in which the muscles are in constant training. For some time I was puzzled to see where the end of the rope had been made fast, for it is certain it must have been made fast somewhere. I, therefore, went down on my knees and examined the floor, until I detected that one of the boards had recently been disturbed. With my knife I was enabled to lift this until I got my fingers under, and then raise it altogether. It was the board that had evidently been lifted when the gas-piping had been put in, and in replacing it the workmen had neglected to nail it. The board was only half the length of the room, having been sawn in the centre for convenience when laying the gas. The half, therefore, was very easily removed, and of course it enabled anyone to get at the cross beams or joists. One of these beams passed just below the window, and I felt convinced that the cord had been made fast round it.

I could not help feeling some satisfaction at having thus solved the problem as to how the murderer got into and out of the house. But still that did not bring the criminal to justice. That he was no ordinary person I felt perfectly convinced for three reasons. (1) Had he been so he would not have taken such elaborate and risky means to reach his victims; (2) His motive was not robbery; (3) By his making a duplicate key. This also showed that the murder was most deliberately planned.

So far, then, my investigations had not been barren of result; but still the clue, if clue I had really got, was of the faintest possible description, and I by no means felt hopeful of running my man down. With these reflections, I was in the act of replacing the board when it occurred to me to strike a match and look under the flooring as far as possible. It must have been some kind prompting of my good genius that moved me to do this, for I could not possibly have given a reason for it. As I held the match down and peered under the boards, I almost uttered a cry, for my eye caught sight of the stock of a pistol. By means of my walking-stick I drew it out. It was an old-fashioned, single-barrel, smooth-bore weapon, and I had an inward conviction that I held the weapon that had killed the old woman. The bullet I had carefully wrapped up in a piece of paper and placed in my waistcoat pocket, and in testing it I found that, although it was flattened somewhat, it exactly fitted the bore. The importance of this discovery could not be over-rated. It was at least a tangible clue. But where was the knife that had gashed poor Lord John's throat so fearfully? As the murderer had concealed the pistol under the boards, why not the knife? I at once went out and secured the services of a joiner, and without telling him of my find, I instructed him to lift the boards. The knife, however, was not discovered. The criminal, therefore, had either concealed it some-where else or carried it off with him.

I have mentioned that on one occasion Lord John was known to have been absent for three days. Now, my varied experience in detecting crime had taught me that the seeming improbable was often the most probable; and, keeping this ever before me as an axiom, I was never disposed to ignore anything that might aid me in my business of bringing criminals to justice. I therefore resolved to try and find out where he had been to during these three days, and I thought that some of his letters might afford the information. Accordingly, I went through his papers, and at last came across the following:

—— Hotel, Newcastle-on-Tyne.

I break the silence of years to tell you that I am lying here very ill, and, being in deep distress, I beg that you will come and see me and render me some assistance, or send me a remittance.

GEORGE

Thinks I, as I folded that letter up again, this is an important link; but who is George? On looking through some of the murdered man's private account books, I found repeated entries, always just before quarter day, of 'George 25 *l*' It was as clear as a pike staff, therefore, that the old man allowed this mysterious George a hundred a year.

The following day I started off for Newcastle, and put up at the
—— Hotel. By dint of patient inquiry I learnt that some months
ago they had had a visitor who was supposed to be an officer of a
ship which had arrived in the Tyne. He was exceedingly ill, and one
day an old man came to see him. But they evidently didn't get on
well together, as the servants frequently heard high words passing
between them in the invalid's room. The old man went away on the
third day, and the invalid soon after recovered, and left also.

My next move was to ascertain what ships had come into the
Tyne about that time, and if any one of them had had a sick officer.
It was not long before I discovered that a small coaling steamer
called the 'Iron Duke' had come in from Barbadoes, that her chief
officer was a man named George Devonport, that he had been ill all
the voyage, and was ashore ill, and was unable to go away with the
ship when she left again. George Devonport was described as being
about sixty years of age, and as hailing from London. His age, therefore, precluded the possibility of his being the son of Lord John,
which struck me at first might be the case, but I felt sure he was a
relation of some sort; and also the *murderer of Lord John.*

I have stated that when I had satisfied myself that an entry to
the house had been effected from above, I was of opinion that the
person who had used this means of entry was one whose muscles
were in constant training. George Devonport was a sailor, and to
scale a rope would be an easy feat for him. How to find George
Devonport was the next problem I had to solve. It seemed to grow
upon me as a conviction that he was the criminal, but I also felt
sure that he had an associate in the person of some woman. That
woman was the one who went to look at the empty house, and took
a wax impression of the key. She was described by the landlord as
a tall, gaunt, rather masculine-looking woman, neatly dressed, and
wearing widow's mourning.

Soon after I returned to Glasgow, and after consulting with the
authorities I caused an advertisement to appear in the 'Times' and
other London papers asking for the heirs or next-of-kin of John
Micklethorpe.

The applicants were to apply to a firm of solicitors in Glasgow, and in a few days these gentlemen handed me a letter worded as follows:

25 —— Street, Chelsea, London.

Replying to your advertisement, I beg to say that I am the half-brother of the late John Micklethorpe, whose real name was Devonport; and as I have every reason to think I am his nearest surviving male relative, I must be his heir in the absence of a will.

I shall be glad to have some particulars from you, and am, gentlemen, yours truly,

GEORGE DEVONPORT

So, so, my good fellow, I thought, I've trapped you at last. No will had been discovered of the murdered man's, and therefore in law this George Devonport would certainly be the heir.

By the next post a letter was despatched to him, asking him to come through to Glasgow without loss of time, and within a week he had arrived. I found him a somewhat different man to what I had expected to see. He was short, rather thick set, with a clean shaven face and a sullen, determined-looking expression of countenance. In reply to the solicitors he said his age was fifty-five. He seemed reluctant to give much information about himself, but was particularly inquisitive as to the amount of property the murdered man had left, and what it consisted of.

On the third day, having arranged with the solicitors to have him at the office, and having procured a warrant in the meantime, I appeared on the scene in company with two constables, and, tapping him on the shoulder, I said, 'George Devonport, I arrest you for the murder of your half-brother'.

If I had had my doubts about my man up to this moment they all vanished now, for he turned deathly pale, stammered out that I was a fool, and then pulling a small phial from his pocket he tried to get the cork out, but we were too quick for him, and subsequent analysis proved that the bottle contained a powerful dose of corrosive sublimate.

In due course he was brought to trial, and I had got such a mass of circumstantial evidence together that his conviction was a foregone conclusion. He was found guilty and condemned to death. The night before his execution he made a full confession of his guilt. He was the murdered man's half-brother by the same father, who had been an eccentric and extravagant country squire, who squandered a fortune on the turf, and getting into difficulties appropriated some money of which he was trustee, and on this being discovered, he committed suicide. John had been well brought up, but George had been somewhat neglected. At their father's death they were both young men, but the prisoner took to drink, and subsequently went to sea. After a voyage he returned. The two brothers had never got on well together, and now they broke out into open rupture, as John was found to be courting a young woman George had made love to. This led to great bitterness, which culminated when John married her. But within a year she gave birth to a still-born child, and died herself a few hours later.

After this George became a very wild and indifferent sort of character, and John, who had been passionately attached to his wife, seemed broken with sorrow, and changing his name, owing to the disgrace his father had brought upon the family, he went north with a servant, a buxom young woman then, who had been engaged by his wife. This was the woman who was murdered with him. Having always been fond of collecting curiosities and antiquated things, he started a business which, combined with money-lending, enabled him to accumulate a small fortune. George, finding out where he was, began to annoy him, until at last John agreed to allow him a hundred a year, paid quarterly. This payment was kept up for several years with great regularity, and for many years they did not meet until that meeting in Newcastle. The old bitterness broke out again, for John upbraided George for his drunken habits, and George accused John of having driven him to drink. Before John went away he told his brother that he should have none of his money, as he intended to make a will leaving it all to a charity. It was then that George resolved to murder him before he could make the will, and with that end in view he came to Glasgow, and lived for some time in a squalid lodging in the west-end of Argyle Street. At length, finding that the house above his brother's shop was to let, he disguised himself in woman's clothes, and by means of the duplicate key gained entrance on the night of the murder. The pistol he had bought some time previously in London from a marine store dealer, and as it had only one barrel, he sharpened up a sailor's jack knife. On getting in at the window by means of a rope, as I had surmised, he disturbed the old woman in her bed, and immediately shot her. The report of the pistol aroused his brother, who came running in in his night-shirt, when George at once seized him, and with the jack knife gashed his throat, but not until after a considerable struggle. Although he was straitened for money, be resolved not to take much away, as he quite expected to get all the dead man's property. He effected his escape by means of the rope, which he carried away with him, together with the jack knife. As he was untying the rope from the beam the pistol fell out of his pocket, and in his hurry to get away he kicked it under the boards. The knife and the rope he flung into the Clyde from Victoria Bridge.

Although he had thus made a clean breast of his double crime, it will be remembered that he died anything but penitent, and on the morning of his execution he refused the ministrations of the chaplain, and stated that after the murder he always carried a bottle of corrosive sublimate in order to kill himself should he be arrested for the murder.

I hope I may without want of modesty say that I was highly complimented by the authorities for having brought this remarkable criminal to justice.

The Lady in the
Sealskin Cloak

usiness of a private nature necessitated my presence on
the platform of the Queen Street High Level Station, Glasgow, one winter afternoon as the 2.10 express from Edinburgh arrived. As this is the fastest of the afternoon expresses, it is a long and busy train, and for some ten minutes or so after it reaches its destination there is considerable bustle and confusion on the platform. I had no particular object in noting the arrivals, but by confirmed habit and long experience I am ever vigilant, and have acquired the power of quick observation, the ability to judge quickly, and arrive at rapid and almost invariably accurate decisions. I need scarcely say that any man who, by instinct or training, cannot acquire these qualities, is totally unfitted for the detective's calling. The art of reading one's fellow-men must be inborn, for, as of the poet, *Poeta, nascitur, non fit,* so of the detective. The instincts of his profession must be with him at his birth, and developed and perfected afterwards by training and experience.

As the train drew up a daintily-gloved hand thrust from the window of a first-class carriage attracted my attention. There was no very definite reason why it should have done so, for the owner of the hand simply indicated that she—it was unmistakably a feminine hand—wanted the assistance of a porter. Nevertheless, my natural curiosity prompted me to move along a little, for the train had not quite stopped, and fix my eyes on the particular compartment of that particular carriage. In the few brief moments that intervened I found myself speculating as to what the owner of such a small and richly gloved hand could be like. Was she young or old, good-looking

16

or ugly? I had not to wait long before my curiosity was gratified. A porter hurried to the door, threw it open, received from the person in the carriage a handsome travelling rug, a costly handbag, three or four yellow back novels held together by a strap, and some other odds and ends. Then with a chivalrous politeness, begotten by the keen expectancy of a good tip, he extended his own brawny and grime-stained paw to assist the owner of the things to alight. I saw a small foot wearing an exquisite buttoned boot, the foot and the neat ankle being in keeping with the hand, make its appearance on the iron step, and in another moment a lady sprang lightly on to the platform. As certain novelists would say, 'Before my astonished gaze there stood a radiant being'. To put it in more prosaic language, I beheld a faultlessly-dressed woman, seemingly about eight-and-twenty. She was not only good-looking, but positively handsome, and her well-moulded figure lost none of its attractiveness by an exceedingly costly and most magnificent tightly-fitting sealskin cloak that reached to the bottom of her dress, and could not have cost a penny less than a hundred guineas.

This superb cloak enhanced my interest in the lady, and I wondered who she was that she could afford to wear such a luxurious and expensive article of dress. As she moved along the platform her grace of carriage and stately bearing proclaimed her unmistakably as being far from a commonplace person. She impressed me at once with the idea that she was a woman of superior breeding. She had very bright, golden colour hair, which was gathered behind in a circular fold. Over the face, as far as the mouth, she wore a light gossamer fall with white spots, and this rather served to emphasise, so to speak, the delicacy of her complexion, which, however, was not wholly the production of nature, for the practised eye detected at once that cosmetics had been called in to enhance nature's charms. The soft, moist, red lips and the delicate peach bloom on the cheeks owed something to the mysteries of the feminine toilet table. She had beauty enough, however, and there was no need for these meretricious aids. But when was lovely woman satisfied with unadorned beauty?

Without making myself obtrusive in any way, I could not help watching this very attractive and conspicuous young woman, and I noted that she had remarkably keen, restless eyes of some hue of blue. She seemed to me to scan with eagerness the hurrying people as if she expected somebody, and there was a certain something in her manner that indicated that she was disappointed.

The porter addressed her, inquiring, no doubt, if she was going to take a cab. I saw her small foot beat the platform with impatience; then she said something to the man, and made a gesture indicating that he was to remain there, and she came back up the platform, sweeping close by me as she went, so that I got a full view of her face. She was obviously expecting someone to meet her, and the someone wasn't there. The crowd had considerably thinned by this time, and when she had taken in a full view of the platform she turned back to where the porter waited, and then, preceded by him, she went towards the cab rank.

As I had leisure on my hands, and feeling an unaccountable interest in this very charming young person, I followed in an indolent sort of way, looking as though I was oblivious of all my surroundings, though very little escaped my observation. As they reached the end of the platform, a small, well-dressed man, wearing a frock coat and tall hat, rushed up evidently out of breath, and accosting her, they shook hands.

'So this is the person she's been expecting,' I thought, 'and he is late. Is he husband or lover, I wonder? Whichever he be, such an imperious young lady will not let him off without a severe chiding.'

She did not indicate anger, however, by her manner, but I saw that she threw a hurried glance all round. I knew the value of that glance at once. If it meant anything at all it meant watchful suspicion, and instantly it raised in my mind doubts whether there were not hawk's claws beneath this dove's feathers. My own naturally suspicious disposition was at once put on the alert, and my vigilance was quickened. The man was dark complexioned, with a Jewish cast of countenance. Over his frock coat he wore a costly overcoat trimmed with fur at the collar and cuffs, and in his button-hole he carried a little bunch of lilies-of-the-valley. Yet, in spite of his fine clothes, it needed no very keen judge of character to determine that he was not a gentleman in the proper sense of the term, and I was equally certain that he was not the lover of that handsome woman, or there would have been more effusive warmth on his part in the greeting. He might have been the husband or— But no matter, I drew my own inferences. Their interview was very short; whatever they had to say they said rapidly. Then, without raising his hat or bowing, he turned abruptly and hurried away, but not before I had impressed his face on my mind, so that I could have picked him out from a thousand others.

For a moment, owing to the abrupt manner in which he left, I thought he would come back again, but that thought was soon dispelled, for she moved on; the porter procured a cab, assisted her in, having first placed her rug and bag on the seat (she had no other luggage). Then the gloved hand was extended towards the opened paw of the porter; the paw closed instinctively on a coin of sufficient value to bring an expression of supreme satisfaction into his grimy face, and the cab drove away, but I had noted the number, and at once wrote it down in my pocket-book.

'Have you any idea who that lady is?' I asked as I sauntered up to the porter with an assumed languid air.

'No, but she's gey guid-looking,' he answered, with a wink. 'She's a real lady tae, for she gave me a half-crown.'

As my and the porter's standard of judging a lady were not likely to be in consonance, I did not venture to dispute him, but inquired if he knew where she had gone to.

'Ay, she telt the driver tae tak' her tae the —— Hotel.'

As the —— Hotel was the grandest and most expensive in Glasgow, I inferred that whoever or whatever my lady in the sealskin cloak might be, she was in the habit of doing things 'swellishly'. As I turned back into the station I could not help a feeling that I had not seen that young woman for the last time.

As I happened to be well acquainted with the manager of the —— Hotel, I dropped in a few hours later, and while discussing a small nip of excellent 'Long John' in his snuggery, I casually asked if he had had many arrivals that day.

'No, we are rather slack just now,' he answered.

'No one of note, I suppose?' I added.

'No. Well, a very stylish and handsome young woman arrived, and engaged one of the best bedrooms and a sitting-room for a week. She came by the Edinburgh express, I think.'

'Oh, who is she?'

'I don't know. Some swell, I fancy. She gave her name as Mrs. Clara Penelope Fitzwilliams.'

'That's upper ten thousandish,' I exclaimed with a laugh. 'Has a classical ring, too, about it.' Then I asked with professional point-edness, 'Is she all square, do you think?'

'Phew! who's to tell? You can't make sure of anyone nowadays. She'd no luggage, and so paid for the rooms in advance. She said she expected a gentleman—a friend of her husband's—to call and see her this evening. I tell you what,' added the manager, as he poked me in the ribs, 'if she were my wife I shouldn't care to let her travel about the country alone. She is too handsome. In fact, she's about as handsome a young woman as I've seen for many a long day.'

'By Jove, I should like to see her,' I said, not deeming it prudent to let the manager know that I had already seen her.

'Well, if she's going to be here I dare say you may have the chance,' was the answer.

In a little while I took my departure, resolving in my own mind to keep my professional eye on this beautiful mystery, for do what I would I could not divest my mind of the idea that there was some-thing wrong about her. She wasn't a runaway wife come to meet a lover; at least, not if the man at the station was her lover, because he was not effusive enough. And if he was her husband, why had she taken the rooms for herself alone, and told the manager she expected a friend of her husband's coming to see her?

'No, no, my lady,' thought I, 'you are queer, and I'll find out something about you.'

Two days after this I was going down Buchanan Street during the busiest part of the day, when I suddenly came face to face with my lady of the sealskin cloak once more. I could not help thinking that if possible she looked handsomer than when I first beheld her at the railway station, while her superb figure, set off to such advantage by the costly cloak, her graceful carriage, and her lofty bearing attracted general attention, and I found that I was not the only one who regarded her with interest, though the interest in my case was somewhat different, I fancy, to that which induced so many men to turn round and stare after her as she passed. If she was conscious of this, and it is more than probable she was, she did not betray it, but seemed supremely indifferent to everything and everybody. As I was hurrying to keep an important engagement with one of my chiefs, I could not shadow her as I should have liked to do. We were destined, however, to meet a little later that same day, but under somewhat different circumstances. It was in Hope Street. A splendid carriage, drawn by a faultless pair of horses, passed me at a smart pace, and, glancing to see who were the fortunate individual or individuals who could thus indulge in such luxury, I once more beheld the sealskin, but this time she was not alone. She had as her companion the Jewish-looking man I had seen her speak to at the railway station. I recognised the carriage as belonging to a well-known livery stable, and the fact of my lady driving about in such style did not tend to lessen my suspicions that she was something different to what she appeared to be.

That evening I dropped in on my friend the manager of the —— Hotel again.

'What do you think of the lady in the sealskin cloak now?' I asked.

'Well,' he answered, with a puzzled expression of countenance, 'I don't know exactly what to make of her. There's something queer about her, I'm sure of that. But she's a lady at any rate in her manners, and she knows how to dine too. She's a first-rate customer, and I only wish she was going to stay for a month or two.'

'Ah, I see you look at it from the *l.s.d.* point of view,' I remarked, a little dryly.

'I am obliged to do that to a considerable extent. Profitable customers are very desirable in our business, and as long as this lady pays for what she has, it is nothing to do with me what she is. But the fact is, you fellows are so deucedly suspicious of everything and everybody, that you think everyone is a criminal who does not get on the housetops and proclaim his pedigree and business.'

I smiled at my friend's argument, as I replied:

'Hardly so, dear boy, but this beautiful creature, who dresses so handsomely and lives so well, is something very different to what she appears to be on the surface. My opinion, in fact, is that she is a sharper.'

A look of irritation passed over the manager's face as I said this, and I saw at once that she had succeeded in winning his good graces.

'I don't believe it,' he exclaimed, a little warmly, in answer to my last remark. 'She is a lady in every sense of the word.'

'Very well, my good friend,' I returned, 'enjoy your opinion. Perhaps I am wrong, but I do not think it. And if I am I shall have to confess that I have lost my power of judging character.'

I saw that he was inclined to continue the argument, and to vigorously defend his own views regarding the enchanting creature who had apparently thrown a spell over him. But argument in such cases was not in my line, and so I cut him short by pleading a pressing engagement, and took my departure.

That evening I looked in at the theatre, and while scrutinising the various parts of the house I was utterly amazed to see that one of the private boxes was occupied by the beauty of the sealskin, the dark Jewish-looking man I had observed at the railway station, and last, not least, my friend the manager of the —— Hotel. Knowing him to be a prudent and cautious man as a rule, and one who was peculiarly sensitive to public opinion, my surprise may be better imagined than described. But when I gazed at the truly fascinating face and the really bewitching manner of the charmer my surprise lessened, for a man must have been singularly strong-willed to have resisted her.

For several days after this—I think for about a week—I was much engaged, and the mysterious lady of the sealskin cloak had passed out of my memory, when one evening, on returning to my home, I found a note from the manager of the —— Hotel. It was worded as follows:

'For God's sake, come here immediately. Something terrible has happened.'

'So my good friend the manager of the —— Hotel has been trapped at last,' I mused as I slipped his brief note into my pocket. For I had no doubt in my own mind that 'the something terrible' he said had happened was in connection with the mysterious beauty of the sealskin. An outsider would have accused me, no doubt, of jumping to very hasty conclusions; but I should, indeed, have been lacking in that essential of the detective's calling, namely, the power to reason *a posteriori,* if I had drawn any other inference. Almost from the first moment I had gazed on the lady I was prejudiced against her, and, to make the reason for this clear to the reader's intelligence, I should have to enter into an argument which would far more than exhaust the space at my disposal. Suffice it then to say that I looked upon Mrs. Clara Penelope Fitzwilliams with unmistakable suspicion: and having noted how the manager had succumbed to her seductive wiles, his brief note was to my mind proof positive that my suspicions had been more than justified. When, therefore, a few hours later I entered his private room I was not surprised by his exclamation:

'I'm in an awful mess. If I had only allowed myself to be warned by you this would not have happened.'

'The enchantress of the sealskin has something to do with this?' I remarked with a solemn face, and yet finding some difficulty in keeping my countenance as I observed his distress. And I experienced a little sense of triumph that I was right in my judgment of the lady, for the detective is human, the same as his fellows, and does not like to find himself in the wrong.

'Yes, confound her,' he exclaimed savagely, as he thrust his hands deep into his pockets, and stood with his back to the fire.

'Well, now, come tell me all about it,' I remarked encouragingly, as I saw by his manner that even now he was somewhat reluctant to confess that he had been victimised, for how could that confession do otherwise than betray his own weakness, and few men like to confess that they have been befooled. He threw himself into a large easy chair, and played a tattoo on the arms with his finger nails, after the manner of a person who is excited, and suffering great distress of mind. For some moments he did not speak, and then with a sort of desperate plunge be said

'I thoroughly believed in that woman, and thought you had done her a cruel wrong in suspecting her of being other than what she seemed; but, by Jove! you were right, and she's the most artful she devil I have ever met.'

I smiled inwardly at this expressive testimony to the correctness of my theorising; but preserving my usual outward gravity in such circumstances, I remarked— 'She has robbed you, then?'

'Yes; but let me explain. A few days ago she showed me a letter purporting to come from her husband. It was written on note-paper bearing a crest and motto, and it pretended to rate her for her extravagance, and it was worded so as to lead to the inference that she had written asking his permission to buy some diamond jewellery. I remember one passage of the letter ran thus: "Although I find it very hard indeed to deny you anything, I cannot help saying that we must be a little more economical for some time, for, as you are aware, depreciation in landed and other property has caused a considerable reduction in my income, a reduction that, though temporary, necessitates some amount of self-denial. However, I will yield to you for this once, providing you do not expend more than a thousand pounds, and for this amount I will send you a draft on the Union in the course of a couple of days." Now, after, reading that, how could I come to any conclusion than that she was genuine?'

'It was clever,' I remarked ambiguously, as he looked at me, as if expecting me to answer his question approvingly.

'Clever! I should think it was,' he cried. 'Well, the following day an assistant came from Mackinnon and Duncan, the jewellers, with a case of diamond earrings, a necklace, a bracelet, and a magnificent gold watch set with diamonds and pearls, the lot being valued at a thousand guineas. I was called in to see the things, and my lady expressed much distress of mind that the promised draft from her husband had not arrived. Of course, the assistant declined to leave the goods without the money, but as she had taken a box at the theatre for that evening, and was very anxious to wear the jewels, she persuaded me to pay a hundred pounds deposit, and this I consented to do on condition that the jewels were handed to me to lock up in my safe until the whole of the money was paid. This was consented to. I paid the money, and took the jewels; but as I was invited to accompany her to the theatre, I handed them to her later on. I went to the theatre, and besides myself in the box there were another young woman and the dark Jewish-looking man who has visited her two or three times. By heavens, if you had only seen how exquisite my lady looked you would not be surprised at her making victims.'

'Nothing ever surprises me, dear boy,' I remarked, 'except that some men are so weak.'

'All right, pitch in to me, I deserve it,' he answered tartly. 'It was pretty late when we came back to the hotel, and, as she complained of a severe headache, she went straight to her room.'

'And did she return the jewellery to you?' I asked.

'No, I couldn't ask her to take it off in the vestibule, and I intended to get it in the morning, but before the morning came the bird had flown. She had let herself out in the dead of night, and left not a scrap of anything behind her that was of the slightest value.'

'She even took her splendid sealskin cloak,' I said, with a smile.

'Yes, the fiend,' exclaimed my friend, with set teeth.

'Hush, call her the beautiful syren,' I remarked, 'for indeed she is a syren to have succeeded so completely in luring a shrewd business man like yourself to your fall.'

'Call me an infernal fool,' he cried bitterly. 'Now you see the position I am in. Besides the hundred pounds I paid, Mackinnon and Duncan say they hold me liable for the value of the articles, as I virtually vouched for the woman's honesty. Of course, as a point of law, they might have some difficulty in establishing that contention, but my reputation is at stake any way, and my directors may be disposed to take a serious view of the matter, and call upon me to resign, which would mean practically discharging me. Now there are two things I wish. I want, if possible, to prevent this wretched affair from becoming public, and I want you to bring all your abilities into play, and if possible arrest the woman before she has had time to dispose of the jewellery.'

'As regards publicity, that cannot be avoided,' I said. 'The arrest of the woman is scarcely less sure, but the recovery of the jewels is another thing.'

As I took my departure I felt that I had to deal with no ordinary criminal. This woman was evidently a swindler of a peculiarly daring and audacious type, and she was allied to confederates of no less ability. On the very face of it the robbery had been artfully matured and planned, and such adepts were not likely to have bungled in anything, and would have taken every means to have insured their safe retreat. The fact of the woman having gone away in the night seemed on the face of it to render it easy to trace her; and yet I was sure it was not a spontaneous act, but premeditated and consequently arranged for. No train went out of Glasgow earlier than five o'clock in the morning, and as these early trains seldom had many passengers, a lady-like, well-dressed woman would be conspicuous. Now, although I did not deem it probable that she had gone by train, at any rate not at that early hour, for she was too 'cute for that, it was nevertheless my duty to institute inquiries. But, as I expected, without any result. At none of the stations had such a woman been noticed. Nor with all the available resources at my command could I get the faintest clue to her whereabouts.

The case was a somewhat peculiar one. I felt that from the first, for they were no commonplace criminals I had to deal with, but evidently a well-organised and rich band of malefactors, who had elevated swindling to the position of an exact science. I was therefore on my mettle, and, quite apart from the professional zeal that moved me, I was desirous of bringing about their arrest for the sake of my good, but weak friend, the manager of the —— Hotel, who was threatened with almost social ruin through the unfortunate affair.

For a whole week I and those at my command exercised a sleepless vigilance, but not the shadow of a trace of the sweet lady in the sealskin could be found. Nor did our daily inquiries by telegraph in other parts of the country encourage us in our search. It really seemed a little short of marvellous how so conspicuous a woman could have so effectually avoided observation. But the fact that she had done so only served to prove that she was a perfect adept in her calling. The heads of the Criminal Investigation Department were of opinion that she had succeeded in getting out of the country. But I did not believe this. I even went further, and declared my conviction that she had not only not left the country, but had not even left Glasgow. I was laughed at for this, but I thought, 'Before I have done with this case you shall laugh on the other side of your mouths'.

Of course, I had very well-grounded reasons for the belief I held. Firstly, the woman left the hotel in the dead of night, and she possessed no luggage beyond what she could conveniently carry. Therefore she had no change of garments, and being elegantly dressed, to say nothing of the costly sealskin, she must have attracted attention had she proceeded to any of the railway stations. Secondly, the unusually artful ruse she adopted to trap the manager of the hotel proved that she was clever and far-seeing beyond the ordinary, and such a woman was not likely to place herself in jeopardy by incautious acts. The sham letter with its crest and motto showed how well planned the business had been, and it was also indicative of keen intelligence. Thirdly, she was not acting alone. Besides the manager of the hotel she had as her companions at the theatre another woman and the dark Jewish-looking man. This was confirmation at once that she was not acting alone, but was in league with confederates as clever as herself; and with so many clever heads at work their plans were not likely to miscarry for the want of forethought. This ratiocination could hardly fail to lead me to the conclusion that Mrs. Clara Penelope Fitzwilliams, as she was pleased to style herself, was lying *perdu* in Glasgow, and she would remain in concealment until the vigilance of the enemy relaxed, when she would make good her escape. And in the meantime she would rely upon her confederates getting clear with the swag.

As I have already stated, my views were not acquiesced in by my superiors, and so I resolved to keep my opinions to myself and work upon a plan of my own, by which I was prepared to let my reputation stand or fall. I knew that there were two other persons, at least, engaged in the swindle besides Mrs. Fitzwilliams. These two were the Jewish-looking man and the female who was in the box at the theatre on the night previous to the disappearance of the lady in the sealskin. The man I could have picked out from a thousand others. The second woman I had never seen, but she was described to me as being good-looking, about twenty years of age, a blonde with blue eyes, and a small wart on the side of her nose. The man had been introduced to the manager as Mr. William Drew, a stockbroker from London, on a visit to Glasgow, and the woman as his sister, 'Miss Nellie'. Now I felt perfectly certain that Miss Nellie was the tool, and would be used accordingly. I therefore kept one eye especially for her, and another for the principals. It was, of course, rather like looking for the proverbial needle in the bottle of hay to search in a great city, containing nearly three-quarters of a million of inhabitants, for a young woman who was described as a blonde, with a wart on her nose. A vast number of women are blondes and have warts on their noses. This particular wart was further stated to be by no means conspicuous or a disfigurement. Nevertheless, I had come from experience to regard the seemingly impossible as highly probable, and so I never felt in any way discouraged when unusual difficulties stared me in the face.

For nearly three weeks I devoted myself with untiring energy to this particular case, but day after day went by and I seemed to be no nearer the solution of the mystery. One night I happened to be prowling about the Broomielaw as the Dublin steam-packet was getting up steam and taking in cargo preparatory to starting on her voyage at eleven o'clock. It was a particularly disagreeable night. A misty rain was falling, and a cold wind was sweeping up the river.

I scarcely know what it was that induced me to linger about the wharf. But linger I did, some vague, shadowy presentiment that something might turn up attracting me. There was the usual scene of bustle and excitement, and a number of passengers began to gather about as the hour for departure drew near. These included the inevitable woman with three or four children and ever so many big bundles to look after; a soldier or two, and a sailor, who had been soaking themselves with the villainous compound sold in the neighbourhood of the Broomielaw under the name of whisky. There were some working men and women, and several cattle drovers and pig dealers. All these people were of an exceedingly commonplace type—people who had to be content with the lees and dregs of life and found living hard. Nevertheless there was not a face I did not peer into according to my wont, and as I read in many of them the story of hopeless struggle, or of vice and craft, of heartaches and bitterness and repining, I sighed a sigh for poor humanity.

The second bell had rung, and the steam was blowing off with a deafening roar. A little crowd of friends and acquaintances had gathered on the wharf, and there was much shaking of hands and some weeping, diversified by farewell nips from flat bottles which had been purchased in neighbouring public-houses. The third bell clanged out, and the roaring steam went swirling away in dense clouds into the darkness of the night. Suddenly I caught sight of two figures as they came out of the shadows of the shed into the flaring light of the flickering gas-lamps. These two figures at once attracted my attention. One was a man seemingly bowed with age, and with long white hair falling about his shoulders. The other, presumably his daughter, was a young woman, dressed neatly in black, and wearing a hat and thick fall. The old man carried a box, and the girl a bundle. Making their way through the crowd, they went up the gateway and on board the vessel. As they passed by the lamps at the gateway I got a brief glimpse of the woman's face, and I saw that she was young, a blonde, and had a small wart upon her nose. Instantly all my instincts were aroused. Were these the people, I wondered, that I was searching for? I had little time for consideration. I might or might not be right, but, as I stated at the beginning of this article, I come to quick decisions, and am quick to act, and I hold by the proverb which says, 'The man who hesitates is lost'. Already the warps were cast loose, the gangway was hauled up, and the engines of the vessel had made a revolution to ease her head off.

'I will shadow these people,' I said to myself, 'and will find out who they are.' At some risk I sprang on board, and in another few minutes we were steaming slowly down the Clyde. I soon found that the old man and his daughter had taken cabin tickets, but I contented myself with the steerage. It was a rough night, and as I knew that those I was shadowing could not escape from me while we were on the sea unless they jumped overboard, I secured a berth and turned in.

The following day as we neared Dublin the weather improved, and most of the passengers were on deck, but, though I searched eagerly, I saw nothing of the old man and young girl, and I learned from the steward that they were in their respective cabins. The vessel reached her destination, and as soon as she was moored my party made their appearance, and mingling with the crowd, went on shore, carrying their small quantity of luggage. My suspicions were now thoroughly aroused. The fact of their coming on board at the last moment, and remaining in their berths till the vessel was moored, seemed to me in themselves suspicious incidents. I noted also that both the girl and the man seemed to shun notice. Of course this would have escaped the observation of an outsider, but my profession had quickened my powers of observation, and the most infinitesimal acts were to me signs of deep import.

When the old man and the young woman got on shore they engaged an outside car, and as soon as they had driven off I jumped on another and told my driver to keep the first one in view, and in due course I saw it arrive at the door of the Royal Hotel, where the boots received the travellers' things, and the car was dismissed. I felt that they were safe now for a little while; and as I had nothing with me but what I stood in, I went into a shop, purchased a railway rug and a small portmanteau, and thus furnished presented myself at the Royal, where I engaged a room. An hour later I strolled into the breakfast room, where my people were seated in a recess enjoying, evidently with keen appetites, a sumptuous breakfast. I secured a table so that I could command a full view of them, and then ordered my own breakfast. Long before I had finished I was convinced that my journey was justified, and I would have staked everything I possessed on my opinion that the old man was not an old man at all, but a young one. He did not eat as an old man eats. His movements were not those of an old man; neither did he laugh, speak, nor act as age does. Therefore I concluded that if they were not the particular people I wanted they were nevertheless lawbreakers of some kind, and I should make a haul anyway, so that my journey would not be fruitless. They had given their names as Mr. Charles Schofield and Miss Schofield, of London.

In the course of the morning Mr. Schofield and Miss went out, and so did I, and I took exactly the same direction as Mr. Schofield and Miss took. Before I had followed them very far I saw them enter a shop in Abbey Street. It was a nondescript sort of shop—dirty as to external appearances, while the small window was filled with a very miscellaneous lot of articles, including old swords and pistols, antique jewellery, gold lace, epaulettes, old clocks, battered silver spoons, teapots and urns, and such like rubbish, all of which no doubt had a market value.

What did my people want in such a place? No good, of that I was convinced. I waited fully an hour before they came out. Then they returned to the hotel, and I took the opportunity to slip away to the chief police station, where I ascertained that the owner of the shop in Abbey Street bore a very indifferent reputation, and was suspected of being a purchaser of stolen goods. On hearing this I felt sure I was on the right track at last, and it was with very pleasurable feelings I returned to the hotel. For the rest of the day I scarcely ever lost sight of Mr. Schofield and his daughter, and when darkness had fallen I saw them go out, the man carrying the box I had seen him carry on board the vessel at Glasgow. They engaged a car, and I another, and as I suspected they would, they drove straight to the shop in Abbey Street. I immediately went at full speed to the nearest police station, and returning with two constables, who were to remain ready for a call outside, I entered. It was some minutes before any one came to me. Then from a little room, the door of which had a glass window screened with a green curtain, the owner appeared—a snuffy little old man, wearing a faded dressing-gown and a skull-cap. I inquired the price of an old watch in the window, and as he went to the window to reach the article out I darted into the room alluded to. Mr. Schofield and Miss were there. Something was on a table in the centre of the room, but the something was covered over with a cloth. I snatched the cloth away, and revealed a quantity of jewellery, which from the description I at once recognised as the stolen property. For a moment the man and girl seemed paralysed with astonishment. But it was only for a moment, and as the man recovered his presence of mind be put his hand behind him. In an instant I had blown a whistle for my assistants, and sprang on my man before he could draw the revolver he carried in a back pocket. But even then he did not yield without a struggle, in the course of which his grey beard came away, and I found that my captive was my old acquaintance, the dark-complexioned Jewish-looking man whom I had first seen weeks ago on the platform at Glasgow. In less than twenty minutes we had our captures, including the proprietor of the shop, safely under lock and key, and, comparing the jewellery with the list I carried, found it was all there with the exception of a small diamond ring. When the man was searched we discovered letters upon him all written in cipher, but addressed to 'John Byron, Esq.,' at a house in a very quiet and obscure street in Glasgow. That night I started back, without even apprising the authorities in Glasgow of my capture, and as soon as I arrived I waited for nothing, but proceeded immediately to John Byron, Esquire's, address, and as a bold stroke I inquired for Mrs. Byron. A respectable-looking middle-aged woman opened the door to me, and I saw immediately that I had realised the old proverb, 'Fortune favours the bold,' for the woman said that Mrs. Byron was ill in bed, and could not see any one. I requested her to go at once and say that a great friend of her husband wished to see her, and when she had mounted the stair to deliver my message I followed rapidly, and waiving all ceremony under the circumstances, burst into the room which I saw her enter, and lying in bed and truly ill was the beautiful lady of the sealskin cloak, and on her finger was the missing diamond ring.

Realising in an instant that something was wrong she uttered a suppressed scream and fainted. The landlady was of course much astonished; and as, from her manner, I was sure she did not know the character of her lodgers, I showed her my badge, and told her I had a warrant for the arrest of the woman known as Mrs. Byron. My first care was to make sure that there was no weapon concealed under the pillows or in the room. Then I assisted to bring the invalid round, and when she had recovered consciousness I said I would remain outside the door while she dressed, but she assured me she was too ill to do this, and so I sent for the divisional police surgeon, who, having examined her, certified that she was suffering from congestion of the left lung, but that with care she might be removed to the prison infirmary, where, in spite of her protestations, we soon had her.

From inquiries I learned that her real name was the somewhat unromantic one of Ellen Smith; and the girl we had arrested in Dublin was her sister. They were the daughters of a captain in the merchant service who had been drowned at sea, their mother having died while they were young. They had been well brought up by an aunt, but had fallen under the evil influences of a Jew named Solomon Boss, *alias* Schofield, *alias* Byron, *alias* many other things, and for several years they had lived by systematic swindling. As no former convictions were proved against the women, Ellen got off with two years' hard labour, and her sister with twelve months. But the man, who was an old offender, was sentenced to ten years' penal servitude; while the man who kept the shop in Dublin was released, as nothing could be proved against him. I was really sorry for the two women, and Ellen's beauty and really charming manner won her numerous admirers, and during the trial she received several offers of marriage from infatuated men. Of course my friend the manager of the ——Hotel was delighted at my success in bringing these criminals to justice, and restoring the stolen jewels to the rightful owners. But, considering Ellen Smith's seductive ways, and her great charm of face and figure, I was not surprised that he had fallen a victim to the lady of the sealskin jacket.

The Tuft of Red Hair

I was busy one morning collating certain documentary evidence in my possession with a view to the prosecution of a notorious begging-letter impostor, when a telegram was put into my hand. It had been despatched from Edinburgh, and was worded as follows:

COME HERE IMMEDIATELY. WANT YOU TO TAKE UP AN IMPORTANT CASE. DON'T LOSE A MOMENT. AMPLE COMPENSATION FOR SERVICES.

Although the sender of this urgent message was a stranger to me personally, he was well-known as a cheap and advertising tailor in a most extensive way of business in the Modern Athens. It is not necessary to mention his real name, but for the purpose of this narrative I will refer to him as Mr. Wilson. I was a little puzzled how to act, for the trial of the begging-letter impostor was to commence in three days, and my personal attendance was all but indispensable, for I had been working the case up, and had all the details at my finger ends. I therefore went down to the central office to confer with my chief, and to ask him if he had any idea why Mr. Wilson had sent for me.

'I don't know,' he replied, 'unless it has something to do with the murder that was committed in Edinburgh the day before yesterday.'

This was the first I had heard of the murder, but I learned then that a peculiarly atrocious crime had been perpetrated two days before, that was on Saturday, and up to that moment no information had been received of the arrest of any suspected person. The result was that a few hours later I found myself in Edinburgh, and I at once sought an interview with Mr. Wilson.

He was a large, rough-spoken, vulgar sort of man, with a great display of watch-chain and rings. He was very voluble in his speech, and had quickly informed me that he had a wife and ten children, that his nearest relative had been his sister, but that two days ago she had been barbarously murdered in one of the old houses in the Canongate. Mr. Wilson was at great pains to impress me with the fact that for many years there had been absolute estrangement between him and his sister, arising originally out of family disputes in connection with property.

It was, alas! the old story of worldly greed and sordid interests being allowed to override natural affection and destroy heart ties. It was not long before I discovered that money was Mr. Wilson's idol, and he bowed down and worshipped it, though outwardly he was professedly a God-fearing man, a rigid church-goer, and a liberal supporter of the church. But his spiritual life, as is generally so with men who take such pains to trumpet their godliness, was a sham, while his carnal life was a great reality. Mr. Wilson was a lover of the fleshpots of Egypt, and he believed not in the mortification of the flesh for the benefit of the soul. Like mine Uncle Toby, he loved to take his ease, and did so so far as his anxiety about the accumulation of worldly wealth would permit him to be easy.

Mr. Wilson, I soon saw, was not so much concerned about his sister's cruel death, though he outwardly professed to be, as he was about her property. It appeared that she had an income of between seven and eight hundred a year, which was derived from real estate, and in the absence of a will to the contrary this property would revert to her brother. But not only had her house been stripped of everything valuable, but neither will nor deeds of the property could be found. If she had made a will no trace of it was forthcoming, and her title deeds had vanished. It was generally believed also that she was in the habit of keeping a considerable amount of cash in the house, but not a single shilling had been found.

'It's just awful to think what has been lost through her pigheadedness,' wailed Mr. Wilson, as he gave me the foregoing particulars. 'For years she has been a disgrace to my family, and has squandered her money in dissipation, and now that she has been called away there's nothing left. It's just awful, awful.' His anxiety about the money disgusted me, but I kept my thoughts to myself. 'Now I want you to leave no stone unturned to recover the stolen deeds,' he went on, 'and to find out if she had made a will'.

I shall use every means in my power to track the murderer down,' I replied pointedly.

'Ay, ay, do,' he replied eagerly, 'but don't forget the property'.

When, much to my relief, I got away from the garrulous Mr. Wilson, I proceeded at once to the scene of the murder. The deceased, although never married, had been known in the neighbourhood as Mrs. Rennie. She had occupied for several years a small flat at the very top of one of the old tenement-houses in the Canongate. In the poor locality in which she had elected to reside she was regarded as being very wealthy and very eccentric. She lived entirely alone, and was much given to dissipation.

On entering the room where the crime had been perpetrated a ghastly sight met my view. With the exception of the body having been placed on the bed, nothing had been disturbed in the room, which bore evidence of the awful death struggle that had been enacted there. Mrs. Rennie had been a powerful and muscular woman, and she had fought desperately for her life. A table was capsized and two of the legs broken off. A chair was smashed literally to pieces, and the long curtains that screened the window had been torn down. The floor, which was without carpet, was like the floor of a shambles, and the struggling feet of victim and assassin had squelched and trodden the blood about until all the boards were marked with gory patches. On one of the walls from about six feet high down to the skirting board was a great uneven mass of blood stain, as if in the awful fight for life the victim had been pressed against the wall while the hot blood was spurting from her wounds. A heavy brass candlestick was lying on the floor. It was blood-stained, and all dented and twisted out of shape, telling too surely that it had been used as an instrument to batter the life out of the wretched woman. Having made a cursory examination of the theatre of the tragedy, I proceeded to an examination of the victim, who had been covered with a blood-stained sheet. Now, I can fairly lay claim to being a strong nerved man, for during the many years I have followed my calling I have beheld harrowing sights enough and to spare, but I started back in horror as I turned down that sheet, and revealed the face of the dead woman. Never before had I seen such a look of unutterable and concentrated horror as had been frozen by death on the marble face. The mouth was open, as if it had been struck rigid in the very act of uttering a cry of terror. The eyes were literally starting from the head, and on the left cheek was a ghastly wound, which had laid the bone bare. The head had been beaten to a pulp, and in parts the brain was oozing out. It was evident that when she had been attacked she had been preparing herself for bed, as she was only slightly attired, and some of her garments had been torn to pieces, and hung in rags about the body. Round the throat and under the ears were large purple marks, showing the pressure of murderous fingers. On the left shoulder was a jagged wound, and there were many wounds and marks about the chest. Two fingers on the right hand were broken, one being torn off with the exception of a fragment of skin. Ribs were also broken on each side, suggesting that she had fallen across the table with her murderer on the top of her. The left hand was tightly clenched, so tightly, in fact, that the nails had entered the palm of the hand.

In age the murdered woman would be under forty. She had a somewhat masculine but not unpleasant type of features, which were of a mould indicating determination of will and strength of character. She had a quantity of brown hair, while her figure was exceedingly well developed and symmetrical, so that in life she must have been a by no means unattractive person.

So much for the physical aspects of this dreadful crime, which was one of unusual atrocity. Some human fiend in a paroxysm of hellish fury had beaten his victim into a mangled mass of torn flesh and broken bones; and the weapon that had been used was too obviously the heavy candlestick which was lying there, mute evidence of the awful fact.

My next step was to make a thorough examination of the room. Near the overturned table were broken glasses, a smashed bottle that had held whiskey, the smell revealing that; some biscuits, a whole lemon and some pieces of lemon, a sugar bowl with sugar, a loaf of bread, and part of a mutton ham. These things were scattered about the floor, indicating that the victim of the tragedy had been partaking of supper before she was attacked, and she had not been taking it alone. I came to the conclusion easily, for there were two plates, two toddy tumblers, and two knives and forks. That fact, therefore, was important. A large wooden chest had been ransacked, the lid having been forced with a poker which had broken in halves, one half lying on the floor, the other inside the chest, which now only contained some wearing apparel all crumpled and huddled together, and much blood-stained. This proved that the murderer and thief had ransacked the chest after the crime. The door of a press stood slightly ajar, and on opening the door I saw evidence of hasty overhauling here, this press evidently having been a receptacle for papers, letters, &c., and these had been tossed on one side, and half a dozen silver spoons had either been overlooked or purposely left behind as being not worth carrying under the circumstances.

On the floor I picked up a crumpled and bloodstained one pound note. The murderer had handled this, and had let it fall by accident, and as it was lying near the chest the inference I drew was that he had found a quantity of notes in the chest, and in crushing them into his pocket had let this one drop.

Having completed my survey of the room I turned my attention once more to the corpse, and made a most minute examination of it. Between the fingers of the clenched hand I observed one or two coarse red hairs protruding. I knew the value of those hairs, and as I could not open the hand I returned later on with a medical man, and with his aid I took from the palm of the dead woman a tuft of red hair, which, being curled and twisted, showed that it had formed part of a man's whisker, and this little bunch had been torn out by the wretched woman in her death agony. Very carefully indeed did I wrap that tuft of hair up in paper and place it in my pocket-book, for it was an invaluable clue to the perpetrator of the crime.

My investigation finished, I arrived at three conclusions.

Firstly. The murderer was a powerful man, for a weakly man could not have subdued such a muscular woman.

Secondly. He had come home to supper with her, and had inflamed himself with drink, which accounted for the savage fury which was evidenced by the mutilated condition of the body.

Thirdly. The murderer must have been well acquainted with the habits of the woman, and have known that she was possessed of valuable property. For it was the hope of big gains that led him to the commission of such a barbarous crime. That is to say, he had not murdered her in a mere outburst of passion, the result of some dispute. It had been a premeditated crime, and I mentally sketched out the scene. The two had supped and partaken freely of toddy. The toddy kettle still stood on the hob. It was a two-pint kettle, but now did not contain more than half a cupful of water. The pieces of lemon, too, when put together, showed that two whole lemons had been used in brewing the toddy, and it was safe to argue from this that certainly not less than eight glasses of toddy had been drunk. The feast finished, the woman was in the act of disrobing herself when the man attacked her with the candlestick, thinking no doubt to stun her at once. Unsteady with drink, however, he had failed, and then had ensued that terrific struggle, until the poor victim had succumbed through loss of blood and exhaustion.

Such, then, was the story of the murder so far as the inanimate things in the room told it to me. The crime had been committed some time between Saturday night and Sunday morning. That much was known. The deed was discovered on Sunday morning about nine o'clock, by a boy who had been in the habit for a long time of leaving a pint of milk. He used to put the can down by the door, but on this particular morning he was surprised to find the door open. He called Mrs. Rennie, but getting no answer thought she had stepped out for a moment, and so he went in to put the can on the table. Then the truth was revealed, and the alarm given. A medical man and policeman were soon on the spot, and the doctor concluded that the woman had been dead for some hours, as the body was quite cold, and the rigor mortis had set in.

In searching for the trail of the assassin I saw that I had little to hope for from the residents in the tenement. They were an ignorant and hard-drinking lot. Mrs. Rennie's rooms were next to the roof. The people below her were a shoemaker and his wife and their unmarried grown-up son. They had all three been the worse for liquor on the Saturday night, and had heard nothing unusual.

I made a careful examination of the stone stairs all the way down. On the landing, near Mrs. Rennie's door, and on six steps of the first flight were distinct traces of blood. These traces had been made by the boot-soles of the murderer as he left the scene of his crime. With my own hands I swept up the dirt of the landing and the steps, and secured it in a paper packet for future use, for I felt it might prove a link in a chain of evidence.

As might naturally be supposed, such a bloodthirsty crime caused intense excitement throughout the city, and for many days the hue and cry was hot, but a fortnight passed and no arrest had been made. This was partly due to the fact that no description, even a vague one, could be given of the murderer, as no one had seen him enter in company with Mrs. Rennie. My own theory, as already stated, was that he was a powerful man with red whiskers. I have given my reasons for assuming that he was strong. That he had red whiskers was conclusively proved by the tuft of red hair in the dead woman's hand.

As the days passed by without bringing any result, Mr. Wilson grew irritable and excited, although I told him that I felt confident of arresting the murderer sooner or later. But he seemed to think that a detective should be endowed with superhuman powers, and be able to nose out a criminal as a bloodhound can scent blood. The most careful search had failed to discover any deeds of the house property, and it was obvious that there was no will, for had there been one in existence, some lawyer would have known of it, and would have come forward by this time. Mr. Wilson knew little or nothing of the habits of his sister, beyond that she occasionally gave way to dissipation. But what he was most concerned about was the loss of the deeds and her money, for he felt convinced that she only spent a small portion of her income and must have hoarded the rest, and that hoard possibly had been accumulating for years. It chanced one day that I was at Mr. Wilson's when a man came into the room where we were to ask Mr. Wilson some business question. My instinctive habit led me to scrutinise him, and I was astonished to find that he answered to the mental picture I had drawn for myself of the murderer. That is, he was a powerful man, he stood about five feet ten and a half. He had broad shoulders and a massive chest, and he had bushy red whiskers. His face suggested that he was in the habit of indulging occasionally in liquor. In other respects there was nothing remarkable about it. He was pale, like most tailors, and had that sad expression of countenance which is peculiar to men who follow his trade.

'Who is that?' I asked of Mr. Wilson when the man had left the room.

'Well, he is one of my best workmen, and I am sorry to say I am going to lose him, for he gave me notice a few days ago, as he is going to join a brother who is in Australia. His only fault is that he drinks a little, and is a most passionate man.'

'What is his name?'

'George Fraser.'

'Is he married?'

'No. I believe not. He lives with an aunt.' Then, looking at me for some moments in mute surprise, he burst into a laugh which was rather expressive of contempt for my stupidity, and exclaimed, 'Surely you don't think Fraser is the murderer?'

'Well, he strikes me as being a man who is not altogether incapable of committing a crime,' I answered cautiously.

Mr. Wilson lapsed into thoughtfulness. Then presently he remarked, 'That man is a clever workman, and has been with me for ten years. I have offered to double his wages if he will stop, but he won't.'

'Did he know your sister?'

'Yes. For three or four years after he came she was in the habit of visiting me occasionally, and sometimes I sent her messages by Fraser. But that is years ago.'

As I rose to go I asked Mr. Wilson if he thought Fraser knew who I was. But he expressed a pretty confident opinion that he did not, and so, having obtained the man's address, I took my departure, with a strong suspicion asserting itself in my mind that I was at last on the track of the criminal, and I justified my suspicion thus: Fraser is a powerful man and has red whiskers. That is one point— a small one I admit, but nevertheless a point. Fraser, after ten years' service, and with good wages which he could have doubled, suddenly announces his intention of emigrating to Australia. That is another point, and a stronger one. Fraser was acquainted with Mrs. Rennie. That is a still stronger point. Fraser, according to Mr. Wilson, drank a little, and was a passionate man. All these points I threw into the balance against the improbabilities of his being the right man, and to my mind they seemed to outweigh them, and so I went direct to his lodgings in a house South Back of Canongate. This was in the immediate neighbourhood of the scene of the crime, and that seemed to me to be another point. He lived up five flats, with an aunt, who let lodgings. Before mounting up I bought a pair of men's boots, which I had made up into a parcel. I inquired of the aunt, who was a woman of about sixty, with a dissipated looking face, if George Fraser was in. Of course I was told no, so I said I had brought him a pair of new boots, and he told me to get his old ones to repair.

The aunt seemed surprised and a little puzzled, but exclaimed:

'I ken naething aboot it. But gin he telt you tae get his auld anes you had best come ben and seek them for yoursel', as I dinna mind which anes he wants done.'

She led me into her nephew's bedroom, a small, ill-lighted place, in which was a deep press in the wall. Opening the door of this press, she showed me three or four pairs of boots on the floor, while hanging up were several articles of clothing. I should have liked to examine these, but did not want to arouse her suspicion, so I took up one pair of boots after another and scrutinised them keenly. One pair only attracted my attention. I saw, or thought I saw, suspicions stains on the leather. I wrapped them up in my handkerchief, and thanking the woman, hurried away. As soon as I could get a cab I drove off to my friend, the late Professor Archer, the celebrated analytical chemist. He had a laboratory in his house, and we lost no time in examining the boots. The dirt from their soles was carefully scraped off and compared with the dirt I had swept up from the stairs and landing of the house where the murder had been committed. This dirt was placed under the microscope, with the result that the Professor expressed a guarded opinion that the dirt from the boots and the dirt from the stairs were identical. But in regard to the stains on the upper leather he was more pronounced, and said they had unmistakably been made by blood, but whether human blood or not was difficult then to say, and a more elaborate and searching test would be required to determine the fact. I felt, however, that I had gained another important link in the chain of circumstantial evidence, and leaving the boots with the Professor, I drove rapidly to the head police office, where I obtained the assistance of two plain-clothes constables, and we proceeded to Mr. Wilson's. I told him briefly I had reason to suspect Fraser of the murder, and intended to arrest him, but in order to avoid a scene asked him to send for the man. This was done, and never dreaming of the trap he was walking into, Fraser came in with a jaunty air. Before he could take in the scene I stepped up to him and said:

'I arrest you on suspicion of having murdered Mrs. Rennie.'

The man staggered back, and his face literally went green. Then he made a movement as if he intended to rush out, but my two assistants sprang on him and in a few moments we had him handcuffed. Then he set his lips hard, and breathing heavily through his nostrils he glared at me and exclaimed: 'You fool, I'll make you pay for this.'

I smiled to myself, knowing that it was an impotent threat of a doomed man, for I felt convinced now he was the criminal. We conveyed him at once to the jail, and during the journey he never spoke. As soon as we had him safely lodged I despatched a special messenger for Professor Archer, and when that gentleman arrived I produced the tuft of red hair I had taken from the dead woman's hand. When Fraser saw this and gathered our intention he became like a furious animal, and his face was horrible in its expression of wrath and passion, and this served to strengthen my conviction that we had the right man. For only a man capable of such fury could have committed such a crime. It took six stalwart warders to master him, and we had to strap him down to a bench.

A comparison of the tuft of hair with the hair on the wretch's face established their identity, both in texture and shade. But we had a surer test than this. The root of each human hair, as is well known, is enclosed in a sort of little sheath. When the hair is plucked forcibly out, this sheath is partly torn out also, with the result of leaving tiny lumps or swellings, and some redness. The redness soon goes off, but a powerful magnifying glass will reveal the tiny lumps for weeks afterwards. And such an examination of Fraser's cheek showed us that some portion of his whiskers had been forcibly torn away. Our next move was to search his lodgings, but we found none of the lost property, as I hoped we might, and an examination of his clothes revealed no blood stains. This was a disappointment to me, but nevertheless I never doubted but what I had got hold of the right person.

In due course he was put upon his trial, and by that time we had collected such a mass of circumstantial evidence as to leave no room to doubt the guilt of the prisoner. A verdict of guilty was accordingly returned, and he was sentenced to death.

For many days after his condemnation he preserved a sullen, brutish demeanour, and seemed to have utterly hardened himself against all attempts to bring him to a sense of his position. But as the day of his execution drew near he gave way to desperate despair, and when at last he came to fully realise the horror of his impending doom, he utterly broke down, though he continued to assert his innocence up to the very night previous to the execution. Unable, however, to endure his remorse any longer with the sounds of the workmen erecting the scaffold ringing in his ears, he sent for the chaplain in the dead of night, and he made a full and circumstantial confession. It appears that he had long carried on an intrigue with the wretched woman, who frequently supplied him with money. He knew that she kept large sums in her house, and had often been tempted to rob her. On the night of the murder they both drank freely, and he wanted her to let him have a considerable sum of money, which she refused. They had words, and suddenly as she stood with her back to him he seized the candlestick and struck her on the head, intending only to stun her. But she turned round and flew at him, and then ensued that sickening death struggle which, according to his own account, lasted for over half an hour. He found several hundred pounds in notes and gold in her box, together with her deeds, and all this property he carried off and buried in a box in a cellar which his aunt rented beneath the house in which he lived, and which she used for storing wood, coal, and other things in. The clothes he wore, and which were very much drenched with blood, he cut into pieces and burned in the kitchen grate; but he forgot about his boots, and had no knowledge of that damning piece of evidence, the tuft of red hair, which the dead woman gripped in her stony hand. His intention was to go to Australia, where he hoped to enjoy unmolested his ill-gotten gains. He had laid his plans well, as he thought; but murder will out, for a Divine vengeance pursueth him who sheddeth man's blood, and I was destined to be a humble instrument in working that vengeance out. The money and the deeds were, of course, recovered from the cellar, and handed over to Mr. Wilson, the rightful heir, on his establishing his claim to them.

The Pearl Necklace

◈

L ate one Saturday evening a young and neatly-dressed girl presented herself at a large pawn-office on the south side of Glasgow, and asked for a loan on a pearl necklace. As is well known, the number of pledges taken in by a pawnbroker in a poor neighbourhood on a Saturday night is very few indeed, as compared with the pledges that are given out. Those that are redeemed are generally articles of clothing that are needed for the Sunday wear, and part of the week's wages are appropriated regularly to this purpose. As soon as Monday morning comes the clothes 'go up the spout' again till the week end. Saturday night, therefore, is always a busy time in these pawn-offices up to the very hour of closing.

In the particular office alluded to they happened to be unusually busy, and a great crowd of unwashed people were clamouring for their bundles when the girl entered. She could not get up to the counter for some little time, owing to the number of customers, and when she did succeed she was attended to by a youth who had been an assistant in that office for about four years.

'What do you wish out?' he demanded of the girl, naturally thinking she had come to redeem a pledge.

'Nothing,' she answered, 'but I want you to give me a loan on this,' putting something on the counter, the something being wrapped in a pocket handkerchief.

The assistant undid the handkerchief, which enfolded a small, common cardboard box, and on lifting the lid of the box he saw a pearl necklace lying on a piece of black velvet. Taking the trinket under a gas bracket the better to see it, he examined it critically and came to the conclusion at once that it was valuable. The pearls were not only large but unusually perfect, and they were set in the finest gold.

'How much do you want on this?' he asked, as he went back to the counter.

'Four pounds,' she answered, after some hesitation.

The man was surprised at the smallness of the amount demanded, as the necklace was exceedingly valuable, and his intention was to take it to his master to examine; but the master was very much occupied, so the assistant asked the girl her name and address, which she gave as Harriet Millar, 119 Greenside Street, and without further questioning he made out the ticket, handed her the four pounds, and the transaction being so far concluded, she took her departure.

On the Monday morning following I was requested to go to the pawn-office in accordance with a request made by the proprietor to my chief at the Central. On arriving at the shop I was at once shown into the proprietor's private room, and without any preliminaries, he said:

'I felt it my duty to send for you, as late on Saturday night an assistant of mine lent four pounds on a pearl necklace. On his showing me this after the shop had been closed I was struck by its magnificence, and as it cannot be worth a half-penny less than three hundred pounds, I feel convinced the person who pledged it did not know its value, otherwise she would never have asked only four pounds on a thing worth three hundred. Moreover, it is so unusual for us to be offered pledges of such value that my suspicions were aroused, and this morning I sent one of my men down to the address given, but he reports that there is no such number in the street, and he could hear nothing of such a person as Harriet Millar. That in itself would hardly be a justification for suspicion, as very few pledgers ever give their correct names and addresses, but what I can't get over is that such a trifling amount should have been asked for so valuable an article.'

I agreed with the pawnbroker that there were elements of suspicion in the circumstance, and on examining the necklace I was no less struck than he had been by its magnificence. I judged it to be of Italian workmanship, and not only were the pearls of unusual beauty, but the setting displayed the very highest art of the gold-smith's craft. I made inquiries of the assistant who took the pledge if he could describe the girl who brought it, but he was rather hazy on the subject, though he thought she would be about eighteen, that she had reddish hair, and was neatly dressed.

There was not much in this vague description to go upon, but, making a few notes, I advised the pawnbroker, in case anyone should come to take the pledge out, to detain the person if he or she could not give a satisfactory account of the possession of so valuable an article, and to lose no time in sending for a policeman. With this advice I left, feeling pretty sure, when all the circumstances were considered, that the necklace had been stolen, and that the thief was utterly ignorant of its real value, otherwise four pounds would never have been accepted for a thing that would have brought a hundred at least.

Two days later, that is to say, on the Wednesday, we received information from Carlisle that on the preceding Thursday a daring burglary had been committed at the residence of a gentleman liv-ing at Wreay, near Carlisle. This gentleman's residence, which was a large, old-fashioned country mansion, was situated in a very lonely spot, and during the absence of the family, who had gone to London to be present at the marriage of a son, the house was broken into, and a great quantity of jewellery, silver plate, and other valuable property had been carried away. The report stated that only four servants were in the house at the time, namely, the butler, a coach-man, the cook, and a chambermaid. The burglary had not been discovered until the return of the family on Monday, as during their absence the greater part of the rooms were locked up. Entry had been effected over the roof of a greenhouse, by which means the robbers had lifted the window of a bath-room, and so got into the house. They then made their way to a spare room containing a safe. In this safe the jewellery and the plate were always locked up when the family were away, a circumstance that the thieves must have known, for they confined their depredations entirely to this room.

With great skill and dexterity the safe had been forced, and its valuable contents carried off. These were estimated to be worth nearly ten thousand pounds. Having secured their booty, the vagabonds went out by the same way they had entered, and no one in the house knew anything at all about the robbery until on Monday, when the butler went to the room to obtain some plate for the family use, and he then found the safe broken open.

We were further informed that up to the hour of sending the report off no clue to the thieves had been discovered; and that they were evidently very expert and practised hands, and probably were part of a gang. We were requested to give information to all pawnbrokers and jewellers in the principal towns of Scotland, and to be on the alert. Then followed a list of the things stolen, and amongst them was:

'A pearl necklace, set in fine gold, of Italian workmanship. A family heirloom of great value. The pearls are unusually large and perfect, and the setting is peculiar to Italy.'

This description left no room to doubt that the necklace which had been pledged on the Saturday night for four pounds was the one referred to. And the fact argued that, however expert the thieves might have been as housebreakers, they had not much knowledge of the value of jewellery, for four pounds would never have been accepted for a thing worth as many hundreds; and this act of stupidity on their part raised my hopes that I should be able to lay my hands on the criminals with comparatively little difficulty if they belonged to Glasgow. But I could not overlook the fact that expert criminals who wish to dispose of the proceeds of a burglary generally go to towns where they are quite unknown, and in this instance appearances favoured the view that the young girl who had pawned the necklace had come into the town for that especial purpose.

As was my custom, however, I began to theorise, and to work the problem out in my own mind to a logical conclusion, with this result —that, as the hour was late when the girl visited the pawnbroker's, she must have passed that night at least in the city or the immediate neighbourhood, and therefore must have left some trace behind her. But it suggested itself to me as a feasible probability that she either belonged to Glasgow or some place not far off. That she was not one of the actual thieves— that is, she had no hand in breaking into the house, but was connected with them. She might be the daughter of one of them, or a sweetheart. That the thieves, or some of them, belonged to Scotland. Otherwise, why did they come so far north from the scene of their operations? If they had been English they would probably have gone south.

I therefore commenced my quest for the malefactors with a firm conviction that they were *habitués* of Scotland, and had their domicile in one or other of the large towns situated within easy distance of the border.

The clue which I had to work from was very slender, for only a vague description of the girl was obtainable. But still I was hopeful, and determined to lose no time in trying to get on the trail of the criminals before it faded. I therefore disguised myself as a Jew pedlar; that is a pedlar ostensibly, but in reality a snapper up of unconsidered trifles; for, as the reader will infer, an *honest* pedlar would hardly be in touch with the criminal classes.

I may be permitted perhaps to suggest a picture of myself in this disguise, stating by the way that nature has endowed me with a very prominent organ of smell, although I have not a trace of Israelitish strain in my composition. An olive complexion, deep set eyes with shaggy eyebrows, and dark hair, are likewise my physical characteristics, so I am enabled to play the *rôle* of the Jew with considerable success. In the instance with which I am dealing I wore a long beard which I prized highly, for it was presented to me many years ago with an assurance that it had proved part of one of the many disguises assumed as occasion required by the world-renowned French detective, Lecoq, in whose footsteps I have humbly endeavoured to follow. A battered, soft, felt hat, a faded and frayed long coat of an undeterminable colour, old and much worn pantaloons, and boots so antiquated that by the natural effluxion of time certain portions of the uppers had parted company with the soles, thereby disclosing the true anatomical proportions of the toes, completed my costume. While as a finishing touch to the illusion I carried a pedlar's box, containing some tapes, pins, thread, &c., and a few articles of very common and very cheap Brummagem jewellery. But amongst these latter I had taken care, for reasons that will presently appear, to include a cheap imitation pearl necklace. This was my bait whereby I hoped to catch some big fish.

Thus attired and equipped, I took my way one Saturday evening to a very low lodging-house in the neighbourhood of the Broomielaw, and which was notoriously the rendezvous of thieves. In a large room, or rather vault, of this place these outcasts and pariahs of society found shelter. A large coke fire in the centre of the vault diffused warmth and noxious gases at the same time, while heaps of straw answered the purpose of beds. This barren comfort could be enjoyed for two-pence a night, while another two-pence secured a hunk of coarse bread and a bowl of soup made from—heaven knows what.

When I entered this den of evil things there were about a dozen men present, ranging in ages from seventeen to sixty. Some were warming their chilled blood at the coke fire; others seated at a wooden bench were wolfing bowls of the steaming concoction yclept soup; while three or four were stretched on the straw smoking.

My entry was the signal for a general start, for these people who make war on society are ever on the alert like wild animals.

'Goot-evening, shentlemens,' I exclaimed to reassure them, as I rubbed my blue nose on my coat sleeve, and stretched forth my other hand over the blazing coke.

A big raw-boned man here rose from the straw, and coming close to me and peering into my face, he asked, with a covert threat:

'Are you a cross-man?' (*Cross-man* is thieves' slang for those who get their living by dishonest means.)

I winked at him knowingly, and with a smirking smile answered:

'I am a very honest shentleman, but I think that property is not divided fairly, and when I finds some men who have more than their share I helps myself to some of it.'

There was a roar of laughter at this, and the big hulking loafer asked if I was going to stand 'a blow out of belly-timber.' (*Belly-timber*, slang for food.)

'Vell, shentlemens,' I answered, 'trade is not so goot vid me. I have padded the hoof (walked) from Carlisle, but trade was not goot, shentlemen. Trust me, it was not.'

With half-closed eyes I watched narrowly through the old horn spectacles I wore what effect my words would have, and I saw significant looks exchanged by three or four of the men gathered round the fire.

'What was the news in Carlisle, cully?' asked the man who had first addressed me.

I knew at once what this question referred to. It meant had I heard any news of the robbery. I did not expect to find those I was looking for here, but I did expect to pick up some information; for amongst the criminal classes the news of a crime spreads like wildfire, and I was perfectly certain that some of these blackguards would be well posted up in the particulars of the burglary at Wreay. I glanced round warily, and then, lowering my voice and speaking very confidentially, I replied:

'I heard that some shentlemens had been on a visit to a country-house at Wreay, and had enjoyed themselves very much, but I do not know who the shentlemens were.'

More glances were exchanged, and then a young fellow remarked:

'I'll bet a bawbee that Rusty Dan was in that treat.'

'Who is Rusty Dan, shentlemens?' I asked, glancing from one to the other.

'What, don't you know Rusty Dan?' cried the young fellow. 'He's Dan M'Lean, of Paisley.'

The hulking man, who had first spoken, looked reprovingly at the speaker, as if to caution him not to be so free with his tongue. Of course this look did not escape my notice, and guessing its meaning, I made a motion as if to open my box, saying the while:

'Oh, I was only curious to know because I met a shentleman—a very nice shentleman—in Carlisle, and I did some trade vid him.'

This had the effect I expected. It aroused curiosity, and my listeners pressed forward eagerly, and I heard one remark to another, *sotto voce*:

'The blooming Sheeny (Jew) has got some of the swag.'

I at once showed that I heard this, and said:

'Vell, shentlemen, I bought a little thing, but I do not think it is very goot.' Here I opened my box, and from an inner drawer produced the sham pearl necklace. This was passed round from one dirty pair of hands to another, and critically examined, and then a man who had not before spoken said:

'It ain't rumbo' (genuine).

'I thought so, too,' I returned; 'but then, you see, I did not pay much for it, and I hope to make some profit.'

'You will have to sell it to a mug (flat) then,' said one.

I laughed as though I was quite prepared to do that, and thoroughly understood my business. I relieved myself of the box, and putting it on a seat sat on it, and ordered a bowl of the soup, which I managed, even at the risk of nauseating myself, to drink.

In a little while the place was quiet again. The majority of the lodgers had buried themselves in the straw, but the young fellow who had mentioned 'Rusty Dan's' name and another man were playing cards with a greasy, dirty pack that must have been carried about in one of their pockets for many a long month. I took a seat near these fellows, and watched the game for some little time, and when they had finished I said to the young man, speaking very confidentially:

'Perhaps Rusty Dan, as he has been out visiting, may have some more lumber to dispose of. If so, I should like to trade. Where is he to be found? '

'Well, he stays in Paisley when he's at home.'

'What like is he?'

'A tall fellow. Pock-marked, and with brick red hair. That's why we call him Rusty Dan.'

I did not ask any further questions for fear of arousing suspicion. But exceedingly pleased with the information I had got, I announced my intention of retiring to rest, and selecting a corner, I made a pillow of my box, and pretended to fall asleep. I passed some hours in the horrible place, and once or twice really did fall asleep. When daylight broke I hurried away, glad enough to get out of the fœtid atmosphere, compared to which the dense smoky fog that then hung over the city seemed pure and delightful.

Hurrying to my home, and changing my dress, I proceeded without loss of time to Paisley, and before long I ascertained that Mr. Daniel M'Lean, *alias* Rusty Dan, occupied a flat with his wife and daughter in a by no means disreputable quarter of the town, and that nothing was known against him. Amongst his neighbours he was supposed to have private means, and he was known to attend race meetings, and was frequently away from home, as he was at this moment when I was so anxious to make his acquaintance. Of course I was by no means certain that this gentleman was the man I wanted, but nevertheless I felt it highly desirable that I should know him, and this for two reasons. Firstly, he was known in the thieves' kitchen at Glasgow, and a man is judged by his associates; and, secondly, his movements seemed to me to be mysterious. I therefore resolved to learn something more about him without loss of time. With a view to this end I attired myself in a manner which was suggestive of a racecourse frequenter—that is, of a betting man— of a questionable class, and proceeded to wait on Mrs. Dan M'Lean.

I found the lady was a very typical personage. She was immensely stout: very vulgar and illiterate, with coarse hard features and small ferret-like eyes. She was attired in an old faded velvet gown, and she wore a quantity of good jewellery, notably, a gold chain attached to a gold watch hung at her waist, a gold brooch set with rubies, and a number of rings, one being a snake ring with diamond eyes.

On my inquiring if her husband was at home, she fixed her small piercing eyes on me, and scrutinised me keenly for some moments. Then she said brusquely:

'No. What do you want with him?'

Here I hazarded a bold answer and said hesitatingly:

'Well, a little time ago I was in Carlisle, and met him there. We did some business together, and he asked me if I should happen to be in Paisley to call upon him.'

'Oh, ay,' she returned, never once having taken her eyes off me, but I was too old a hand at the business of criminal hunting to flinch beneath a gaze, however piercing it might be. Then she seemed to hesitate for some moments, but after a little reflection asked, 'What is your name?'

I pulled out a well worn and dilapidated leather card-case (part of my stock-in-trade), and taking a card out, on which was inscribed, 'James M'Kinnon,' I handed it to her. She read it, and seemed to be a very long time in doing so, but at last said, 'Will you come in a bit, Mr. M'Kinnon?'

Of course I accepted the invitation, and followed her into a small, fairly well-furnished parlour, where a young girl was sewing some braid on the bottom of her dress, from whence it had been partly torn off. She appeared to be a little confused as I entered, and dropping her dress rose to her feet. In an instant I had taken stock of her, and felt sure I was looking on the girl who had pawned the necklace. She was between eighteen and twenty, had reddish hair, rather coarse features, and a neat figure, while there was that expression of low cunning in her face which is so marked in those who from their earliest childhood are brought up in an atmosphere of falsehood and deceit.

'This man's named M'Kinnon, and he knows your father,' said the woman coarsely.

'Oh!' was the girl's only response, as she dropped into her chair again, and, lifting up her dress, resumed the sewing of the braid; but I noted that every now and then she scrutinised me from under her drooped lids. The mother also took a seat, and motioned me to do the same, and when we were both seated, she said:

'What business did you have with Dan?'

'I bought a little swag from him,' I answered, and at these words I saw the eyes of the two women meet, and a peculiar expression came into their faces.

'What was the swag?' asked the mother.

'Only a few odds and ends, but he told me we might trade better if I called here.'

The mother and daughter seemed to consult each other with looks, then the girl said:

'Well, my father's away now.'

'Where is he?' I asked quickly.

'He's gone to the Manchester races,' she answered; then as she suddenly thought she had committed herself, she added, 'Well, he will have left there by this time, and I don't know where he'll be.'

'When will he be home?' I asked.

'Can't tell,' said the girl curtly.

'Perhaps in a week, perhaps two weeks; we never know,' put in the mother.

As I saw that these people were not disposed to be in any way communicative, and as I had already obtained some valuable information, I rose to go. The elder woman accompanied me to the door, and as she held the handle in her hand she said with great abruptness:

'Look here, mister, is your name really M'Kinnon?'

'Why do you doubt me?' I returned with intentional ambiguousness.

'Well,' she began, dwelling on the word well—'I don't think you are quite on the square.'

I laughed and answered:

'You'll see when your husband comes back,' and then I wished her good-day and took my departure, for I felt that further parley would be a mistake. But I resolved not to lose sight of these people. I was perfectly sure that they suspected me, and I deemed it not improbable they might try to warn the man, wherever he was. I therefore planted myself in such a position that I could watch the house, for I thought if they did anything they would do it soon. Nor was I mistaken. In the course of an hour I saw the girl come out. She was dressed in a neat bonnet and shawl, and after pausing a moment to glance up and down the street, she hurried away, and in a few minutes I was on her track. She went straight to the telegraph office, and I waited until she came out and had got out of sight. Then I slipped into the office, and making myself known, demanded to see the telegram, which was shown to me. It was addressed to Henry Reid, at a public-house in Edinburgh, and I happened to know that this public-house bore an evil reputation, and was the resort of a low class of betting men and touts. The message was worded as follows:

'The drains are up; you had better not come back yet; we'll write you.'

I felt sure that 'the drains are up' was a pre-concerted phrase to express danger, and that Henry Reid was Dan M'Lean alias Rusty Dan. I knew I was on the right scent, and I quickly wired a cipher message to my chief, and in the course of the evening I received word that Dan M'Lean had been arrested in Edinburgh, and, my plans having been all arranged, I proceeded to arrest Mrs. M'Lean and her daughter. On searching their house, we found a few articles of the jewellery that had been stolen from Wreay, and various other things, which we had reason to believe were the proceeds of burglaries. M'Lean turned out to be the head of a notorious gang of thieves, and he had for a long time been able to carry on his work successfully, as he pursued his avocations far from home. The Wreay burglary had been planned and instigated by him. He was ultimately sentenced to a long term of imprisonment, and his wife and daughter to shorter terms. Nearly all the stolen jewellery and plate were recovered, which, together with the pearl necklace, was, of course, restored to its rightful owner. As I was curious to know how it was that such an experienced thief as M'Lean had parted with so valuable an article as the necklace for such a trifle of money, I visited him immediately after he was committed, and put the question to him.

'Well, I had never seen anything like it before,' he answered, 'and knowing it would be dangerous to get it valued at a jeweller's, I sent my wench to Glasgow to spout it. She was to ask four pounds, and if the money was readily lent I meant to get the thing out again, and pawn it somewhere else for more.'

'And why didn't you do that?'

'Because I knew that the beaks had got a list of the things that were nabbed, and I felt it would be dangerous,' he responded sullenly.

'Ah, you made a great mistake, Mac,' I answered in a mock sympathetic tone, 'for, not only did you lose the chance of potting a big sum of money, but your lagging is due entirely to that precious pearl necklace.'

A River Mystery

It was said by one of the Greek philosophers of old that man could imagine nothing in connection with human life that had not happened. I have often been struck with this saying when, in the course of my professional career, I have been called upon to unravel some unusually tangled thread of romance and mystery, and in nearly all cases of murder, where the crime is not committed for the mere sake of vulgar robbery, there is generally a considerable amount of romance about them. Most people nowadays like to be thought practical, and if any unfortunate writer of books happens to depict incidents that savour too much of romance, he is at once pounced upon by the noble army of reviewers and mangled. Of course there is romance and romance. There is the romance of the Court of King Arthur and the Knights of the Round Table, and the romance of Edgar Poe's marvellous story of Hans Pfaall, in which a man ascends to the moon in a balloon, and the immortal 'Thousand and One Nights', to say nothing of scores of others of a like kind which one could instance. But the authors of these productions never intended them to be taken seriously, and certainly it was not these sort of things the philosopher alluded to when he said man could imagine nothing in connection with human life that had not happened. The romance I mean is the romance which connects itself more or less with the life of nearly every individual who comes to man's estate. In ninety-nine cases out of every hundred this romance is never heard of, but occasionally some peculiar circumstance or series of circumstances brings this romance, as we are pleased to term it, into prominence, and we exclaim in surprise, 'Is it possible such things can happen?' Now, it is well known that nothing in connection with our poor little human affairs tends to shadow them in mystery and romance so much as Death, when it is allied with crime.

I have been tempted into the foregoing remarks *apropos* of one of the strangest romances of real life I have ever had to deal with. And I am bound to admit that, were the facts and details of the case not on record, I should hesitate to tell the story, lest I laid myself open to the accusation of being a romancer in the sense implied by a polite gentleman, who was asked what sort of a person so-and-so was, and answered: 'Well, sir, romance is so natural to him that he only speaks the truth by accident.' The story I have to tell may read like the nightmare fancy of a disordered imagination, but, alas! it is too surely a page from a real life's history—a page blotted and stained with tears and reddened with human blood.

Let me begin my narrative in the dramatic style, and say:—It is night, a summer night, when the heavens are palpitating with a myriad stars, and the odour of a thousand flowers is borne upon every zephyr that blows. A day of heat has been succeeded by a night of beauty, and panting humanity lolls about to catch each cooling breeze, which, blowing up the river, comes with a grateful freshness. The great city of Glasgow, with its toiling thousands, seems to be sinking to rest—that is, such rest as a great hub of human beings can ever know; for, after all, it is only a brief lull in the throb and beat of its passionate life that comes to a city during the silent watches of the night.

The whirr of the day's wheels hardly ceases before the clarion of morn arouses the toilers again. But it is some little distance from Glasgow where, if I may term it so, the prologue of this mystery begins. The scene is that part of the Clyde where one begins to get clear of the filthy river, and the breath of ocean comes uncontaminated to one's nostrils, while around is a picture in which nature in her wildness just touches the margin of so-called civilisation—that is, the civilisation of dirt and grime, of the foulness of human hives, of great sewers pouring out their pollution and death, and tall chimneys vomiting to the very heavens dense clouds of damnable sulphurous fumes, which produce mirk and misery, and cloud the brains as much as they choke the lungs.

It is that part below Greenock where the river widens out, and the entrance to the Holy Loch suggests to the jaded toiler health and repose and pleasant scenes of wood and fell. Here you begin to realise that even the Clyde cannot pollute the sea, for here there is a smell of brine, and the seaweed clings to the rocks, and the water is limpid, and at night one can see it flashing into phosphorescent gleams. Here on this summer's night a boat, apparently without an occupant, floats alone. I say apparently, for, as will presently be seen, the boat had an occupant. The tide is setting up, and so the boat drifts along towards the upper reaches of the river. It rises and falls with the swell, and the water gurgles about it, and the stars watch it, and the night wind toiling in from the ocean seems to blow over it with a wail.

It is strange that a boat should be drifting like this at such an hour, and the very fact of its being there uncontrolled by human agency is suggestive of some mystery. Presently a large steamer creeps up, coming from the sea, and picks her way cautiously to an anchoring place off Greenock, until the light of day shall render it safe to enter the narrow part of the river. The boat is drifting in her very track, and soon the man on the lookout on the bows of the steamer reports that there is 'something on the water ahead.' The steamer's course is just slightly altered, for at this time of the year holiday folk on calm nights are fond of boating, and will drift about even during those hours when sleep seals the eyes of most people.

So the look-out on the steamer, perceiving that the something ahead is a boat, hails it with a warning cry, but there is no response. The great vessel proceeds on slowly, very slowly, and again the boat is hailed, but no answer comes back, and the supposition naturally is that it is a boat that has got adrift from some of the quays, and that is not a matter the steamer can concern herself about, and so she would have passed on had not the officer on the bridge perceived, from his height, that the boat was not tenantless. Some person seemed to be lying asleep in the bottom—yes, asleep! But it was the sleep that only the trumpet of the Angel of Doom could break, though the officer did not know that then. He therefore shouted with all the strength of his lusty lungs, but the only response was the echo of his own voice from the hills opposite.

There was evidently some mystery here that must be solved, so the engines of the steamer were stopped, a boat was lowered and pulled towards the waif, and then it was discovered that there was an occupant in the drifting boat; that occupant was a woman, but she was stone dead. Such a ghastly freight could not very well be taken on board the larger vessel, so a rope was made fast to the boat with its silent passenger, and it was towed astern. And when the steamer dropped anchor off Greenock information was conveyed as soon as possible to the proper authorities that the vessel had picked up some strange flotsam. Thus, then, may be said to end the prologue to the startling drama, and what follows must be dealt with in a more prosaic manner.

The boat was towed ashore, the body carried to the dead-house by the police, and the police surgeon, Dr. John Macleod, was immediately called upon to make an examination. That examination revealed the fact that the woman was dead, and also that she had been murdered. The front of her dress was soaked with blood, and when the clothes were removed, a bullet wound was observed just over the heart. Of course no *post-mortem* examination was made then, but by probing with his finger the doctor determined that without doubt the bullet had gone into the heart.

How did the woman meet her death? That is, did she shoot herself, or did somebody else shoot her? Was it murder or suicide?

It was murder!

The proofs of this were to hand. The front of the woman's dress where the bullet had entered was singed and burnt, showing that the muzzle of the pistol had been held close to her. Now, if she had held it herself the pistol must have been found in the boat, for instantaneous paralysis would ensue on the firing of the shot, and the woman, assuming that she held the weapon herself, could not have thrown it overboard, for, of course, she was shot in the boat; it would, therefore, have fallen in the boat, but there was no pistol there. She herself was lying face downwards, and her position made it clear that she had been sitting on the after thwart when the fatal shot was fired, and the person who fired had been sitting on the midships thwart, possibly had been rowing. That the murderer had been so sitting was incontestable, because the dress would not have been burnt if the muzzle of the weapon had not been held close to the body, and any one sitting farther off could not have held the pistol near enough to produce this result.

It happened that at this time I was staying at Greenock with some friends, preparatory to proceeding to the Highlands for a brief holiday, and it further happened that Dr. John Macleod was a very dear old friend of mine, and he and I had been together the previous evening. It was therefore but natural that he sent for me as early as possible, and when I joined him he said:

'Well, old fellow, here's a job for you. The river has given us a mystery during the night, and murder has been done.'

I at once went with him to see the body. It was a sad sight, all the sadder because the victim was young and beautiful. It is no mere expression to say that she was beautiful, for seldom indeed had I looked upon a more perfect face. Her age was between twenty-two and twenty-five. She was very dark, with a splendid mass of hair, done up in a heavy plait, and fastened behind. Her teeth were perfect, her mouth small, as were also her ears. Her skin was white and without a blemish, her feet and hands small, the latter being delicately formed, and giving no indication that they had ever performed manual labour. She was handsomely dressed. She wore well-fitting bronze leather buttoned boots, and spun silk crimson stockings. Her underlinen was all fine and of the best kind, and it was marked with the name 'Marie.' Her dress was silk, being adorned at the neck and cuffs with real lace, and she had worn round her shoulders a light black lace shawl, which was found in the boat stained with blood. So far these things proved that she did not belong to the toiling classes, but moved in a superior station, and this tended to increase the mystery.

Having taken stock of her clothing and personal appearance, I tried to work out some theory for the motive of the crime. It wasn't robbery!

On her engagement finger she wore a valuable ring set with pearls and rubies, and it fitted so loosely that it could easily have been slipped off. In her ears she had small gold drops set with pearls, and she also wore a valuable gold watch and chain. I roughly valued all these items at fifty pounds, therefore it was not to possess himself of her gew-gaws that the murderer killed her. But in addition to these things there was something else on her poor body, which to me professionally was of infinitely more value than all the other things put together. This was a small, gold, round locket about the size of a penny. It was fastened round her neck by a tiny gold chain as fine almost as a piece of thread. On the lid was engraved a monogram, 'M and R' interwoven, and round them a true lover's knot. The locket itself contained the portrait of a young, handsome looking man, blonde, with a mass of curly hair, china blue eyes, and a long, drooping moustache.

I studied this portrait for some time; and I asked myself:

'Is the original of this the murderer?'

Perhaps he was or perhaps he was not, but at any rate I knew the value to attach to that portrait, and so I carefully took charge of it.

In the poor girl's dress pocket was a morocco leather purse containing a sovereign and half-sovereign, some silver and a broken ring, but not a scrap of paper of any kind. In a pocket, however, in her petticoat were a needle-case and a draper's bill, with the name of a well-known London firm on it. The bill was receipted, and was for four pairs of silk stockings, a dozen cambric handkerchiefs, two silk neck handkerchiefs, and some ribbon.

Of course I took charge of that bill, thinking it might afford a clue. But more important still, in the same pocket was an ivory memorandum tablet, and written on it was this:

'August 25. To see Dick, and insist on some settlement.' The date then was August 27. Therefore this memorandum probably had reference to some appointment two days previously. Dick, too, was an abbreviation of Richard. The name on the girl's linen was Marie, and the monogram on the locket 'M and R'; those letters surely stood for Marie and Richard, and had been engraved when love was a paradisiacal dream to the two young people. Now, on the ivory tablet was written, 'To see Dick, and insist on some settlement.' Did not the word *insist* unmistakably point to something unpleasant? Love does not need to be insisted upon to perform its obligations; and so, interpreting for myself, I said, 'There had been a rupture between these two people. Dick's love had cooled, and the unhappy girl felt it was necessary to insist on something being done. Therefore Dick holds the key of the mystery.'

In the boat nothing was found save blood. The oars were gone, but subsequently they were picked up near the mouth of the Holy Loch. On the stern of the boat was the name of a Gourock boat-hirer, but when he was applied to he stated most positively that that particular boat had not been hired from him on the night of the crime. Therefore the boat must have been stolen, and this fact proved to my mind that the crime had been premeditated; because the person who stole the boat away knew that if he went to hire a boat in the ordinary manner, the person with whom he negotiated would be able to give some description of him, and so, to obviate that, he took the boat clandestinely.

It will have been seen from the foregoing that nothing was wanting to shroud this little tragic drama in seeming impenetrable mystery, and yet I was not without hope that I might be successful in clearing away some of the shadows and letting the light of day shine where now all was dark. For, although I am not a particularly sensitive man, I confess to a display of deep emotion as I gazed on that beautiful girl whose young life had been cruelly extinguished, and I felt it was my duty to use my poor abilities in trying to mete out just punishment to her slayer.

A *post-mortem* examination of the girl's body revealed one thing and proved another. It proved that the doctor was right about the direction of the bullet, for it had absolutely gone right through the heart, producing instantaneous death. Cases, of course, are on record where a bullet has lodged in the heart and death has not followed immediately, but that has been where certain important vessels have escaped rupture. In this instance the heart was literally torn in halves. The revelation was that the girl was in a condition when, in the course of a few months, she would in all probability have been engrossed with maternal cares.

Here, then, was a motive for the crime. This poor girl had loved not wisely but too well. It was the old, old story. Alas! how old, how pitiable. She, in blind trust and faith in the man who had won her heart, had surrendered that which is a woman's brightest jewel. Then came the awakening, bringing neglect on his part, anxiety on hers—anxiety that increased as the signs of maternity became unmistakable. And the sequel—she begging, praying, insisting to have her honour saved; he trying to shrink the onus of his great responsibility, until at last, stung into madness by remorse and shame, he had recourse to the dreadful alternative of slaying her, in the hope that the grave would save him from the fruits of his sin, and that his crime of murder would remain for ever a mystery. It needed not the gift of prophecy to determine that the foregoing were the elements of the story, for the dead girl's state was too surely eloquent of a state of wrong and shame.

Then I felt sure also that the false lover was a man moving in a good social position, for a poor man would not have left upon the girl's dead body something like fifty pounds' worth of jewellery. And she, poor thing, had evidently been gently nurtured, for the soft white hands showed that she did not belong to the ranks of the toilers with muscle and sinew.

Although I had often seen the bodies of dead men and women and children, no one that ever I had looked upon had moved me to so much emotion as did this beautiful girl. For one of such exquisite mould and feature, with every attribute of that divine loveliness which the poet weaves about his ideal woman, to be cut off in the prime of her youth by disease would have been inexpressibly sad; how much more sad, then, when in the fullness of robust health, and with long years of rich life apparently lying before her, she was suddenly hurled into the darkness of death by the murderer's bullet!

These were my thoughts as I turned away from the grim dead-house where her sweet body lay, and began to weave plans to trace and track her slayer.

I had arranged to take a brief and much needed holiday; but now stern duty bade me stay, so I abandoned the pleasure I had anticipated, and at once set to work to unravel this tangled skein of human mystery.

I felt sure that the dead girl was a foreigner. Her dark hair, her olive complexion, and her white pearl-like teeth pointed to a sunnier clime than that of the British Islands. Then, again, her linen was marked *Marie*, and that was essentially a French name.

My first step was to communicate with the firm of London drapers whose names were on the receipted bill found in the dead girl's purse. They remembered the transaction to which the bill related; and the spun silk stockings which the girl was wearing at the time of her death they recognised as having been purchased in their establishment; but beyond that they knew nothing. It was an ordinary transaction, and when the lady had made her purchase the things were done up in a parcel, and she took them away with her. I saw there was no clue therefore to be got out of that affair, and that I must look for a clue elsewhere.

On removing the portrait from the locket I found the name of an eminent photographer in the West End of London; and this gave me hope that he would be able to supply me with some items of information about the original. There was also a slip of paper in the locket. It was folded up into a tiny compass, and on unfolding it I read the following beautiful lines of Tennyson, penned in an exceedingly neat, lady-like hand:

> O Love, O fire! once he drew
> With one long kiss my whole soul through
> My lips, as sunlight drinketh dew.

The writing, while unmistakably feminine, was remarkable as being unusually small, and every letter perfectly formed.

Alas! how utterly absorbing must have been the love of the poor girl whose hand traced those burning, passionate lines; how like an ideal dream her life at that time; how like a glimpse of Paradise the life that this love pointed to! But it was a dream only, and it had lured her to a pitfall wherein was Death.

The photographer remembered taking the photograph a year before this time, and a reference to his books showed that he had sent a proof for approval to Mr. Richard Gumbrell, then staying at —— Hotel, in the same district of London.

The name struck me as being an exceedingly uncommon one. The hotel people could give me no information beyond the fact that a gentleman of that name had stayed there, and, singularly enough the London Directory had not a single Gumbrell amongst its many thousands of names.

Such, then, was the extent of the information I was enabled to obtain in London. But the report of the murder brought forth a Glasgow hotelkeeper, who recognised the murdered woman as a lady who had stayed at his hotel for two days as the wife of Mr. Davies, and Mr. Davies, the hotelkeeper had no doubt, was the original of the portrait in the locket. It was noted in the hotel that Mr. and Mrs. Davies did not seem to be on the best of terms, and on the morning of the day they left one of the chambermaids heard them in altercation in their bedroom. They had no luggage except what they could carry themselves, and when they left Mr. Davies said they were going through the Trossachs. That night the dead body of the young lady was found in the boat drifting at the mouth of the Clyde, but all inquiries failed to trace the movements of the man after he left the hotel. He had managed most effectually to lose himself.

I should have been lacking in the faculty of perception if after this I had had any doubts that the handsome blonde young man with the china blue eyes, who had been photographed as Mr. Gumbrell, and in Glasgow had taken the *alias* of Davies, was the slayer of the girl Marie.

So far the story, as I had read it at first, turned out to be correct: and Richard Gumbrell, *alias* Davies, had been the lover of Marie, and had foully murdered her. But the mystery was a mystery still, and it really seemed at this time as if there was not much likelihood of clearing it up. Poor Marie was consigned to a humble grave in the cemetery at Greenock, and it was for the future to reveal whether her cruel and cowardly murderer would stand for judgment for his crime before the bar of his fellow-men, or carry his dark secret with him to the bar of the Eternal Judge. He had certainly been clever in destroying his traces, and if he did not blunder later on, the chances were that he would escape man's vengeance.

About two months later my attention was drawn to the following advertisement, which appeared in some of the London daily papers:

> Notice.—If Miss Marie Albert does not remove her things from —— Terrace, South Kensington, and pay the amount due within fifteen days from the appearance of this notice, they will be sold to defray expenses.

Such intimations as these are common enough, especially in the great world of London, and this one would hardly have attracted my attention if it had not been for the Christian name Marie. The surname Albert is also French, and, therefore, I felt it to be my duty to make some inquiries at —— Terrace, South Kensington, with a view to discovering if the Marie Albert advertised for, and the young woman who was sleeping so soundly in the Greenock Cemetery were one and the same person.

I found the house a highly respectable one, and the tenants were in the habit of letting apartments, mostly to young ladies who were studying at, or had business connections with, the Kensington Art Schools. On showing them a photograph of the dead girl they instantly recognised it as that of Marie Albert, and they were inexpressibly shocked when they heard of her terrible fate. So far this was progress, and yet it seemed as if it would give us no further solution of the mystery. The lady of the house, whom for convenience sake I will call Smith, informed me that she knew little of Marie Albert, who had occupied apartments there for about three months, but what she did know was all in her favour.

She was French by birth, but had been in England for some time. She was very accomplished, very quiet, very lady-like and very lovable, with the disposition, as Mrs. Smith described it, of an angel. Of Marie's private affairs, however, the landlady knew nothing, for she was singularly reticent. She seemed to suffer from fits of dejection, and occasionally wept a good deal. When she first went she appeared to be well supplied with money, but the last month she had borrowed a little from her landlady. When she went away she stated that she was going to visit some friends in the country, but would be back in three or four days. She only took with her a handbag, but when she left the house she passed for ever from Mrs. Smith's sight. That it was not her intention, however, to do this was evident; and I was enabled to add another leaf to the sad story. She had gone to meet her false lover, for on the ivory tablet found in her pocket was written:

August 25. To see Dick, and insist on some settlement.

She had left her lodgings on August 24th, and on the night of the 27th her body was found in the drifting boat on the Clyde. 'Dick' had therefore inveigled her to Glasgow. Why? on purpose to kill her; otherwise why had he taken her so far from her home? He had an object, too, in taking her to Glasgow. He thought it would be less likely that she would be identified. Like most criminals, however, he overlooked some important points. He should have made away with the locket, all her jewellery, and cut the name out of her linen, then in all human probability no more would ever have been known about her. But it takes a wonderfully constituted man to preserve his presence of mind after committing a murder, and I knew as well as if he had told me that Richard Gumbrell, after he had shot Marie, was too confused to remove the things I have spoken of. All his thoughts were concentrated on his self-preservation.

My next step was to examine the things the poor girl had left behind her. There was a considerable amount of exceedingly good, and even elegant, wearing apparel, including dresses, petticoats, linen, the latter all marked 'Marie.' There were a number of books, including a Roman Catholic Bible, a much annotated Shakespeare, a few of Dickens's novels, and several French works. But all these things had little more than a passing interest for me, as they revealed nothing; but I had greater hopes of a small writing-case, the lock of which I had to force, though my hopes were in a large measure doomed to disappointment. There were a few letters without date or address, and signed 'Dick.' They were very brief, and, as will be seen, did not reveal much. The first ran:

(1) Dear Mignon,*—Do not be too impatient. All will be well. You know how cautious I have to be, lest the old man should smell a rat. If he did I should be ruined.—Always your own, Dick.

(2) Cara Mia,—Wherefore your distress? Have I not told you all will be well? Can you not trust me? Do you doubt my love? For heaven's sake be patient! You know well enough that a false move on my part would mean ruin. Wait and hope. The day is at hand when we will part no more.—Trust me for ever, Dick.

(3) Beloved Marie,—What is the meaning of your last? Are you determined to ruin me? Can you not wait yet a little longer? How often have I told you that I am not master of my own actions? But you know that yourself, and you also know how terribly severe the governor is. I cannot afford to quarrel with him. If I were independent of him I would take you to-morrow. For God's sake do not drive me mad, but be patient.—Semper fidelis, Dick.

(4) Marie,—There must be an end to your importunities; therefore meet me at the old trysting-place on the 25th, nine A.M. sharp. Bring a few odds and ends with you, and we will run away for a few days, and discuss our future. Till then adieu, Dick.

These were all the letters. It will be observed that number four commenced 'Marie', without even the prefix of dear. He had thoroughly lost his temper by this time; and reading between the lines of the older letters, was it not plain to see that she, poor girl, feeling her position acutely, had been urging him to marry her to hide her shame, and at last in letter four he had come to the resolution to get rid of her? Singularly enough there was only one other letter in the desk. It was written in French, and was from a young lady in Paris.

*Mignon is a French pet name.

But there was a diary, which was, indeed, sad reading. It was not a mere commonplace diary recording commonplace events, but it was a record of the writer's emotions, and it revealed the workings of her heart. The greater part of it had no direct bearing on this case, and therefore it would be irreverent to print it for the mere gratification of curiosity. But the following few passages evidently relate to her connection with Dick, and the beautiful sentiments they express render them worthy of being rescued from obscurity. I should state that the entries were in French:

I have been wondering to-day if it is the doom of all women who love to suffer. I fear so, and yet, why should it be? Should not women cultivate cynicism more than they do? Would it not save them from many a pang? And yet a cynical woman is an abomination. The noblest attributes of a woman are patience and endurance. Her nature should be in harmony with all living things, and she should have a heart big enough to feel in sympathy with everything that breathes the breath of God's life. And how could it be so if she were cynical? No, it were better that she suffered and died than developed cynicism.

Is it not possible that the dreams we dream in the innocence of our youth should have realisation in later years? It is a bitter reflection that life should be but as a Dead Sea apple—fair to the eye, but ashes within. Ah! if only love were allowed to guide all our actions, how different would life be! The darkness of living arises from falsehood, uncharitableness, from misplaced confidence, and love that is unrequited.

It is a terrible reflection to think that woman's love for man should so frequently be her ruin. Love is a part of a woman's being, and yet more often than not it throws over her the shadow of death, and in return for the love she gives she receives the adder's sting. Must this ever be so? Will the day never dawn when man will recognise that the love of an honest woman is so precious a thing that to trifle with it is a deadly sin? How bright would the world become if men and women were always honest with each other!

and what an Elysium in truth it would be to women if men would come to recognise that they are not merely as flowers, to be plucked and worn a while, and then flung into the dust.

☞

I awake from dreams to reality, and the reality is maddening. My honour, my hopes, my love, all are discarded by him to whom I have surrendered my heart, my very soul. And yet surely he cannot be deaf to the prayers that I breathe to hint in the name of heaven. He cannot be so callous, so dead to honour, as to crush me down with my shame. No, no; I will not believe it. He will yet save me; he will yet place me in a position where I may say proudly, 'I am an honest woman.'

This was the last entry, and it was pitiable to read it in the light of actual facts—the facts of the lonely, drifting boat; the *post-mortem* examination in the dead-house; and the humble grave in Greenock Cemetery. Can it be doubted that the 'He' referred to was 'Dick'? And Dick had proved that he had a devil's heart; that be could be callous; could be dead to honour. And he had not hesitated to sacrifice this dear woman when he found her in his way.

Although this diary and the letters had revealed something, they had given me no clue to 'Dick.' He was as much a myth as ever. My next step, therefore, was to apply to the lady in Paris whose letter I had found in the desk. But here again I met only with disappointment. The dead girl and this young lady had been schoolmates, and Marie had kept up a correspondence with her old friend, who, however, knew little of her later movements. But she was enabled to give me this information.

Marie Albert was a member of a very good family resident in Bordeaux, and her parents had tried to force her into a marriage with a wealthy man greatly her senior, and for whom she entertained the greatest abhorrence. As her people insisted on the marriage, she ran away, and from that moment her friends lost all trace of her. Her friend in Paris knew she had gone to London with a view, she believed, of trying to get a situation as a governess, for which she was singularly qualified, being well educated and speaking English fluently. Her letters to her friend, however, gradually became more laconic, then ceased; and the later ones seemed to breathe sorrow. But Marie Albert was a very reticent girl, and knew how to keep her affairs to herself.

It will be seen that the progress made in unravelling the mystery was not much up to this point. We had learned something about the murdered girl's history; but that something was little enough, and in the meantime where was 'Dick'?

I have on several occasions in the course of these records expressed an opinion that if criminals were more cautious about small matters, and paid more attention to detail, they would escape more frequently than they do. But it is an incontrovertible fact that most great criminals have been brought to justice through some small oversight on their part. In the present instance, if 'Dick' had destroyed the locket, and cut out the name from her linen, he would have made the mystery a still greater mystery.

I am well aware, of course, that many people have an idea that a detective is, or ought to be, endowed with supernatural powers, which enable him to see what others cannot, and that if he fails to track down some particular individual who has rendered himself notorious, he is lacking in the essential qualifications of his calling. This is a grave error. The astuteness of the detective comes from a keen perception, a natural ability to analyse motives, and to draw deductions from logical premises. He must thoroughly understand the laws which govern cause and effect, and be capable of following up effects to their causes. These are, if I may say so, the inborn qualities of the detective, and without them he can never hope to succeed. But, like all faculties, they have to be trained, and to fit him for his position he must acquire a perfect knowledge of the human heart; he must know to what wickedness it is capable of lending itself, and how innately bad it is. And when he has learnt this all-important lesson he must make himself acquainted with all the various phases of human cunning.

I have offered the foregoing remarks in a somewhat what apologetic vein, for it may be thought that in failing to arrest Dick I had displayed an inaptitude for my profession. But once let a criminal with some astuteness get a fair start and he may for a long time baffle his pursuers. I had been baffled but not beaten; but I had often been baffled before but had always won in the long run, and I felt sure I should win in this case. It was not, however, until four months later that I saw chances of my hopes being realised. Then I noticed in a fashionable paper which devotes itself to chronicling the marriages and movements of fashion an announcement of the marriage of 'Richard Gumbrell, second son of Jeffrey Gumbrell, Esq., of Warwickshire, to Annie, only surviving daughter of Charles Drinkwater, Esq., of London and Simla'.

Then followed a description of the marriage, the dresses, the bridesmaids, &c., and it wound up with saying that after the breakfast the happy couple started for Eastbourne for the residence of the bridegroom's brother, preparatory to going on the Continent to spend their honeymoon.

My heart pulsed much more rapidly as I read that, and I asked myself if this Richard Gumbrell, who had married the only surviving daughter of Mr. Drinkwater, was the man I was seeking? If so, alas! what mockery to speak of the 'happy couple'.

My first course was to proceed to the Warwickshire village, where I found that the Gumbrells were people of excellent standing, and I learned beyond all doubt that Richard Gumbrell was the mysterious 'Dick', the man with the china blue eyes, and blonde hair and moustache, and the murderer of poor Marie Albert. I learned also that Marie had been in the service of the family for two years as French and music teacher to the three daughters, and that there had been much unpleasantness between Richard and his father, owing to what was considered a flirtation on the part of the pretty teacher and the son, ending at last in the girl being discharged.

I found that the villagers were still full of talk about the marriage; it was considered such 'an excellent one', the young people were so 'peculiarly suited', and then, from the monetary point of view, it was regarded as 'a splendid match', for Annie Drinkwater had brought her husband a large fortune, and the Gumbrells were comparatively poor. Mr. Drinkwater was an Indian merchant in very extensive business, and had a magnificent estate in Simla, where the young people were going to take up their residence.

I felt very sorrowful as I journeyed in all haste to the pretty town of Eastbourne, for, alas! the blow would fall with terrific force on each family. But duty is duty, and dead Marie Albert's blood still cried aloud for vengeance.

It was night when I arrived at Eastbourne, and a cold bitter rain was driving in from the sea, and the surf broke on the shore with a sullen moan.

Mr. Jeffrey Gumbrell, the brother, had long been resident in the town, as he suffered from bad health. He lived in a large house in the fashionable quarter, and when I arrived the mansion was ablaze with light, for a ball was being held in honour of the marriage. Under these circumstances, and in order to spare the feelings of both families as much as possible, I resolved to defer the arrest till the following day, for I had no fear that my man would escape me. But he did. Late that night a rumour ran that Mr. Richard Gumbrell had mysteriously disappeared, and his bride was in a terrible state of alarm. He could not have left the town, because he had been seen after the last train had gone. What, then, had become of him? It was soon to be revealed. The wind was blowing in from the sea and the tide was rising; and when the grey dawn stole up from the east, it revealed something floating in the water, a something that was thrown forward and drawn back again as if in mockery. In company with some boatmen I went out to this something. It was a man in evening dress, and the man was Richard Gumbrell, and Richard Gumbrell was stone dead.

How came he into the water, he who was newly married, whose wife was beautiful and wealthy, he who was one of a 'happy couple'? I say, how was it that, on this night of all nights and in his festive garments, this young man, who to all appearance had a life of perfect happiness before him, had gone down into the darkness of the grave? The mystery was a mystery still. The grim sisters, who spin out human destinies, must have lashed him with scorpions. He could not have known that I was on his track; but the coroner's inquiry revealed the fact that from the moment of his marriage he seemed to change and become a prey to melancholy. And on this night he had said to his bride that he felt as if he were going mad.

It was an awful blow to all concerned, and though 'Dick' had evaded man's justice, the spirit of poor murdered Marie Albert must have felt that the crime was most amply revenged.

No particulars were ever forthcoming of the murder, and the details of the crime were known only to the river, and the river keeps its mysteries.

The Skeleton in
the Cupboard

◈

George Peddie occupied the important and responsible position of confidential clerk and teller in the Royal Bank, where he had been for twenty-two years, having entered the bank in a humble capacity at the age of fifteen. He was a member of a highly respectable family, and at one time his father had been rich, but bad times and unfortunate speculations ruined him. He had placed his children well, however, but George, being the youngest, did not get so good an education as the others, and he had to turn out earlier than they had done, owing to his father's reduced circumstances.

George was a smart lad, and the second year the manager of the bank promoted him. So he had gone on rising gradually, and at the end of twenty-two years he was a confidential clerk with a salary of seven hundred a year.

Now, seven hundred a year was not a very big salary for a proud and ambitious man, perhaps, but George might have got on very well with it, might even have ranked as a well-to-do man amongst his acquaintances, had it not been for a skeleton in his cupboard. It is said that we all have our skeletons, but George's was a particularly gruesome one. Its mouldering bones were forever jangling in his ears. It confronted him at all times. If he invited a few friends to a quiet little feast, there at his board sat that grinning thing. His friends of course didn't see it, but he did. It took good care that he should never lose sight of it. If he was a guest anywhere his skeleton went with him. Even in the church on Sunday it sat beside him; and when in the summer he took his three weeks' holiday, that wretched, maddening thing accompanied him. He could not shake it off, possibly because, for one thing, he lacked resolution and firmness. He was rather an easy-going sort of fellow, and he could not muster up sufficient moral courage to fall to and tackle that skeleton until be had broken it into a thousand pieces, and had flung the pieces to the four winds of heaven.

Of course the foregoing is metaphor, but by metaphor we can express great truths, and make graphic that which otherwise might be obscure. George Peddie's skeleton was to him a terrible reality, and it must at last have tortured him into something like insanity, otherwise he surely would not have forfeited his honour, sullied his good name at the bank, and after twenty-two years of service, and when he was earning an income of seven hundred a year, with the prospect of ultimately reaching a thousand, have stood confessed a thief. Yet so it was, and at the age of thirty-seven George passed from a position of honour to the felon's dock. It was a common enough story. One false step, and then *facilis descensus Averni*. George's skeleton drove him into sin, and his sin found him out at last.

As already stated, George occupied a position of trust and responsibility. But something at last caused suspicion; suspicion begot mistrust, and a general auditing of the accounts of the bank was ordered, with the result of discovering a deficiency of no less than between six and seven thousand pounds. This was a big deficit, and the question was who was responsible for it? The various departments were overhauled, and stood the ordeal all save one. That one was George Peddie's, and investigation proved the fact that for a long time he had been carrying on peculations until they had reached the aggregate of nearly seven thousand pounds.

To everyone in the bank the revelation caused blank astonishment. George Peddie a thief! Impossible! But it was not only not impossible; it was absolutely true. There was no mystery, no obscurity about it. All was plain as a pike staff. George had robbed the bank to the tune of several thousand pounds, and all that remained to be done was to render him up to justice, and let justice smite him.

Now, I had nothing to do with this case, for it was not one that needed any unravelling. But it chanced that I knew George Peddie. I had been numbered amongst his friends. I had sat at his mahogany, had smoked his cigars and drank his wine. I knew his handsome wife, and knew how he worshipped his only child, a fairy-like, graceful little girl of eight, with laughing blue eyes and rippling golden hair that seemed to have in it some of the sun's glory. I knew Mrs. Peddie, who was George's junior considerably, to be a proud woman—as proud as she was handsome, fond of dress, show, gaiety, and company. I had no knowledge at that time what George's income was, but, in common with all his friends, I thought it must be something very nice—indeed, considerably over a thousand a year—otherwise how could his wife and daughter dress as they did? how could three servants be kept? how could he entertain his friends in the liberal manner that he did? how feast them on champagne and the delicacies of the season? Therefore, when I heard of his arrest, I was thunderstruck; and then I recalled an answer he had once made to me on my happening to remark incidentally what a lucky fellow he was, with only one child, a handsome, fascinating wife, and all the comforts and some of the luxuries of life.

Never shall I forget his answer, and the look that accompanied it—a look of the most utter distress, of unmitigated woe.

'Ah, my God, old fellow' he exclaimed, 'if you only knew the skeleton I have in my cupboard.'

I laughed heartily and derisively. Fate *seemed* to have been so kind to him that it was difficult to believe that the familiar household curse tortured *him*. But how little we really know of the inner life of those even with whom we are most familiar. It was, alas! too true. George had his skeleton, as will presently be seen.

As soon as the news reached me that he had been arrested for robbing the bank, I hurried off in a now official capacity to see him in prison, for he who has no pity for his fallen friend is unworthy the name of man; and I have the Arab's sacred regard for the bread and salt—that is, he of whose hospitality I have partaken should be served even at the risk of my life.

'George, this cannot be true. I'll not believe it,' I cried in an outburst of grief as I noticed the awful haggardness of his face, his sunken eyes, and the expression of blank despair.

That expression was not the expression of a hardened criminal, but of a man whose heart was broken, and whose brain was tortured.

'Yes, yes,' he moaned, 'it is true, quite true. I am a thief. But it's the skeleton that has done it.' Then, as he beat his head with his hands, he exclaimed with a passionate wail of pain, 'Oh, Eva, what will you think of me, my beloved darling! When you come to realise the disgrace I have brought upon you, will you not curse me?'

Eva was his daughter. One of the sweetest children it has ever been my lot to be acquainted with, and I was perfectly well aware that he idolised her. Therefore, his passionate outburst of intense distress did not surprise me; and, further, it served to convince me that his wrong-doing was not the result of any inborn criminal instincts.

George Peddie had been forced into crime by circumstances and not by inclination. I was resolved, therefore, to try and get a glimpse of his skeleton, and I probed him until I learned the following pitiable story, which I give in my own words:

At the age of twenty-seven George had married Miss Annie Duncan, who was seven years his junior, and the second daughter of John Duncan, the once wealthy shipowner.

The Duncan family were of mushroom growth. John Duncan's father, an ignorant and illiterate man, had kept a sailor's slop shop near the docks, but he managed to scrape a few pounds together by screwing in every possible way, and he gave his only son John some education. When he died he left this son a hundred pounds. It was regarded as a fortune for such humble people, but John, though humble in origin and position, was not humble in mind. He craved for riches, and was determined to have them. He married young, and his wife brought him a dowry of two hundred, and, with that and what he had himself, they set to work to build up a colossal fortune, and in the process of time John became a great shipowner, and was said to be worth over a million of money. Then this family, who had had their origin in the gutter, set up their carriages and horses, coat-of-arms, grand house, butler, and all the etceteras.

Their children were educated in grand style, and with the most extravagant tastes, and all of them were as proud as Lucifer, and about as heartless. But a change came in the course of time. Gigantic losses brought the family down a peg or two, and they had to reduce their establishment, but their pride was not lessened.

George Peddie about this time made the acquaintance of Annie Duncan, a singularly handsome, but most extravagant girl. It was well known that George, although poor, was of very good family. He was a dashing, handsome, young fellow, and he and Annie fell in love. Of course her parents would not hear of such a thing as *their* daughter wedding with a penniless man. He was scouted and flouted, and even Annie turned her back upon him. But he was infatuated. He would not give her up. He persevered and persevered. He pursued his object with dogged persistency; he gave her no peace, no rest, until at last his constancy prevailed, and she agreed to a secret marriage. The marriage was kept from the parents for nearly a year and a half until longer concealment became impossible, and then, when the secret was revealed, how the Duncans did rave. No terms were too harsh; no name too bad to apply to George. However, the young couple set up housekeeping on their own account in a small way. But after the birth of their child, Annie began to change. The estrangement from her parents was hard to bear, but perhaps not so hard as the comparative poverty she now had to put up with. Patrician tastes had been instilled into her, and she had lofty ideas and most extravagant habits. She could not understand being denied anything, for even though in her later days at home her father's wealth had been reduced, there was still enough left to let the children do much as they liked.

It was only to be expected that when the romance of courtship and marriage had worn off that Annie Peddie should find her changed position galling. It was a new experience to her to have to scheme this way and that way in order to spin out the slender income. Of course a cautious and less pretentious woman would have found no difficulty in managing her little household on five hundred a year, which was George's salary at that time. But Mrs. Peddie did not possess the virtue of self-denial. Her wants must be supplied whatever else went short. And so there sprang into existence that gruesome skeleton which haunted George night and day. Mrs. Peddie never ceased to reproach him. She accused him of having dragged her into the marriage, and she tortured him with her tears and reproaches. But he, brave fellow as he was, bore it all patiently and silently. He had a smile and good word for everyone, and men envied him, for did he not seem so happy? Had be not one of the handsomest wives in the town? and to all outward appearance there was not a single note of discord between them.

In order to gratify his young wife's tastes as much as possible he had his At Homes and social gatherings, and a man who was so genial and bright in his disposition as George was could not fail to have troops of friends. And so there was never a vacant seat at his festive board, and the splendid dresses of his charming wife were universally admired. And all this time, when George was laughing the loudest his skeleton was goading him the most.

Festivity is well enough, but festivity is costly, as the poor fellow soon began to find out. But he lacked resolution. He had not the strength of mind to tell his wife she must dispense with two of her servants; that she must wear less expensive dresses, and keep less company, and that she must assist in the kitchen and with the house-work. Imagine the amount of courage required to tell such a woman that. George could not for the life of him do so, and so the skeleton grinned horrible, and went on for ever rattling its bones in the poor fellow's ears; but he endured it, and at last that ghastly skeleton tempted him to his fall. His income was too small to meet the many demands upon it. Yet bills must be paid, but how? It seemed hard that he every day of his life should be handling thousands and tens of thousands of pounds, when a few paltry hundreds would clear him of his difficulties.

This was a fatal argument, and no man ever used it yet and put it into effect but he dug himself a grave or riveted the felon's chains about his limbs. But George's skeleton had become maddening with its haunting presence. For it sat down with him at his table, and rose up when he rose up. It lay down with him at night, and followed him to the bank, or in his walks abroad. And all this time his silly heartless wife could not see it, and every complaint she made set the skeleton grinning. So her poor weak husband yielded, and the bank money was gradually carried away. Always, of course, in the fatal belief that before long it would be replaced; that something would turn up; that a fortune would fall down from heaven at his feet, or something like that. At any rate the peculations went on. The horrible skeleton had to be kept quiet. And so Mrs. Peddie dressed as usual; the three servants were kept on; the company rather increased than decreased; the wines were as good as ever, and duns were unknown at the door of George's pretty villa.

But, alas, at what cost of wear and tear of brain and heart was this deception kept up! George himself alone knew. And, added to the skeleton, the sword of Damocles swung over his head, and when he got up in the morning he never knew whether that day was not destined to see the fall of that ever menacing sword.

Of course the end came at last, as it was bound to come sooner or later. Concealment was no longer possible, and George passed from his position of honour and trust to the criminal dock.

Such was the heartbreaking story, and there was not a word of it but what was true. And the sequel was an amount of human misery that to contemplate makes one shudder.

On the Duncan family the blow fell with terrific force, and their great pride was shivered down into the dust. For many days Mrs. Peddie seemed to be threatened with brain fever. Not from grief and sorrow for her wretched husband, but from wounded vanity. And though George begged and prayed her to go and see him she never went near. To her it seemed a monstrous thing that he should make such a request. Had he not brought disgrace enough upon her without asking so dainty a creature to go to a prison to see a felon? Some women might have been weak enough to do that, but thank heaven she wasn't one of them. She had made sacrifices enough in becoming his wife, and now as a thief he had no right to expect her to degrade herself still further by going to him.

All the facts, as I have stated them, I placed before the bank directors, who, taking them into consideration, and pitying George's human weakness, pleaded for him at the trial, with the result that his punishment was mitigated, and he was only sentenced to two years' imprisonment. But it was in its moral effect as terrible to him as if it had been twenty. At the end of his term he emerged a prematurely old and broken-down man. His hair had turned snow-white, and his once plump, fresh-coloured face had become withered and yellow.

When he once more stood a free man, it was also as a widower, for Retribution had been impartial. Mrs. Peddie had taken the blow to her pride so much to heart that she became reckless, and tried to drown the voice of conscience with alcohol. As she was naturally delicate, and utterly unused to hardship of any kind, she fell ill, and her lungs became affected, and six months before her husband was released she passed away. This was a dreadful sorrow to him, for, with all her faults, he loved her. But still he had his child, who was now more beautiful than ever, and she clung to him.

A few sincere friends, who knew how good George's heart was, got together a sum of money to give him a fresh start in life. The Duncans did not contribute a penny. Moreover, they tried hard to keep the child from him, but in that they failed. She went with her father to California, and the last I heard of him was that he was managing a dry goods store in San Francisco, and doing well. The skeleton was laid, but the haunting ghosts of memories had taken its place; but they were sorrowing and pitying ghosts, and would walk with him until his time came to go down into the darkness of the grave.

The Gentleman Smasher:[*] A Strange Story

A good many years ago very great annoyance and loss were occasioned, not only in Glasgow, but various other towns of Scotland, by an enormous amount of bad money that found its way into circulation. While some of the coins were so clumsy as to excite surprise how any one could be taken in with them, others again were such excellent imitations that even practised eyes were deceived. Amongst these spurious coins was a considerable number of sovereigns and half-sovereigns, but the great bulk of the money consisted of sixpences, shillings, half-crowns, florins, and five-shilling pieces; the latter, however, being comparatively rare. The complaints about these coins were many and bitter, and, of course, there was the usual outcry against the police that they were not doing their duty. The authorities at length determined to try and lay their hands upon the smashers, and I was deputed to take the case in hand.

I knew from experience that the work before me was not of an easy nature. Of course, if a person was detected in the act of passing bad money he or she might at once be given into custody; but there was always the difficulty to prove that the person uttering the coin knew that it was spurious. Habitual smashers were also exceedingly careful not to have two bad coins in their possession at the same time, so that in case of arrest, and unless the antecedents of the utterer were doubtful, the probabilities were that no conviction could be made, and the capture got off. If one can manage to get hold of

[*]A smasher in thieves' slang means a passer of bad money.

the originators—that is, the manufacturers of the spurious coins—
it is another thing, and some big hauls have occasionally been made
in that way. And in the course of these narratives I shall relate a
very remarkable ease of the capture of a gang of coiners. As a rule,
however, the manufacturers are not the utterers, but they dissemi-
nate the coins either by selling them at a low price to professional
utterers, or employing a staff of their own to pass them. Now, given
intelligence and ordinary caution, there is no class of crime that
can be carried on with greater comparative safety than passing spurious money, although the penalties in cases of conviction are unusually heavy, as the offence is one committed against the govern-
ment of the country, and there are and have always been special
Acts of Parliament dealing with it.

In pursuing my inquiries my first step was to get together an
entire set of the duffing coins. There was not much difficulty in
this, as such a large number had been put in circulation. On examining these coins, which represented value to the extent of ten
pounds, and ranged from threepenny pieces to sovereigns, I was
struck by the great difference in them. Some were exceedingly good
imitations, others were exceedingly bad, while some were new, and
others old. These facts proved that they had not all been made from
the same dies nor at the same time, and I therefore came to the
conclusion that they emanated from a gang of professionals, and
were got rid of by an organised system. This conclusion seemed to
me to receive confirmation by the evidence I was enabled to collect; and the coins were for the most part passed among small shopkeepers in poor neighbourhoods, and usually on Saturday evenings
when business was most brisk.

Beyond ascertaining the above facts, my vigilance and inquiries did not result in anything at the time. But one Saturday night a
half drunken woman tendered a spurious florin in a public-house
in exchange for a gill of whisky. The assistant who took the coin at
once saw that it was spurious, for it happened to be a particularly
bad specimen, and he questioned the woman as to where she had
got it from. Her answers being unsatisfactory, she was given into

custody; and when I heard of this I began to think I had got a clue at last to the principal culprits. The woman, however, stoutly protested her innocence, vowing that she had received the florin amongst change for a pound note.

On making inquiries I found that although she bore anything but a good reputation there was nothing against her. She lived in a wretched neighbourhood, and was ostensibly a widow, with one daughter about three-and-twenty. This daughter, however, did not live with her, but kept a little shop in another part of the town, and professed to buy and sell second-hand female apparel. This young woman went by the name of Margaret Dowie, and passed as the wife of a man who was at least double her age. By trade he was a rivetter, but had not been known to do any work for a very long time. Notwithstanding this, he never seemed short of money, while his wife dressed in a manner that was far beyond her station. She was rather a well-favoured young woman, and knew how to make the best of such charms as nature had endowed her with.

After an interview I had with her about her mother, I came to the conclusion that 'she knew a thing or two,' and was as cunning as a fox.

In spite of all our efforts, however, we could not obtain an atom of evidence against the old woman, and she was of course discharged. But after this it was noticed that for some time no more coins were put in circulation, and I concluded that the arrest of the old woman had acted as a warning at headquarters, and more caution was being used. To my own mind this fact proved beyond doubt that there was an organised system in force for getting rid of this money, and spies and agents kept the principals informed of all that was going on.

Several weeks passed, and we had no complaints, and then the smashing commenced again. Various paragraphs in the papers cautioned the public against these spurious coins, but this did not stop the coins being passed. It only made the criminals more cautious. Renewed complaints were also heard from neighbouring towns, so that it seemed pretty evident that the operations of the band had pretty wide ramifications. The means that were taken to get rid of the coins made it exceedingly difficult to get any clue. A small shopkeeper, for instance, would find on going over his money at the end of the business day that he had a bad half-crown, florin, or other coin, as the case might be. Annoyed at his loss he would in all probability try to pass the coin off on somebody else, and so for a time it was kept circulating about. The operations of the thieves were directed principally against these small traders, as there was less danger of being found out, though occasionally a duffing sovereign or half-sovereign was passed off in a big store.

It chanced that about this time I was asked by a friend of mine to accompany him to a social gathering at the house of a gentleman of whom I had heard, but had no personal knowledge of. This was a Mr. Andrew Stevenson, who lived out at the west-end of the town, and who some time previous had made himself conspicuous by exposing a certain notorious advertising quack who for many years had been preying on the public. Mr. Stevenson's services in this case were publicly recognised, and he was presented with a purse of money. His son was well acquainted with my friend, and in sending the invitation to him requested him, if he cared to do so, to bring a friend with him. Thus it came about that I was invited. By arrangement I joined my friend at his home, and as we proceeded to the Stevensons' I asked my companion what sort of people they were, and also requested him not to mention my calling.

'Well, I don't know much about the family, though I've known Jim, that's the son, a considerable time.'

'What does he do?' I queried, more out of curiosity than for any other reason, and it being a confirmed habit of mine to ask questions.

'I'll he hanged if I know,' was the laughing reply, 'and I don't think anybody else does. He is a sort of respectable mystery. He's always well dressed, and seems to have plenty of money.'

'Does a bit on the turf, may be?' I suggested.

'Perhaps. In fact, I should say it was very likely, for he's rather horsey in his talk. But he's one of those sort of fellows that are as deep as wells, but, unlike wells, you can't pump anything out of him.'

I began to feel more interested, for I knew that people who had no visible means of livelihood must either have private means or prey in some way upon their fellows.

'I suppose the family's pretty well off? 'I remarked after a pause.

'Oh, I think so. They live in rather a swell house. The old man seems a queer old buffer, though.'

'Has the queer old buffer any other children? '

'Yes. Two daughters.'

'Young? '

'Yes.'

'Good-looking? '

'Umph. So, so. But, by Jove, they dress like duchesses.'

My interest in the Stevensons was now thoroughly aroused, but I was prevented asking further questions as we had reached our destination. It was a large semi-detached villa with extensive garden back and front. Plate-glass windows, an imposing doorway with portico and fluted pillars, and a profusion of flowers in boxes on the window-sills, gave the place quite a mansion-like appearance. We were admitted by a woman servant who, however, had been hired for the occasion, and we were shown into a reception-room of quite noble proportions and exceedingly well furnished, while a dozen splendid etchings hung on the tastefully papered walls.

I was at once presented to Mr. Stevenson and his son and daughters. The host was a man of about fifty-five; exceedingly well preserved, and very gentlemanly in his manner and appearance. The son struck me as being rather vulgar and deceptive, nor was I particularly struck with the young women. They were, to my taste, a little too *prononcées*, as the French would say, and they displayed an amount of self-assurance which was repellent. The father, however, was a really charming man. He was well-informed, had a fund of anecdote, was lively in his conversation, and seemed to have more than a smattering of knowledge of a great many subjects. I found also that he was a perfect connoisseur of etchings, and as I had a weakness that way myself, we warmed to each other. On going in to supper, I was struck by the magnificent display. The room itself was exceedingly large, and was splendidly furnished, while the walls were adorned with a number of first-class prints, mostly sporting subjects; and front this I concluded that my friend was right in his assumption that the family had horsey proclivities.

The table was arranged in a very elegant manner, while the supper was all that could be desired. There was no sham about it; everything was good. The wines were more than good—they were super-excellent—while our host was the soul of the company, and enlivened the festive board with joke and jest.

The guests, however, not only astonished me but set mc pondering. I can best describe them by saying they were a seedy lot. The women were loud, the men coarse, and I wondered how such riff-raff came to be gathered together in such a stylish house. Many of them seemed utterly out of place, and their performances with their knives during the supper proved that good breeding was conspicuous by its absence. Their conversation, too, was not such as one expects to hear from the lips of ladies and gentlemen gathered round a gentleman's board.

By the time supper was ended several of the guests were hilarious, and showed by their manner that they had done more than justice to the host's excellent liquor. We now adjourned to another room on the ground floor, for a carpet-dance. In this room there was further evidence of the host's taste and easy circumstances. There were several valuable oil-paintings on the walls, and a superb mirror adorned the mantelpiece, while two costly Sèvres vases stood in recesses.

As I had never been able, owing to some physical inaptitude or maybe mental obtuseness, to master even the elementary stages of the terpsichorean art, I asked to be excused from joining in the dancing, and I was content to sit and look on. Naturally my thoughts were busy during this time, and I could not help speculating on the contrast between my host and his guests, and I wondered how it was that a man so refined and polished as himself associated with people who were so much his inferiors in point of breeding.

Suddenly I was startled from my reverie by a face that I felt sure I had seen before. It was the face of a young woman, not a particularly good-looking face, and yet not altogether a bad one. It was one of those faces that please on the first hurried glance, but won't bear looking into. There were details in this particular face that were not pleasing. I was necessarily a physiognomist. It was part and parcel of my profession to be so, and it was my habit—some people have called it an unpleasant one—always to study faces. I therefore began to analyse the face of this young woman, and that analysis was by no means favourable to its owner. She wore a very low-neck dress, and a quantity of cheap jewellery; and she was be-rouged and be-powdered. It was not these things, however, that attracted me. But the face was familiar; where and when had I seen it? I have the faculty of never forgetting a face when once I have looked upon it, and now I racked my brains to try and remember where this young woman and I had met before. That I knew her by sight I was absolutely convinced; and somehow or other it ran in my head that my meeting with her had not been under circumstances favourable to herself.

'But surely,' I thought, 'a woman of doubtful position would hardly be a guest under this roof.'

This reasoning did not satisfy me, and seizing an opportunity, I crossed to where my host was sitting, and, pointing to the young woman, asked who she was.

I thought that he looked at me rather strangely as he replied:

'Oh, that's Miss Florence Kinnaird. She's a friend of one of my daughters.'

Having given me this information, he turned to one who was seated on his other side and entered into conversation. I took this as a hint that he did not wish to be questioned further on the subject, and so I went back to where I had previously been sitting in a recess. I had chosen this corner because, as a non-dancer, I was out of the way, and it afforded me a good view of the room.

For some moments after I got back to my seat I began to think that I had made a mistake about Miss Florence Kinnaird, but as I watched her glide round to the dreamy music of a waltz I was more than ever positive that her face was familiar to me. And I puzzled and puzzled over the problem until I mentally exclaimed 'Eureka!'

It was the face of Mrs. Margaret Dowie, the keeper of the second-hand clothes shop and daughter of the old woman who had been arrested on suspicion of passing bad money.

I confess that this discovery almost took my breath away. It came as a revelation, and at once my professional faculties were fully aroused. What did this mean? I thought. Was Mr. Stevenson wilfully deceiving me? or did he really believe this be-rouged woman to be Miss Florence Kinnaird? If so, then she was wilfully deceiving him, and there was a mystery somewhere that required fathoming, and I determined to try and satisfy myself as to how Mrs. Margaret Dowie, alias Miss Florence Kinnaird, came to be a guest under Mr. Andrew Stevenson's roof.

'It is a strange world, my masters, and there are strange people in it.'

I came to the conclusion that the Stevensons, as well as their guests, were to be classed amongst the strange people.

I will not dwell upon the details of the rest of the evening's proceedings. One thing seemed clear, these people had come together to enjoy themselves, and they did it. And after the manner of their kind they made it the occasion for unlimited eating and drinking. The party did not break up until about four in the morning, and there were manifest signs both amongst the males and females that the drinking part of the entertainment had been indulged in not wisely but too well.

I was particularly struck with the fact that there were no cabs or carriages waiting for any of the guests, who paired off or went in threes or fours their respective ways. I had made it my business to keep my eye on Miss Florence Kinnaird, and I saw her go away with a very vulgar sort of man, whose gait indicated a certain alcoholic haziness of vision. This couple had a special interest for me just then, and I followed them.

As I anticipated, the young lady and her swain pursued their way to the quarter of the town where I had first made her acquaintance; and as she drew near her second-hand clothes shop she stopped at a street corner and seemed desirous of getting rid of her escort, but he on his part seemed no less desirous of remaining with her. They stood arguing the point for some considerable time, and their argument occasionally waxed warm. At last she lost her temper, but she allowed him to embrace her in a very effusive and affectionate manner. That interesting little incident over, he staggered off and she hurried to her shop, letting herself in with a latch-key.

Of course there was now no longer room to doubt that she was the person I took her to be, namely, Mrs. Margaret Dowie, or, at any rate, the lady who chose to thus style herself. And yet she had been to a West End house as Miss Florence Kinnaird. My detective olfactory sense instinctively began to smell out something very fishy, and I resolved that before I was much older I would know a good deal more about Mrs. Dowie, as well as about Mr. Andrew Stevenson. On the following day I commenced to give practical shape to this resolution, and directed my attention to discovering something about Mr. Stevenson's antecedents and his past history. All that I had learnt in the course of a week, however, was that he had lived in his present house about five years. Where he had come from nobody seemed to know, nor did anybody know from whence he derived his income. He was supposed to be a man of means, but he was heavily indebted in the neighbourhood, and I found that amongst his creditors there was not the slightest doubt about his stability. In fact, the prevailing opinion was entirely in his favour, and he was considered to be a gentleman in the truest sense of the word. His wife was said to be dead, and it was thought that the children had been somewhat neglected in the bringing up.

I was by no means satisfied with the information I had obtained. There was some mystery surrounding Mr. Stevenson and his family, and I confess to a strong dislike for a mystery of that kind. I do not mean to say for a moment that folks should get on the housetops and proclaim their private affairs for the gratification of idle curiosity; but I do think honest people should not live in a manner which is suggestive of laborious study to conceal something in their careers which they are afraid the world shall see.

Mr. Stevenson bore the reputation of being a gentleman. To some extent I knew, from personal contact with him, that the reputation was not altogether undeserved, as far as his manner and bearing went. But there were other elements antagonistic to this which aroused my suspicions. For instance, he lived, as I discovered, chiefly upon credit, and he kept up his position by fostering a belief that he was a man of means. But my logic would have been very poor if I had not argued to myself that a man who supports such a position by the credit extended to him by his fellow men is not a man of means, though he may be, and usually is, a mean man. Then, as regards Mr. Stevenson, junior, although it was obvious that his father had to subsist to a large extent on credit, and seemed to be constantly depriving Peter of his rights in order that the clamour of Paul might be stopped, the young man was not known to follow any fixed employment. He did not go out much in the fore part of the day, but generally towards its close, and usually he did not return home till late. He had certain haunts amongst the public-houses of the city, where he was considered to be rather a fast young man, with a liberal supply of cash, which enabled him at times and not infrequently to play billiards for considerable sums of money, and indulge his taste for champagne.

Then, again, while it was a rare thing for visitors to be noticed at Mr. Stevenson's house during the day, there were generally plenty of callers after dark.

The foregoing particulars about represent all that I was enabled to learn of Mr. Stevenson and his interesting family. But so far from satisfying me, they only served to whet my appetite for more. In other words, I was by no means content, and I could not avoid the feeling that there were certain doings of Mr. Stevenson which were shrouded by a veil, and in the interest of society generally it might be as well to tear that veil aside and let the light shine a little on his daily path.

About a week later, one wet and dismal evening, when a drizzling rain was falling with maddening persistency, and the streets of the city were covered with slimy unctuous mud, a dilapidated, restless-eyed, blue-nosed, half-starved looking man entered the second-hand clothes shop of Mrs. Margaret Dowie, alias Miss Florence Kinnaird. He was a slouching man, whose general appearance was suggestive of an incessant struggle with life. As he entered the shop which was redolent of the odour of mouldering garments, he cast furtive glances about him, and pulled his threadbare coat about his neck as if desirous of concealing the fact that his laundress had not returned his only shirt.

'Are you Mistress Dowie?' he queried, in a squeaking voice, as that interesting lady, *sans* rouge and powder, now appeared from her inner den.

'Yes. What do you want?'

'Well, ma'am,' pursued the squeaky-voiced blue-nosed man, while he looked about him suspiciously as if he had been hunted, and he feared his pursuers might be at his heels; 'well, ma'am, I've been recommended to you as one who might be disposed to do a little business.'

Mrs. Dowie's eyes brightened in anticipation, and she fixed them on the dilapidated man's face as if trying to read him. Then brusquely:

'What's your business?'

He lowered his squeaky voice to an asthmatic whisper, and producing from somewhere in the inner depths of his ragged coat a piece of cloth rolled up, he said, as he slowly unrolled the cloth:

'Can you do anything with these?'

The 'these' referred to consisted of three sovereigns, two half-sovereigns, two crown pieces, four florins, half a dozen sixpences, and nine shillings. If all this money had been genuine it would surely have been strange merchandise to want to sell, but every coin of it was spurious.

Mrs. Dowie opened her eyes to their fullest extent, took up the piece of cloth and its contents, and said, 'Come here,' and followed by the shabby man, she went into her den, shutting the half-glazed door that separated it from the shop.

'Where did you get these?' she asked, as she examined them critically.

'Well, ma'am, that ain't of no consequence,' he replied with a sniffle. 'I've come by 'em honestly,' and he grinned significantly, 'and if we can trade I'll bring you a lot more.' The good lady turned them over and over, she rung them on the table, she tested them with her teeth, and finally examined them through a magnifying glass. There could be no doubt about it, she was a keen judge of such things. At last she said:

'I'll give you a sovereign for them.'

The man grumbled and haggled about the price for some time, but as she would not spring a single shilling more he accepted the sovereign, and the business being closed, and promising to bring more of the same sort of articles, he slunk out of the shop in the same hang-dog manner he had entered it.

Reader, the man who engaged in that little transaction of selling imitation coins was your humble servant.

'I've gained an important point,' I said to myself, as I left, and hurrying to my home I changed my costume, and returned to the street in which the second-hand clothes shop was situated. I watched the shop until it closed for the night, and about half an hour later Mrs. Margaret Dowie came forth, muffled in a cloak and sheltering herself from the rain with a substantial umbrella.

She took her way to the West End; I followed and saw her enter the house of Mr. Andrew Stevenson. That was all I wanted for the time being. My suspicions were confirmed, and so I went home and slept the sleep of the just.

Every one of those coins was marked, and a week later one of the sovereigns, a shilling, and a five-shilling piece was brought into a district station by a woman who kept a greengrocery shop. She could not tell exactly when she had taken the shilling and five-shilling piece; but she distinctly remembered receiving the sovereign in payment for some apples the preceding afternoon, and the person who presented it was a young woman who, from the description, I felt sure was one of Mr. Stevenson's daughters.

I now had ample justification for proceeding to legal measures, and I applied for and obtained a search warrant to search Mr.

Stevenson's house, the result being that we found spurious coins of all kinds representing about five hundred pounds of value. As Mr. Stevenson could give no satisfactory reason for being in possession of so large a quantity of money, he was arrested, as were also his daughters, his son, and Mrs. Margaret Dowie and her husband. We collected an overwhelming mass of evidence which proved that for years the Stevenson family had lived by passing bad money. They were not manufacturers of it, but simply smashers.

Their business was an extensive one, and they collected the coins by means of agents, of whom Mrs. Dowie was the most active and valuable. These agents were well-known to the pariahs of society, who got the money from the coiners; paying a small price for it, selling it to the agents at a profit, who, in turn, sold it again, of course at a profit, to the Stevensons, who took all the responsibility of passing it, and they evidently found it a very lucrative business. Mr. Stevenson, I discovered, came from a good family. He had been at college, but had failed to take a degree. For some time he followed the calling of a teacher, but it was too exacting and the pay too meagre for the gratification of his æsthetic and luxurious tastes. He loved comfort and ease, and so embarked in the smashing business, but only to learn that sooner or later the Hand of Retribution seldom fails to smite the wrong-doer. These people, as well as Mrs. Dowie and her husband, were sentenced to various terms of imprisonment, but I felt that they were only part of a very dangerous gang of criminals, and I was ambitious of unearthing the most dangerous of the lot—and that was the coiners themselves. How I ultimately succeeded in doing this I shall relate in a future article.

How I Snared the Coiners

In my story under the heading of 'The Gentleman Smasher,' I promised to relate on a future occasion how I succeeded in ultimately netting the manufacturers of the spurious coins, and I will now redeem that promise.

It goes without saying that if there were no makers of bad money there would be no passers, or, in thieves' slang, 'smashers'. The material has to be produced before it can be put into circulation. The making and passing of bad coin is, in fact, a perfectly organised business. The producers are generally artizans with some knowledge of chemistry and science. Then there are the wholesale agents; that is, people who buy the duffing coins in large quantities at a certain price, and who sell again at a slightly higher profit to the smaller fry by whom it is disseminated. In some instances, as in the case of the Gentleman Smasher to wit, the wholesale agents prefer to be their own disseminators, as, though there is more risk, there are much greater profits. The prices that are paid for bad coins will seem to the public astonishingly high, for it is generally within thirty per cent. of the face value. Thus, a man who succeeds in passing a bad sovereign will only make six shillings profit, and besides, he has usually to purchase something in order to get the bad money off. The cost of production of a really good imitation of a sovereign is from six and sixpence to seven shillings, so that the manufacturers make about the same, or a slightly higher rate of profit than the agents, but then they also run more risk.

The business of a coiner requires a considerable and somewhat costly plant, so that those who embark in the enterprise require capital to begin with. Quite apart from the necessary tools, which are numerous, a certain amount of pure gold and silver is required, as well as dies, moulds, a milling machine, an electro-plate bath, certain chemicals and acids, and a powerful electric battery. The base of all duffing coins is copper, with sufficient brass amalgamated to give it stiffness and the necessary 'ring'. As is well known, it is no proof that a coin is bad if it bends, as many shopkeepers who have resorted to this test have found out to their cost, for anyone damaging a good coin by bending it can be compelled to replace it. Nor would the weight be any test of its genuineness save for one thing; careless coiners generally err on the side of overweight. Now, it is almost needless to say that when a gold coin leaves Her Majesty's Mint it is never by any possible chance over the prescribed standard weight. The process employed for getting the exact weight, even to the thousandth part of a grain, in a coin of the realm minted at Her Majesty's Mint is an exceedingly delicate one, and that is precisely the point in which makers of bad coin fail. For genuine coins are weighed with perfect scientific accuracy. It will thus be seen that if shopkeepers and others had the means of accurately weighing base coin it would be more frequently detected than it is. But that is the great difficulty. A rough test, of course, would be to weigh a suspected coin against a genuine one of the same face value, but after all it is but a rough test. Now every one is perfectly well aware that the test universally resorted to in everyday life is to ring a coin by bouncing it on a counter, table, or the floor. But even this is not an infallible test, for a perfectly genuine coin may sometimes, through a defect, ring dull. In nine eases out of every ten, however, the coin that has not the ring may be rejected as a duffer. Manufacturers therefore give great attention to this sound, and that is the primary cause why well-made imitation coins cost so much to produce, because the ring can only be got by a nice amalgamation of copper and brass, and both of these are expensive metals.

The most common coins manufactured by coiners are sixpences, shillings, florins, and half-crowns. Occasionally they turn out five-shilling pieces, but not often; and half-sovereigns are preferred to sovereigns. Duffing sixpences and shillings, if well made, are very easily passed, and on that account are preferred by the humbler members of the 'trade'. Publicans more than any other class of people, perhaps, suffer the most by taking bad money; and they are generally victimised on Saturday nights and holidays when business is brisk, and barmen and barmaids haven't much time to notice critically the coins they receive.

The foregoing particulars *apropos* of what I have now to relate. When Stevenson, the 'Gentleman Smasher,' and his interesting family were arrested, I tried various means to get from them information that would enable me to capture the manufacturers. But I failed, and one of the most striking peculiarities of habitual criminals is their staunchness to each other. This staunchness is known in their own slang as being 'jannock'. One thief will refer to another as 'a jannock fellow'. That is one who won't turn traitor. The Stevensons proved themselves unusually jannock, for though they might have got somewhat lighter sentences by betraying their confederates they wouldn't do so.

For some time after the conviction of these people the smashing ceased in our neighbourhood. The detection and conviction of such experts as the Stevensons naturally alarmed the circulators, who kept their stock in hand or took it elsewhere. As a matter of fact the latter was the case, and about six months later we received an intimation from Scotland Yard that a large quantity of spurious coin was being put into circulation in various parts of the country, and there was good reason for believing that the manufacture of the coin was being carried on in Glasgow. Consequently, I received instructions to use every means to root out the rascals from our midst. I at once set to work, but I was not rewarded with any success. But this failure only served to arouse in me a determination to succeed ultimately, and with this end in view I resorted to stratagem, and became incarcerated as a 'lag' in the same prison as the Stevensons, and I was put into a cell next to that occupied by young Stevenson.

The object of this movement on my part will be readily guessed. I was desirous of getting the necessary information from the convict, but I could only hope to succeed in doing this by assuming the character of a convict myself.

A new-comer in a prison is always welcomed by those who have been incarcerated for any length of time, as he can give them news of the outside world, and to most convicts not the least trying part of their imprisonment is the deprivation of all knowledge of the doings of the world beyond the gloomy walls that hold them fast. Consequently, a man who is just brought in is welcomed. It is necessary to state, however, that convicts are not allowed to speak to each other. At least, that is a rule of all criminal prisons, but it is a rule that is frequently evaded, although to be caught in the act of speaking is to insure being punished. Nor is it easy, owing to the vigilance of the warders, to get more than a few words in at a time, and the result of this enforced silence is that various codes of signals have been invented by the law-breakers in order to carry on conversation, and some of these codes are singularly ingenious. Now, I knew a sufficient number of these codes to lead me to hope that I should be able to establish communication with my neighbour.

The morning after my arrival I went out to exercise with the rest in the prison-yard, and I was purposely placed behind young Stevenson, and the last in the gang. After we had turned out I saw him scrutinise me, and when we had taken two or three turns round the yard, he inclined his head slightly, and speaking over his shoulder, asked in low tones:

'What are you in for, cally? '

'Smashing,' I answered.

'What is the number of your lodgings? '

'Forty-seven.'

'Bono, you are next to me,' he exclaimed, 'mine's forty-eight.'

A warder, who was of course in my secret, here stepped forward, and with great sternness, warned us against talking, saying that if we did it again we would have three days' bread and water. When the warder had retired, Stevenson whispered:

'Can you code?'

'Yes,' I answered.

One of the commonest codes in use by ordinary criminals is what is known as 'finger-nail telegraphy'—that is, by tapping with the nails on the wall of the cell, and it is really astonishing how light a tap can be heard if the person to whom you are telegraphing puts his ear to the wall. Of course the taps have to be very gentle, or the warders would detect them. Then, again, the taps have to be made on various parts of the wall to convey any meaning. For instance, one tap is made to represent various letters, but this could not be done if only one spot was struck. So this is the *modus operandi*.

A man taps once, and the person in the next cell makes a mark by wetting his finger and dabbing it on the wall about the spot where his neighbour has struck. The first tap always stands for A. A tap half a yard from this, on the operator's right, consequently the listener's left, would be B; half a yard to the operator's left, C; below, D; above E. It will thus be seen that by this very simple plan five single taps are made to represent five letters of the alphabet. The next five letters are indicated in precisely the same way, excepting that two deliberate taps are given instead of one, so that we get up to the letter J. For the next ten letters two sharp taps following in quick succession stand for K, then two must be counted slowly before L is struck, then three are to be counted before M, and so on increasing one each time up to T. The next letter, U, is made by three sharp taps; V three taps to the right, W three to the left, X three above, Y three below. Z, which is not often used, is represented by the common method of drumming with the fingers— that is, beginning with the little finger, and following with the other three without pause.

This code requires a certain amount of practice, and some acuteness of hearing; but convicts soon learn it, and after that they can, with a little attention, carry on a very considerable conversation. Of course those who cannot spell resort to other means of communication, but they are always at a disadvantage, as so many signs are required. I ought to mention that the key letter is always struck whether used or not. For instance, in opening a conversation you give the A tap. Then any letter between F and J must be preceded by the second key letter, which is F, and the keys, be it remembered, are always sounded at the starting spot.

After Stevenson and I had been taken back to our respective cells I lost no time in opening up correspondence with him, and I found that he was far more expert in using the code than I was, owing, no doubt, to his having had more recent practice than I had had.

Almost invariably the first thing an old lag asks a new-comer is, what has he been convicted for, and what his length of term is.

I struck a sympathetic chord at once in my neighbour's breast by telling him that I had been 'nabbed' for 'smashing' a 'yellow-un' (sovereign) and a quantity of 'jingles' (shillings).

'Where did you get them from' was his next question, and which I had anticipated would be put.

I informed him that I had bought them from a 'sheeny' bloke (Jew) known to the 'fraternity ' as 'Scotch Moses'. This man was a notorious character, and had been frequently convicted as a receiver. He was not liked by the brotherhood, as he was known to take every advantage and to cheat whenever be got the opportunity; and, strange as it may seem, there is a recognised law of honour amongst thieves, and one thief who cheats another generally gets tabooed.

Stevenson wrapped back that I must be awfully green to have anything to do with Scotch Moses, and I told him that I was only an apprentice to the trade, and I did not know where to go to; and I asked him if he knew a good 'firm' that dealt in the 'raw material.'

'Yes,' he answered; 'you should go to Jim Connor, in the —— Wynd.'

'Is he bono?' I asked.

'He is the biggest maker north of the Tweed,' was the answer.

I need not attempt to describe my feelings when this information was given to me, and, as may be readily supposed, I did not prolong the conversation much after this, and an hour later I left the cell and was making my way into the city. But I had changed my character now, and from the convict had passed into a stable hand, with a general horsey appearance. Of Jim Connor I knew nothing, nor could I get any information about him amongst my colleagues. He was, in fact, absolutely unknown to the police. The —— Wynd did not bear a very high reputation, though there was nothing particularly black against it. Pursuing my investigations in its noisome precincts, I found that Jim occupied a flat at the top of one of the oldest houses, but no one seemed to have the least idea what his calling was.

After mounting up several pairs of stairs, I arrived at Jim's residence. An obtrusive looking and highly polished brass plate was fixed to the door, and bore the inscription, 'Mr. James Connor'. After ringing the bell, I waited some minutes before the door was opened. Then a neatly dressed and quite a good-looking young woman made her appearance. I noticed that she eyed me keenly as she asked my business. I told her I wished to see Mr. Connor, and she told me her father was busy then, but she would take a message if I wished.

'So you are Mr. Connor's daughter? ' I asked.

'Yes.'

I glanced about in a restless sort of way, and then, in little more than a whisper, I said:

'I've been doing two months in quod, and worked along with Jim Stevenson. He told me that your father was good for business, and I want to buy some goods from him.'

She showed no surprise, and answered coolly:

'If Jim Stevenson sent you I suppose it's all right, but you had better come in a minute.'

She showed me into a very comfortably furnished room, and left me. Twenty minutes later the door opened, and a man entered. He was between fifty and sixty years of age, with iron grey hair, a clean shaven chin, and a determined expression of face. He was a powerfully built fellow, well dressed, and he would have passed for a respectable mechanic in his Sunday attire. But I observed in his eyes the restless, searching, furtive expression peculiar to the criminal classes.

I briefly told him what I had told his daughter, and that I had been recommended to him by Jim Stevenson. He asked me my name and what I did. I told him that I had been a stable hand in the service of a gentleman in Ayrshire, and that I had been nabbed for doing a bit of smashing, but that I was going to travel now, and that I had about five quids (sovereigns) to invest. He asked me what coins I wanted, and I said that as I was rather new to the business I would be guided by him. He thereupon recommended me to take a good supply of shillings and sixpences, and a few yellow-uns, 'wholes and halfs'. He asked me for the five pounds, which I handed to him, and he left the room, returning shortly with the following coins—all new—which he handed to me:—Forty shillings, forty six-pences, five sovereigns, ten half-sovereigns, and twenty florins. Altogether representing value to the extent of fifteen pounds. He called my attention to the excellence of the make, which I was not slow to notice, and he advised me to be very careful in smashing them, and not to pass too many in one neighbourhood.

I told him I had a pal who was anxious to do a bit of business, and had about ten pounds to begin with, and that I would bring him up, and I asked what was the best time to come.

'About eight o'clock in the morning,' he replied.

After a few more words of caution from him I took my departure; and I thought that on my next visit he might not be quite so amiable.

It had struck eight the following morning when I and four stalwart colleagues in plain clothes climbed the stair leading to Jim Connor's house, while two more companions remained below. On reaching the top flat I and a companion went forward, while the three other fellows remained on the stair just out of sight, and ready for a rush. The door was opened by Connor's daughter, and we entered and were shown into the little parlour, and as soon as the girl had departed to tell her father I slipped out, opened the door cautiously, and admitted my companions. A few minutes later Jim entered, and before he could properly grasp the situation we had him fast. It was neatly and adroitly done, and when the fellow found himself trapped he uttered a tremendous oath, and tried to snap the darbies with a jerk of his powerful arms, but the irons were too strong for him. In his coat pocket we found a small six-chambered revolver, each chamber loaded.

'Yes, curse you,' he exclaimed, as we took this little instrument from him. 'If I had only known your little game some of you would have got pills, you bet.'

I laughed and told him not to excite himself, as it wasn't good for his health. Then three of us proceeded to search the house. In one bedroom we found a very old bedridden woman, Jim's mother, who seemed too senile to understand anything, so we left her, while we continued our search in another bedroom where a stout young fellow and a woman were in bed. They were Jim's son and daughter.

They were naturally much astonished by our unceremonious entry, and they both seemed to be suffering from a debauch. We allowed the man to put on his clothes, then we handcuffed him, and the daughter coming forward at this moment, we arrested her and put her into a bedroom with the other woman.

At the back of the house we found a suite of three small rooms, opening one into the other, and fitted up as perfect workshops for carrying on the business of coining. No tools nor apparatus were wanting, and besides quantities of metal used in this illicit trade, we found coins of all kinds, representing nearly five hundred pounds of value. In fact, the capture proved the most important of the kind ever made in the city, and, as we subsequently learned, there were some eight or nine members of this precious family engaged in the work, which they had profitably carried on for a number of years.

We did not succeed in netting the whole lot, but besides Jim, his daughters, son, and daughter-in-law, we secured his brother, who did the outside business as 'traveller'—that is, he beat up for customers.

The poor old bedridden woman was well taken care of, but she died a few weeks later; and when Jim was informed of her death he manifested the most intense and genuine grief, and exclaimed in broken-hearted accents:

'You can hang me now, if you like.'

This passionate affection for his mother was as unusual in a man of his class as it was touching, and showed that there was still one soft spot in his heart.

In due course the prisoners were sentenced to various terms of imprisonment, and I was heartily congratulated on having been successful in snaring this dangerous gang of criminals.

The Record of a Strange Adventure

◈

It is necessary to preface this story with a sort of prologue, and relate some particulars of a daring burglary at Thames Ditton. As most of my readers will know, Thames Ditton is a charming rural district on the south of the River Thames, and opposite Hampton. The houses in the neighbourhood are, for the most part, villas of a superior description, in the occupation of London merchants and stockbrokers, with a sprinkling of artists and journalists. One of these houses, a large detached building, standing in extensive grounds, and the residence of a wealthy stockbroker, attracted the attention of burglars, and one night during the temporary absence of the family the place was skilfully entered, and an immense amount of valuable property carried away. This robbery aroused a great deal of interest at the time, for the owner of the house was very well known, and the things stolen amounted in value to several thousand pounds. These things consisted, for the most part, of silver plate, jewellery, clocks and watches: but two very valuable engravings and four oil-paintings—one by the famous Herring—were also carried off. Every means imaginable were taken with a view to the capture of the thieves, and the owner of the stolen property offered a reward of five hundred pounds for the recovery of the pictures alone. But, notwithstanding this, no trace of them was ever obtained; and, though a few arrests were made, the prisoners were speedily discharged for the want of evidence against them.

Although I had nothing to do with the case, I took a good deal of interest in it, and watched anxiously to see if the authorities would succeed in laying their hands on the malefactors. But they did not, so in the course of time the affair faded out of the public memory—even the watch dogs of the law had their attention diverted by other matters—and the 'great burglary at Thames Ditton' was relegated to the long list of undetected crimes. About a year later, however, Scotland Yard was once more put on the alert by the following mysterious advertisement, which appeared in the agony column of some of the London daily papers:

Knave of Spades: be careful. Remember Thames Ditton!

To the outsider there was nothing in this to arouse suspicion, but the authorities 'smelt a rat', as the saying is, and instinctively they associated the advertisement with the burglary. The result was that some of the ablest of the London detectives tried to find out who the advertiser was, but they failed. All they learnt was that the advertisement had been handed in by a woman, though no description, or at the most a very vague one, of this woman was forthcoming. So the detectives could get no clue, and the matter was allowed to rest again.

A little more than two years after the robbery I was making my way along Argyle Street late one bitter November night. I don't know whether it is absolutely possible for a sane or wakeful person to be in a state when he can positively say he is thinking of nothing, for it is difficult to define nothing in this connection. An Irishman tried to give it definition by saying it was a footless stocking without a leg. That wasn't bad for the Irishman, but it is more conspicuous for wit than logic. But though on this occasion I might say I was not thinking of anything in particular, yet I am of opinion that it is pretty certain I was thinking of something. Perhaps as the driving rain beat in my face, and the storm-blasts of icy wind chilled me to the marrow, I may have been dreaming and sighing for the blue sky and brilliant sunshine of southern lands. It was indeed an awful night. The rain was swept along the street by the pitiless Arctic gusts like a waterspout. The streets were all but deserted. Even the 'drunks and disorderlies' were *non est* for once, and no wonder, for even a cur dog would have found shelter somewhere from such a storm.

Suddenly, as I forged along with bowed head, my arm was tightly gripped by someone, and a wheezy, rusty sort of voice said:

'You are Donovan, the detective?'

With a jerk I freed myself from the grip, and, turning sharply on the speaker, beheld a creature in the shape of a woman. She was a tall, gaunt woman, whose few sodden clothes clung to her as they would have clung to a stick. So few clothes had she on, and so thoroughly soaked and drenched were they, that all the irregularities and outlines of her figure were clearly discernible. She had an old ragged shawl over her head, and she held it about her throat with one hand, which I noticed was white and corpse-like, as well it might be, for I, who was well clothed and well protected, suffered from the severity of the weather. How terrible, then, it must have been for this famine-stricken being! For the pinched and sunken frame testified too surely to the want of proper nourishment. I could not see her face for the shawl she held about it, and so I asked somewhat sharply:

'Who are you? and how did you learn my name?'

She broke into an awfully bitter laugh, that wasn't a laugh so much as a wail of despair. Then a fit of coughing seized her that was dreadful to hear, and when she had recovered from it she said:

'I am a living corpse, and shall soon be a dead one. That's who I am, and that's all you need know about me. As to how I know you is not of the slightest consequence. I do know you, and that is enough.'

I was struck by her manner. It was not of a thing of the gutter; and the voice, though cracked and guttural from disease, seemed to indicate that the speaker had known better days: and yet there was something about it that made me shudder, for it was too surely the voice of the living corpse she had described herself. It was the moan of a human wreck—of a sinking derelict that was breaking up and drifting out to the dark ocean of the Unknown.

'Well, what do you want with me?' I asked kindly, moved to pity by her forlorn and wretched condition.

'I want you to avenge me,' she answered.

'What do you mean?'

'Come with me, and you shall know.'

'Why should I go with you, seeing that you will not tell me who you are, nor what you want with me?'

'Are you afraid of me?' she asked, with, as I thought, some irony in her tone.

'No,' I answered, 'and I do not think I should be afraid of any man or woman living.'

'Then come with me.'

'Not an inch till you tell me what you want.'

She drew a little closer, and as she did so the light from a neighbouring lamp fell upon her, and I saw then that her wet face was like putty, and her eyes deeply sunken, with heavy, black rims underneath.

'Did you ever hear of a burglary that took place at Thames Ditton, near London?' she asked in what seemed almost sepulchral tones.

The startling question at once drew me out of myself, as it were. It was like crying 'rats' to a ratting terrier. Instantly I was all on the alert with my ears pricked up, while wind and rain were for the moment forgotten.

'Yes,' I answered eagerly, 'what about it? But come into the shelter,' I added, as I took hold of her bony arm, and drew her into a doorway.

'Oh, don't trouble yourself about me,' she said with appalling bitterness. 'The rain cannot do me any more harm. I am dead, except that the thing that was once my heart beats; but it will stop soon, then you can shovel me into the paupers' hole, and I shall speedily be forgotten.'

I began to think that she was not in her right mind, and I tried to soothe her by saying:

'Do not talk so despairingly. I see that you are ill, but it seems to me you want food and warmth. You are soaked through and through now like a sponge in water, and you had better come with me to a respectable lodging-house I know of. You shall get a good meal and be well dried, and tomorrow I will endeavour to take steps to put you in the hospital.'

Once more she laughed an awfully bitter laugh as she exclaimed:

'You are the first person who has spoken kindly to me for years: but I neither want food nor warmth. My feelings are all deadened. I live only for one purpose—revenge, and that is why I stopped you to-night.'

As I was not disposed to argue with her, I said:

'Very well, but what about the Thames Ditton robbery?'

'The man who had the most hand in that,' she answered, 'is an accursed brute known amongst his associates as "The Knave of Spades." '

I started again as I heard this, and asked eagerly:

'Did you ever put an advertisement in the London papers?'

'Yes,' she answered, 'I did. That man has destroyed me, body and soul. He is a Samson, and, like Delilah of old, I am going to betray him into the hands of his enemies.'

'Where is he now?' I exclaimed.

'Not far from here, where he is lying insensible from drink. He has fearfully abused me to-night, as he has done on scores of previous occasions. He threw me out of the house, bad as the night is, and I was intending to end my misery by going into the Clyde. But the sight of you coming along changed my intention. I have often threatened him, and now I'll have my revenge. I have been weak before but I'll be weak no longer.'

'Do you say he is insensible from drink?' I asked.

'Yes; if he were not no man would ever take him alive, for he has the strength of a horse, and is a desperate ruffian. You can get him easily now if you'll come.'

I was somewhat in a quandary as to how I ought to act. If I went alone I might fail to secure this 'desperate ruffian': and yet, as the hour was late, I should have some difficulty in getting assistance for a time. Besides, if I dallied, the chance of capture might pass. I therefore told the woman to lead the way, and I would follow. Without another word she started to go north, I at her heels. She seemed so weak and tottering that I half expected to see her whirled out of my sight by the fierce gusts of wind. But she held her way, and in about a quarter of an hour she stopped at the entrance to a close that was in total darkness.

'It's up a stair out of this close,' she whispered. 'The place is a nest of vipers, and we must go cautiously.'

I knew that the place was a nest of vipers, as she had aptly described it, and I deemed it but prudent therefore to wait some minutes until I saw the policeman on the beat. To him I briefly stated what I was after, and asked him to get hold of his comrade on the next beat, and tell him to hurry to the nearest station and send up two or three men. I also got from him a pair of handcuffs, as I did not usually carry such things with me. Then, as the man went away to execute my orders, I told the woman to lead the way.

We groped along down the dark close for some yards until we gained the entrance to a stair, up which we began to mount. All was silent as death, save for the wind that wailed dismally up the stair-way.

We mounted to the third flat; then I struck a wax vesta, and saw the woman fumbling in her pocket, from which she produced a latch-key, and opened the door.

'You go in,' she whispered. 'He's in the room at the bottom of the passage there.'

I lighted another match, and told her to go first. She seemed disinclined to do this, and wanted to go out again, but, as I began to suspect treachery, I told her to go and open the door at the bottom of the passage. This she did, and I kept close to her. The opening of the door revealed a large room, fairly well furnished. A petroleum lamp was burning on the table, and I noted that some oil-paintings and engravings hung on the walls, and I recognised them at once from the published description as the pictures that had been stolen from Thames Ditton. I no longer doubted now that the woman had put me on the right track, so I relaxed my vigilance over her, and entered the room, and she slipped past me and went out again.

On the same side of the room as the door, and, consequently, not visible till one entered, was a deep recess containing a bed, and on this bed a man, partly dressed, was lying. He was a remarkable man in every way; and the woman might well describe him as a Samson. He was dressed in a flannel shirt, trousers and stockings, but no boots. He was a tremendous fellow, quite six feet high, with massive limbs and a tremendous chest. He was intensely dark, and had a heavy black moustache and beard, while his chest, which was exposed owing to his shirt being torn open, was a mass of black hair, and I saw that such parts of his arms as were exposed were also covered with hair. His eyes were opened, and he seemed to be gazing vacantly into space. They were small, glittering black eyes, and I recalled the woman's words, that the place was a nest of vipers. 'And surely,' I thought, 'this man is the chief of the vipers,' and I understood from his appearance why he had been dubbed the 'Knave of Spades.'

In my eagerness to secure this extraordinary fellow I sprang towards the bed with my handcuffs in my hand, but I had made a mistake in supposing that he was helpless. A sudden instinct of danger had aroused him, as a savage animal when half asleep is aroused by the approach of danger. Like a flash of lightning he was on top of me, and I went down beneath his weight, the handcuffs falling out of my hand. So sudden had been his movement that I was quite taken off my guard, and now found myself helpless beneath this ponderous brute. Breathing stertorously, and growling with passion, he seized me by the neck and commenced to bang my head on the floor. I knew then that I must fight for my life. Neither of us had spoken a word, and as far as I was concerned it was not the moment for speech. I managed to get my right arm free, and with all the force I could command I struck him a stinging blow in the face, and immediately the blood spurted from his nose into my face and eyes, half blinding me.

I was under a disadvantage in every possible way, for he had me in his powerful grip beneath him; moreover, I was encumbered with a heavy wet overcoat, while he had only his shirt and trousers on. I felt at that moment, and have always been convinced of it since, that my life hung by a hair, for this half-mad giant would have strangled me. But help came from a quarter I had not counted on. The woman—the living corpse—had crept back, and seeing how matters stood, she seized the handcuffs that were lying on the floor and struck the man over the head. With a blood-curdling oath he released me and sprang at her, exclaiming, 'So this is your doing?'

In an instant I was on my feet, threw off both my coats, and went at him, for he had the wretched woman pinned against the wall, and was strangling her. I seized him round the waist, and dragged him away, and the woman slipped to the floor an inert mass, while blood oozed from her mouth.

Still keeping my hold, we struggled desperately, and I dragged him towards the door. He swore and cursed, and groaned and panted: vowing by heaven and hades that I should not leave the room alive. But though I had not the physical strength nor weight that he had, I felt that he would have all his work now to overpower me. Putting forth his power, he dragged me back into the room and made for the fireplace, where there was a poker. I guessed his design, and with a supreme effort swung him round, and we both fell, but this time he was underneath, and face downward. He succeeded, however, in getting his hands on the floor, and by this means, owing to his great strength, he raised himself up and threw me off. I gained my feet, however, as soon as he, and once more we were locked in a deadly grip. In our struggle we crashed against the table, sending it over with the lamp, which smashed, and the oil took fire, while the deadly fumes of the burning petroleum rose in dense clouds. It was an awful moment, and I felt that the poor, wretched woman, lying insensible on the floor, would be burned to death. I appealed to him to save her. But this only made him madder, and he exerted his Herculean strength to throw me on the flames. I was not a chicken, however, and the desperate situation lent me additional strength, and once more I succeeded in striking him on the face, and I got him to the doorway. Then I heard heavy feet on the stairs, and knew that succour had arrived. I shouted out, and in another few moments two powerful policemen bounded up, and in a minute we had the 'Knave of Spades' ironed, though not without a struggle. Then I rushed into the room, which was filled with choking, blinding smoke, and seizing the insensible woman in my arms I struggled out and down the stairs. I was almost suffocated myself, and suffering from suppressed excitement. But I reached the street, and the cold wind and rain refreshed me. I staggered with my burden to a doctor who I knew lived here, and when the door was opened I bore the poor creature into his consulting-room, and giving the doctor my name, and requesting that he would bestow every possible attention on the woman, I hurried back. The fire had been extinguished by the neighbours, and the 'Knave of Spades' was in a collapsed condition, for he had lost a great deal of blood, the wound on his head, where he had been struck with the handcuffs, being of a serious nature.

Leaving one of my men in charge of the place, I, with the help of the other, conveyed the ruffian to the station, and saw him well secured. Then I sent more men to his house to bring away the pictures, and I went to the doctor's to inquire about the woman, and I was shocked to learn that I had carried him a corpse. Being far gone in consumption and exceedingly weak, the fumes of burning petroleum had suffocated her.

The rest may be briefly told. The 'Knave of Spades', whose proper name was John Wilson, proved to be a notorious thief who had been twice before convicted; and he was handed over to the London police. He was clearly proved to have been the ringleader in the Thames Ditton burglary, and being tried for the crime at the Central Criminal Court, he was sent into penal servitude for twenty-one years.

He would tell nothing about the poor woman whose life had been wrecked by him, and all that we could find out was that her name was Mary. She was buried at my expense, and on a slab of white marble I had this simple and touching epitaph carved:

Sacred to the Memory of Mary.
'Though my sins be as scarlet Thy blood can wash me clean.'

The Robbery of the London Mail

In the old coaching days robberies from the Royal mails were comparatively common, for the roads were lonely and unprotected, and lawless bands of ruffians roamed about the country and made the mail coaches their special prey. But when the iron horse had run the lumbering vehicles off the road a new era was inaugurated, and it seemed as if the vocation of the mail robbers had gone for ever. Nevertheless, many robberies of the mails did take place, and perhaps the most daring and extraordinary of them all was that which I am now about to relate.

A good many years ago, one very stormy December night, the London train, with less than the average complement of passengers, and a very heavy mail, steamed out of Glasgow on its way south. It was Saturday, on which day the mail is unusually heavy, owing to the winding-up of the week's business, and on that night almost invariably large quantities of valuable securities, as well as money, are carried to the Metropolis. It had been a very wild sort of day, and towards the evening snow began to fall thickly and the wind rose to the force of a gale. It was due to this no doubt that the passengers were so few. In the first-class there were not more than a dozen, and amongst these was a tall, military-looking gentleman, who was accompanied by a footman, who rode second-class, while the gentleman himself travelled in a first-class compartment alone. He was a very striking-looking man, with a florid complexion, relieved by a heavy white moustache and white hair. He was faultlessly dressed, and wore over his frock coat a heavy overcoat of rough cloth, trimmed with massive fur at the collar and cuffs. It was noted that before the train started the man and his master walked up and down the platform in spite of the bitter wind that was sweeping it, and seemed to be in deep and earnest conversation. Although the railway officials and porters had no idea who the gentleman was, they paid him great deference and attention, for they did not doubt he was a 'swell of the first water,' and that handsome tips would be forthcoming for service rendered. Nor were they mistaken, for the servant, by his master's order, dispensed largess with a liberal hand. The only luggage the gentleman had was a bundle of rugs, a hat-box, and a small portmanteau; and this absence of anything like a quantity of impedimenta fostered the idea that he was a military man.

The train steamed out of the station punctually to time, and very soon was thundering along at tremendous speed in the very teeth of the howling storm.

The travelling post office was in charge of an official and four assistants, and they were to be strengthened at Carlisle by the addition of two more men. As soon as ever the train left Glasgow the doors and windows of the post van were shut, and the men set to work with great heartiness to reduce what seemed to be chaos to order. About an hour after leaving Glasgow and when nearing Carlisle, it was suddenly discovered that one of the most important of the mail bags had been cut open, and, with the exception of about half a dozen letters, the whole of the contents extracted. The utmost consternation at once seized upon all those in charge, and nearly everyone felt perfectly certain that the bag was intact when the train left Glasgow. But, if that was true, then there was some inexplicable mystery in connection with the robbery.

I have said that 'nearly' everyone was certain, and this requires some explanation, because there were only five people altogether in the van, namely, the officer and his four assistants. Now the chief and two men were quite certain, but the other two could express no opinion as they had no distinct recollection of having seen that particular bag, and they expressed themselves as rather inclined to believe that it had been tampered with in Glasgow. The names of these two men, it may here be stated, were George Mitchell and Walter Hardy. The first named had been in the service five years, and, being exceedingly clever and smart, had been rapidly promoted. Hardy, who was quite a young man, not more than two-and-twenty, had only had six months' experience, and was being trained by Mitchell.

Of course, nothing could be done until the train reached Carlisle, and as soon as it drew up, information of the robbery was at once given, and the electric wires were set in motion, but, unfortunately, it was found that there was some interruption, due, no doubt, to the storm, which had increased in severity. In fact, it was admitted to be the worst storm that had visited the country for many years. Owing to the electrical interruption, nothing, of course, could be done then. But it was decided that George Mitchell should remain in Carlisle and go back to Glasgow by the down mail, which was due at Carlisle early in the morning. As soon, therefore, as the other bags had been taken in, the train steamed off again; and just as its tail lights were disappearing the military gentleman's servant came tearing out of a refreshment buffet and rushed after the train. Of course he was too late, and he manifested the greatest amount of distress and concern at having so stupidly missed the train, saying that he would be sure to lose his place, for his master was terribly strict. Of course the porters and the station-master manifested much sympathy with the unfortunate servant, and incidentally he was asked who his master was, and he replied that he was Major Templeton, a retired army officer, very wealthy and somewhat eccentric. The station-master thereupon offered to send the servant south by a goods train which passed there at three o'clock in the morning; but the servant, while expressing gratitude, said he might as well be hung for a sheep as a lamb now, and that the night was too stormy and cold for him to subject himself to the discomforts of a luggage train, and he should therefore engage a bed at an hotel.

As no one could offer any objection to this arrangement, the man proceeded to the hotel, where George Mitchell had already gone and was refreshing himself with some hot whisky and water and cold beef and bread in the dining-room. The military gentle-man's servant took advantage of this to join him and do likewise, and they were the only two people in the room. Having finished their supper, they drew their chairs round the blazing fire, and or-dering some steaming toddy, smoked cigars and made themselves comfortable previous to retiring for the night. They sat together till two o'clock in the morning, and then separated.

The day following the robbery I was ordered to investigate the circumstances, and do everything possible to capture the thieves with their booty. Of course I was only told the bare facts of the case—that is, that between Glasgow and Carlisle one of the mail bags, which was known to have very valuable contents, was found to have been cut, and the contents stolen. The mystery was, where had this been done? It seemed almost impossible it could have been done in transit.

As soon as George Mitchell got back to Glasgow I was placed in communication with him, but he could only give me the story of the theft as I have stated it.

I found Mitchell to be an exceedingly sharp and shrewd fellow, and I thought be would be of great assistance to me in helping to unravel the mystery. It fortunately happened that the thieves had had everything in their favour. First, the storm; secondly, the inter-ruption of the telegraph; and, thirdly, the day following the robbery being Sunday. As was my habit I began my work at the very source, and I endeavoured. to learn every detail of the incidents appertain-ing to the starting of the train, and I was particular to inquire what passengers travelled in it. These questions led to my being informed about the military-looking old gentleman and his servant, and I at once felt deeply interested in these two persons. I sought another interview with Mr. Mitchell, and asked if he had noticed the gentle-man and his servant, and his answer was that he was too busy when the train was preparing to start to notice anyone except such people as he had to deal with officially. But he mentioned that the servant had missed the train at Carlisle; that they supped together in the hotel and that the man had told him that his master was a military officer.

This piece of information at once set me pondering, as well as raised my suspicions, and I deemed it my duty to learn something more about the servant and his master, for I was convinced that the robbery had been effected by means of a conspiracy, in which several persons were concerned. I separately interviewed every one who had had any hand in conveying the mail bags down to the railway station, as well as the Post Office authorities themselves, and each and all was and were positive that the bag was intact when put into the van. I ascertained that the bag in question had been in the van about half an hour before the train started. That of course would afford ample time for dexterous robbers to operate, and they were greatly facilitated in their operations by the fearful night, and the few people on the platform:

This was the theory of the officials, but it was not mine. They were convinced that the bag had been cut in the station. I was convinced otherwise, although I did not say so then, but I made a rule of never overlooking the possibilities involved in any theory. I therefore examined their theory carefully.

But I could find no circumstance which warranted me, according to my way of thinking, in coming to the conclusion that the letters had been abstracted in Glasgow, though I did see much which seemed to justify me in assuming that the robbery had been committed in transit.

Nothing possibly could have happened worse in the interests of justice than that that day should have been Sunday, while the breakdown of the telegraph system only added to the difficulties. But, in spite of all this, I was not disposed to rest on my oars. A stern chase is ever a long chase, and the more start I allowed the robbers the more difficult would it be to get up to them. I hope I shall not be accused of repeating myself if I venture to say again that both by nature and training it was my habit to act quickly in all emergencies, and I had seldom had a case in which quickness of decision was so imperative as in this one. It was impossible, of course, to determine at that moment the amount of the loss, but the officials of the Post Office knew that the bag that had been robbed was the 'registered letter bag', and there would be a large amount represented by drafts, cheques, bills, bonds, and actual money.

Now it was astonishing what a perfect unanimity of opinion there was that the robbery had been effected in the Glasgow station, and no one was louder in asserting this opinion than George Mitchell. He repeated it over and over and over again, and seemed to be exceedingly anxious that no other opinion should be entertained.

I have already said that I held different views, and my reasons for doing so I shall presently explain. When the matter had been well discussed at the Post Office, I astonished everybody by announcing my intention of starting immediately for Carlisle.

'But there is no train until tonight,' cried one gentleman, who was high in position, and thought he had a right to speak dictatorially.

'I am aware of it,' I answered.

'Besides, what's the use of going to Carlisle?' exclaimed another gentleman who had a very exalted opinion of his own abilities. 'You don't expect that the robbers are feasting themselves at Carlisle, do you?'

'No, sir, I do not,' I answered quietly.

'Then, what's the use of going there?'

'That is a question I must claim leave to pass unanswered,' I said. 'I have my own way of conducting my own business, and I must act according to my lights.'

I saw at once that the course I had thus decided upon did not give satisfaction by any means, but I was firmly convinced in my own mind that I should find my clue at Carlisle or nowhere at all. And so I was content to be thought a fool until the triumph was mine; then the laugh would be on my side.

'But how are you going to Carlisle?' asked the gentleman who had first spoken, and who seemed quite annoyed at what no doubt he considered was my pigheadedness.

'Well, sir, I wish you to give me a written request to the railway people to run me down on an engine. Being Sunday morning, the line is clear, and we can cover the journey in a little over an hour.'

At first he seemed disposed to flatly say no to this request, but he evidently thought better of it, and somewhat sullenly assented. But as he wrote out the necessary order and tossed it to me he remarked—

'Of course you will understand, Mr. Donovan, that we shall hold ourselves free to employ other assistance if it seems to us desirable to do so.'

'Oh! by all means do so,' I observed with a smile. 'You have put the case in my hands, and I am simply doing what seems to me right. Of course I may be wrong, and it is for you to exercise your own discretion. I have now another request to make, and that is that Mr. George Mitchell may accompany me.'

This request caused more astonishment than did that for the special engine, and no one was louder in protests than Mitchell himself. But I urged my wish with persistency, and pointed out that the young man might be of considerable use; so at length consent was given, and, as he was only a subordinate, he had to obey orders.

These preliminaries having been settled, I proceeded without loss of time to the station, where I was fortunate in finding a powerful engine with full steam up, as some necessary shunting work was about to begin. As a little delay in that, however, would make no material difference, the engine and tender were placed at my disposal; and, as the telegraph wires were in working order again, news was flashed along the line that the engine was coming, and that it was to be kept clear.

This mode of travelling, of course, was not quite as luxurious as a first-class carriage or even a post van, while the gloom of the morning and the icy atmosphere rendered it anything but pleasant. For our accommodation some of the coals were shovelled back from the front of the tender, and boards covered with sacks were placed for seats. As soon as these little details were settled the signal was given, and with a shriek from the engine we steamed oat into the murky atmosphere. The cold was intense, and the landscape as bleak, desolate, and weird as anyone could possibly imagine. As we cleared the station, and George Mitchell pulled his topcoat up about his throat and ears, he said with a growl—

'Well, I may be mistaken, but it strikes me you are going on a wild-goose chase.'

'Possibly,' I answered, 'but we shall see by-and-by. I have always been of the opinion that it is never safe to prophesy until you know.'

It has been my fate to make a good many queer journeys in the course of my professional career; but seldom, indeed, have I been called upon to endure a more uncomfortable one than that Sunday morning ride on the engine from Glasgow to Carlisle. My companion Mitchell did nothing but growl from the time we left, until with a shriek the engine rushed into the Carlisle station.

I have stated that I had formed a theory about the robbery which was in direct opposition to that held by the officials. They were strongly of opinion that the letters had been stolen from the bag in the Glasgow station, while my opinion was equally strong that they had been stolen in transit; and I will now give my reasons for thinking so.

George Mitchell himself had furnished all the details of the crime, and he was foolish enough to say that his chief and two of his colleagues were sure that the bag had been cut on the journey between Glasgow and Carlisle; but that he himself and his assistant, Walter Hardy, were as sure that the theft been committed while the train was waiting in the Glasgow station. He repeated his views so often, and manifested such anxiety to get those views accepted, that I asked him at last upon what grounds be felt so positive that be was right. And to this he could give me no more satisfactory answer than—

'Because neither I nor my assistant Hardy have any recollection of having seen the bags intact in Glasgow.'

Although of course Mitchell did not think it, his answer was singularly weak and utterly illogical, while he set his statement and that of an irresponsible youth against the chief and two experienced hands. Now I ascertained that the official in charge that night had been thirty years in the service, and was one of the most experienced and trusted men on the road. So I argued to myself that it was not in the least likely that he could have been mistaken. At any rate he was infinitely more likely to be right than Mitchell, and the result was I began to suspect that Mitchell himself had had a hand in the conspiracy.

Of course I did not tell him nor anyone else what my suspicions were at that moment. Had I done so I should have shown a lamentable want of tact and discretion. But I proceeded at once, silently and surely, to spread my net to snare him, in case I should prove to be right; and I resolved not to lose sight of him if possible. Hence my reason for requesting that he might be allowed to accompany me to Carlisle.

After we had refreshed ourselves with some hot coffee, and bread and butter which we much needed, we proceeded to the chief police office, where I managed to have a few private words with the superintendent, and I requested him to detain Mitchell as long as possible on a plea of getting information from him; and while this little plan was being carried out I slipped away and returned to the railway station, where I directed my energies to endeavouring to find out something about the movements of the presumed servant of 'Major Templeton'. Of course he could not get south by train until late that night, when the up mail passed, and the people at the hotel where he slept did not know where he had gone to. He went out soon after Mitchell had left for Glasgow. I obtained, however, a very accurate description of him from a singularly intelligent and observant waiter, and when I asked this man if he had formed any opinion in his own mind about the gentleman's servant, he shrugged his shoulders, and said—

'Well, I wasn't altogether favourably impressed with him.'

'Why?'

'Well—it struck me there was something queer about him.'

The dash represents a long pause my informant made before uttering the remainder of his answer, and it convinced me, as a student of human nature, that he not merely spoke words, but gave utterance to a conviction that had been well thought out.

I did not question him further. There was no need to do that. He could not have told me anything more, and what he had told me only served to strengthen my own feeling that Mitchell and the supposed servant were in collusion.

My business now was to find out where he had gone to. Although it was Sunday, I should have been prepared to stake a fortune, had I possessed one, on the statement that he had not gone to church; while, as for walking about for pleasure, that seemed equally absurd to suppose, for a wet, sleety, clinging snow was still falling, the cold was intense, and the streets and roads were like rivers of greasy slush; and however enthusiastic a sightseer that young man might have been, I am sure that the barren, shivering, dripping, fog-enshrouded country round about would hardly have tempted him forth from the cosy comfort of the hotel fireside.

Where had he gone to then? and why had he gone? To those two questions I resolved to have answers before I was many hours older. As I have mentioned, I had got a very good description of the man from the waiter; even to a small wart on one side of his nose, and I was hopeful that, being Sunday, a stranger would be more conspicuous going through the streets, and it might therefore be able to more easily trace him. I began by making some inquiries amongst a party of railway porters who had been engaged all the morning shunting. Of course my inquiries were directed to eliciting if they had observed a man like a gentleman's servant about the station, and one of these porters told me that he had been asked by such a man if there was a livery stable in the town, and the porter had directed him to one.

This little item of information set me pondering, but, need I say, it only served to confirm my suspicions, and I lost no time in going to the livery stable to ask if my man had been there, and received the reply that he had, and had hired a horse and gig.

'Did you ask where he was going to?' I queried.

'Oh, no. He said he was a stranger in the town, and wanted to pass the time away by driving about a bit.'

'Did he say when he would be back?'

'In the course of three or four hours.'

'Was it a good horse?'

'Yes. The best we had in the stable. He said he wanted one that could go well, and as we saw he was a gentleman's servant, we felt sure he would be used to good horses, and so we gave him a mare that can lick anything on the road in this part of the country.'

'I'm sorry you gave him that mare.'

'Why?' exclaimed the man quickly, and becoming suspicions by reason of my questions.

'Because I am very anxious to see him on important business, and he may lead me an awful wild-goose chase,' I answered with a smile, thus allaying the man's fears.

'Now, tell me,' I went on, 'have you anything else in your stable that could keep the tail of that wonderful mare in sight in a stern chase?'

'Well, yes, I almost think we have. There's Patsy, an old Irish hunter, and if you only get his metal up he'll go like steam.'

'And have you a light gig?'

'Yes.'

'Good. Now, have Patsy ready harnessed in the gig in half an hour's time, when I will come back. I have a call to make first.'

The livery stable keeper looked at me with a puzzled air, and there was an expression of doubt and suspicion in his eyes, so I said—

'You can keep a secret?'

'Yes.'

'Very well, then; I have some reason to think that gentleman's servant is up to some mischief. Here is my card. You will see that I am in the detective service. It is my duty to follow your other customer, and find out his business if possible. Therefore, I trust you will give me your fastest horse and lightest gig.'

'Never fear but I'll do that,' answered the man. 'Patsy's been in since Friday night, and if you let him go I don't think there's much that will keep in front of him. And though the mare has a faster pace, Patsy can stay longer, and would keep his legs when the mare would drop.'

This information was welcome, for I had not a doubt now that that Patsy would have to be put on his metal. No doubt the reader will ask why I thought so, and I will at once satisfy the very natural curiosity. The gentleman's servant had not gone out for pleasure. Of that I was firmly convinced, for there could be no possible pleasure in driving about in such beastly weather. Therefore he must have had a deep design, and I made a guess what that design was. He was either going to meet some confederates, or going to search for the missing letters. And let it be understood at once that I did not for a moment believe him to be what he represented himself to be, namely, a gentleman's servant; nor did I think that he had missed the London train the night previous by accident. I was too old a bird to be deceived with such poor chaff, and I was prepared to stake my reputation in support of my idea that he knew all about the robbery. Such robberies as that were never effected single-handed. It was necessary there should be a concerted plan, and consequently two or more persons were required to carry the plan out. Of course, if I was right in my theorising, the man had not driven south, because the letters had not come even as far as Carlisle, therefore he had gone north, and if I overtook him at all I was sure it would be on the north road.

Having arranged with the livery-stable keeper, my next step was to go back to the police station. I found that George Mitchell had left. He grew impatient, and, of course, the superintendent could not detain him against his will. Having arranged for an experienced member of the force to join me about a quarter of a mile out of the town, I hurried back to the hotel, where, as I expected, I found Mitchell. He was not the man to put himself to much personal discomfort or inconvenience. In fact, he was toasting his toes over a roaring fire, was puffing the smoke from an Habanna, and had a glass of steaming toddy beside him.

'Well,' he exclaimed jauntily, 'what success?'

'Oh, not much, if any,' I replied.

'Aha!' he cried exultantly, 'I told you you were coming on a fool's errand. The best thing you can do is to join me in a cigar and whisky hot. This blazing fire has infinitely more attraction for me than the dreary, wretched streets. Ugh!' he added with a shudder, 'the infernal weather is enough to make those who cannot get comfort go and drown themselves, though for my own part, if I wanted to commit suicide in such weather, I should prefer to be roasted to death, for the water would be so cold.'

He laughed loudly at his own poor and ghastly joke. Then I answered him deliberately—

'Possibly I have come on a fool's errand, but duty with me is duty, and, though you may, I cannot afford to be studying my personal comfort when there is duty to do.'

'Ah,' he observed with a sneer and a smack of the lips, 'you are too conscientious.'

'My conscientiousness is the secret of my success in my profession, sir,' I returned. 'But I mustn't waste any more time. I shall see you later on.'

As I left the room I thought to myself— 'You are either a fool or a clever rogue, Mr. Mitchell, and before the day is done I will endeavour to determine in which category you are to be classed'.

On getting back to the livery stable, I found the gig and Patsy ready. He was a powerful, big-boned, and clean-limbed horse, with a nervous eye, and all the indication of 'go' in him. Although reduced to harness now, he had still some of the lingering fire of the hunter in him. He started off with a bound, but I kept him well in hand till we cleared the town. I picked up my man at the spot indicated, and we got on to the great north road, which, for many miles, runs beside the railway, or nearly so.

Now my theory was this. George Mitchell and young Hardy had worked together, and had, at some spot previously agreed upon, thrown the letters out, and the 'gentleman's servant' had gone to get them. The more I dwelt upon the circumstances of the case the more I was convinced I was right; and in reasoning the matter out it was impossible to avoid coming to the conclusion—firstly, that the letters had been put out some distance from Carlisle; secondly, the spot chosen would, for obvious reasons, be a lonely one. Mitchell of course was very well acquainted with the line, and I did not doubt that the 'servant' had also gained an accurate knowledge of it.

If I was right, the fellow would lose no time; and as he had got a good start I gave Patsy his head and let him go his pace, and he did go! The road was in a bad state, but that told as much against the other fellow as against us. However, Patsy had about thirty-six hours' rest in him, and was eager for the fray. The mud was tossed up by the wheels, and flew about us in a shower, and the bare hedges and dripping, naked trees flew past us at express speed. Fortunately we had the road to ourselves. So Sunday favoured us in that way. But it was an exciting drive, and I felt somehow as if it was a race for my professional reputation.

For mile after mile we kept on, but without coming up with our man. On leaving the town I noted the impress of wheels, and every now and then I examined the road to see if that impress continued, and it did with never a break, and I was sure that the wheels that had marked the ground were those of the vehicle driven by the man I was so anxious to come up with.

After some miles the road and the line part company, but meet again further on. In about two hours and a half we had covered twenty-five miles, and had reached a very wild and lonely part of the country, and where a narrow lane, fringed with dense pine woods on either side, branched off from the main road and led towards the railway.

I got down and examined the ground, and saw that the soft mud of the lane showed newly made tracks of wheels; so we proceeded cautiously now, keeping our eyes about us. For nearly two miles the lane was tortuous, and afforded no long view ahead, but presently there was a bit of straight road that gradually rose to an arch over the railway, then dropped down on to a dreary moorland on the other side. Suddenly I pulled up Patsy with a jerk, and almost threw him on to his haunches, for I saw in a wooded hollow to the left of the bridge a horse and trap standing, and I could scarcely repress a cry of delight. I held a hurried consultation with my companion, and we decided that it would be better for us to proceed. We were both in plain clothes, and we and the horse were covered with mud, so that we thought it not improbable that we might be taken for farmers.

We went on slowly now, and when we came opposite the hollow a man suddenly started up from under the archway of the bridge. That man was the 'gentleman's servant.' Of course he did not know me, and so I asked him if he could give me a light for my pipe, and while he was fumbling in his pocket for matches, I got down, and with a sudden movement threw myself on him, and before he could offer any resistance I had him handcuffed.

He was utterly dumfoundered. If a man had dropped from the clouds and arrested him he could hardly have looked more amazed, and well he might, for the spot was as lonely as one could conceive. It was desolation, and save for the railway that spoke of civilisation it might have been some uninhabited region of the earth.

Close to the railway arch was a heap of paper ashes, and I guessed at once that the villain had been burning the letters. Nor was I wrong. Nearby was a large piece of sacking and a leather strap; and some unopened letters and packages were still lying on the sacking, which had been used to envelop the things when thrown out at this bridge. The man's pockets were bulky with money, articles of jewellery, bonds, and other securities representing many thousands of pounds.

The only remark the fellow made was to curse his ill-luck, and to express with a round oath his regret that he had not had time to put a bullet through me. That he had the means of doing this was proved by a revolver in his pocket.

With the straps that had been used to fasten the bundle of letters, I doubly secured his arms, and having gathered up everything in the shape of letter or package, we put the rascal in the trap we had come in. I got up alongside of him, while my companion took charge of the other vehicle, which brought up the rear, and thus we drove back to the town, and lodged our man in gaol. I then proceeded to arrest George Mitchell, who was scarcely less amazed than the other fellow had been; and a few minutes later I had announced my capture to the officials in London and Glasgow by means of the telegraph. The next day I was informed by wire that young Hardy had also been arrested, and a little later 'Major Templeton' was likewise in the hands of the police. He proved to be a man by the name of Andrew Wilson, who had at one time moved in a very good position in society, but had ruined himself on the turf and had already suffered imprisonment for forgery. His 'servant' was a John Renton, a returned convict. This precious pair of rascals had skillfully planned the robbery, and had corrupted Mitchell by the payment of fifty pounds, and he in turn corrupted the youth Hardy. The boy had cut the bag, and Mitchell had made the letters and packages up into a bundle with the canvas and strap he had specially provided. He was enabled to do this, as he had a compartment to himself in the post van. The spot chosen for throwing the bag out was singularly suitable. Firstly, the bridge was a good landmark, and that part of the country was very wild and lonely; and, secondly, an exceedingly sharp curve rendered it necessary for the trains to slacken speed at this spot.

When the gang were brought to trial the evidence was overwhelming, for young Hardy turned Queen's evidence, and by this means escaped punishment, though, of course, he lost his situation. The others were sentenced to long terms of imprisonment; and as Mitchell heard his doom, he, no doubt, thought that, in taking that engine ride on Sunday morning from Glasgow to Carlisle, I had not gone on such a wild-goose chase as he was pleased to think at the time, or rather affect to think. But it is unquestionable that he never dreamed he would be proved to have had a hand in the crime; in fact, the rascals believed they had had their plans so well that detection was all but impossible, but they received practical illustration of Burns's lines—

> The best laid plans o' mice and men
> Gang aft agley.

All For Love's Sake

◈

O ne morning I received a message from the managing partner of one of the largest drapery firms in the city of Glasgow, asking me to call upon him at my leisure, as he wished
to see me on important business. As I always had leisure for important business I lost no time in complying with the request, and on
inquiring for the manager I was at once shown into his private room.
He received me very graciously, and then proceeded to inform me that
his object in sending was to ask me to try and detect a person in his
employ who for some time had been carrying on a series of petty thefts.
Although he described them as 'petty thefts', he explained that he did
so only in a relative degree, for in the aggregate a very considerable
loss had been sustained by the firm.

Having listened without interruption to his story, I asked him if
he had reason to suspect any particular individual.

'No,' he answered scratching his head. 'That is where the puzzle is. My partner and I have used our best endeavours to fix the
guilt, but without success.'

'What class of goods are they principally that have been pur-
loined?' I asked.

'Well, that again is another puzzling part of the affair, for the
thief has been perfectly impartial, and he has given attention to
most of the departments in the establishment. Nor has he confined
himself to goods, as small sums of money have been missed.'

'You have a good many departments, I suppose, sir?' I asked.

'Yes.'

'And have those in which you sell your heavier stock suffered in
like degree?'

'No, I believe they have been quite exempt.'

'That shows,' I answered, 'that the thief has confined his attention to such things as he could conveniently carry away. Can you
enumerate the things you have missed?'

'Oh yes. They are dress pieces, laces, shawls, ladies' stockings,
some of them very expensive silk ones; ladies' handkerchiefs, ribbons, jewellery—for we have a jewellery department as well; gloves,
they have been carried off, I might almost say, by wholesale; but
the theft of the gloves has now stopped.'

'Were they always ladies' gloves?'

'Always, I think.'

From other inquiries I made I learned that the firm employed
about two hundred people, and about one hundred and twenty of
these slept on the premises. The business was of a very miscellaneous character, even groceries forming part of the trade.

'Some of our people,' continued the manager, 'have been in the
employ a great number of years. The business has gradually increased,
and as it has increased, so we have added to our staff. Now, we have
been very reluctant to cast suspicion on anyone, and so we have kept
this matter to ourselves, hoping that we should be able to pounce
upon the delinquent, and weed him out from the good ones.'

'You speak of the thief in the masculine gender,' I remarked.
'Have you any particular reason for that?'

'Oh no; none whatever. Why do you ask?'

'Because the fact of the articles stolen being principally feminine things, would seem to point to a female hand.'

'Ah, true,' he said. 'I never thought of that before.'

'Or otherwise,' I continued, 'the thief is some young man who may
have been doing the handsome at your expense to his sweetheart.'

This alternative seemed to puzzle the worthy manager still more,
and he scratched his head and knitted his brows in a very comical
way, exclaiming at last—

'Well, the fact is, Mr. Donovan, we shall have to place ourselves in
your hands, in the hope that you will solve the problem. Now, what do
you propose to do?'

'I propose to become one of your people for a time,' I answered.
'In what capacity?'

'In any capacity. Can you make me a sort of shop-walker, or some thing like that, and shift me about from department to department without causing suspicion? I should like to assume the character of a very stupid person, with whom you must always and openly be finding fault; and that also will be an excuse for you trying me first in one place and then another.'

The manager laughed heartily as he tumbled to my little plan; and all the details being settled, it was arranged that I should start on Monday morning, it being then Friday. Accordingly I took my leave, and on the Monday following I duly entered on my new sphere of action.

Now, I had in the course of my career played many parts, but it was a novel one I had thus undertaken, and the character of a draper's assistant did not altogether sit well upon me.

The first thing that the manager did was to take me round and introduce me to the various heads as Mr. Alexander Nicolson, from the Isle of Skye. That in itself was sufficient to beget a certain amount of contempt for me on the part of those knowing Glaswegians, who are pleased to believe that all Highlanders are more or less stupid, and that the islanders of Skye are particularly more so. Of course this is a fallacy, but it is a fossilised belief amongst a certain class of Lowlanders, and nothing can root it out.

I did my best, by assuming a certain amount of awkwardness, to sustain the character, and I was conscious that I was not only an object of curiosity on the part of those it came in contact with, but some of them indulged in a quiet sniggle at my expense. And before I had been in the establishment three days, I found I was the laughing stock of the place; and three or four times a day I was openly rated by the manager for standing gaping and staring about me 'like an idiot.'

At the end of the week I was no nearer the solution of the problem than I had been six days previously. I had seen no one whom I could conscientiously justify myself in suspecting. But of course I wasn't going to give in, and so on the following Monday morning I found myself installed in the gloves, ribbons, handkerchiefs, and parasol department. The most of the assistants here were females, there being only four young men.

The Monday, Tuesday, and Wednesday of that week passed without anything occurring to arouse my suspicion, but I was successful in thoroughly sustaining my character for stupidity, and I became the butt for the very small wit of a dandified young fellow, who, I learned, had been in the employ about two years and was from London. His name was George Barrington, he was about six-and-twenty, he dressed with a great regard to his personal appearance, his wages were fifteen shillings a week and all found. This young man was so infatuated with a sense of his own importance that he regarded me with contempt that was almost too deep for words.

On the Tuesday a young lady had come into this part of the shop, and been served by Barrington with a pair of gloves. He was evidently well acquainted with her, for he shook her hand, and seemed very pleased to see her. She was a remarkably pretty girl, younger than he was, probably about twenty. She was a blonde, with fair wavy hair, and a delicate complexion, with deep blue, almost purple eyes. She was dressed well, even fashionably, though not in any way loud. I noticed that she had small feet and hands, and wore particularly neat boots and gloves.

The probabilities are I should not have taken in all these details had it not been for Barrington shaking her hand. That act attracted my attention and caused me to watch them, with the result, judging from her face and his, that they were lovers. Of course there was nothing extraordinary in that, for many young ladies, with the caprice peculiar to their sex, choose their lovers from amongst drapers' assistants. But what struck me in this case was a very noticeable disparity in the appearance of this young man and woman. She had the air and general appearance of refinement and gentility. Her style, her dress, her manner seemed unmistakably to point to her moving in a very different station in life to what he moved in.

She was as superior to him, in fact, as a gold sovereign is to a brass farthing.

When she had gone I remarked jocularly to him—

'You seem very sweet on that young lady?'

'A fellow has a right to be sweet on the lady who is going to be his wife,' he replied proudly.

'Oh indeed; that's it, is it?' I answered. 'Well, you are to be congratulated, for she's a remarkably pretty girl; and if she's as good as she's pretty, you are in luck's way.'

'I believe you, my boy,' he exclaimed, and he seemed so consciously happy and proud that I could not find it in my heart to think evil of him.

On Thursday morning the young lady came again. The department was rather busy, and there were a good many people being served. Barrington, who had been attending to an old lady, left her, turning her over to one of his shopmates, and he at once went to the young woman, who purchased some handkerchiefs and a parasol. The transaction took a long time, for neither seemed in a hurry to bring it to a conclusion; but I kept my eyes on them the whole time, and when at last they could not make the slightest pretext for prolonging the interview, she rose to go, and he put out his hand to hers and I saw him pass something to her. It was something small, and seemed to be enveloped in white tissue paper. I saw her palm close upon this something, while her face reddened a little; then, with a look of love in her eyes, she left the shop.

Here is a little matter, I thought to myself, that I must get to the bottom of, and in a few moments I managed to slip away, and, going outside, it was in time to catch sight of the young lady as she turned a street corner, and I at once followed her.

She continued her way westward, and at last entered one of the large tenement houses near the park. I hurried up, and was in time to hear a door on the fourth flat close. The plate on the door bore the name Mrs. Walker. I waited for about five minutes, and then rang the bell, and the door was at once opened by a servant.

'Is Mrs. Walker at home?' I inquired.

The servant informed me that she was, and invited me in, showing me into a well-furnished parlour, where she asked my name.

'Well, Mrs. Walker won't know me,' I said, 'but say that I wish to see her on a matter of business.'

In about ten minutes a very stately and ladylike woman, middle-aged, dressed in mourning and wearing a widow's cap, entered the room. I at once rose and bowed.

'Excuse my intrusion, madam,' I said, 'but I believe you have a daughter.'

'Yes, my only child. But, pray, inform me who you are and why you ask?'

'Firstly, will you permit me to see her in your presence?'

'Oh, certainly!' the lady answered, and, ringing the bell, she told the servant to request 'Miss Annie' to come in.

In a brief space of time Annie entered, and, as I had expected, I looked again on the young woman I had followed from the draper's. She had divested herself of her bonnet, cloak, and gloves, and there could be no two opinions as to her good looks.

'I understand, Miss Walker,' I began, 'that you, are acquainted with a Mr. George Barrington?'

'Oh yes,' she answered, while the colour rushed into her pretty face.

'Mr. Barrington and my daughter are engaged,' said the mother proudly.

'Oh, indeed!' I exclaimed, in seeming surprise. 'Well, I may at once say that I have a very particular reason for asking you a few questions about Mr. Barrington, and I do so by desire of his employers.'

'We shall be happy to answer any questions we can,' said the mother, evidently without suspecting what my object was.

'Have you any idea what his means are?' I asked.

'I believe he is very well off,' Mrs. Walker said.

'But his salary is only fifteen shillings a week,' I returned.

'Oh yes; but then his father is a comparatively rich man, and allows his son two hundred a year; and George is only in the shop to get a good knowledge of the various departments, and his father is then going to set him up in business.'

'Will you kindly tell me how you know this?'

'Why from George himself and also from letters that he has frequently shown us,' said Mrs. Walker, beginning to evince alarm, and she added quickly, 'I hope there is nothing wrong?'

Without answering the question, I addressed myself to Miss Walker, and said—

'It is necessary that I should ask you a question, miss. You were in the shop a little while ago, and as you were about to leave Mr. Barrington handed you something wrapped up in paper. Will you please to tell me what it was?'

I saw her grow pale as she said—

'Oh yes; it was a brooch.'

'A brooch?'

'Yes; it's my birthday, and he gave it to me for a birthday present.'

'It's painful for me to have to arouse your suspicions in any way, but I will ask you to let me see the brooch.'

Without another word she jumped up and left the room, and the mother, who had now become agitated, remarked—

'I hope, sir, there is nothing wrong?'

'I hope so, too,' I returned prevaricatingly.

In a few moments the girl came back, and handed me a small cardboard box, saying—

'I've scarcely looked at it yet.'

I removed the lid, and lying on a bed of snow-white cotton wool was a beautiful gold brooch set with rubies and pearls, and I saw immediately it was valuable.

Handing my card to Mrs. Walker, I said—

'I shall be compelled to take this brooch away for a little while, in order to prove that it has been come by honestly. But I may at once say—in fact, it would be cruelty not to do so—that there are good grounds for suspecting that Mr. Barrington has for some time been robbing his employers.'

Poor Annie uttered a cry, and Mrs. Walker burst into tears, and exclaimed—

'Well, I have sometimes wondered how George could make so many handsome presents to Annie, and especially such things as silk stockings and silk handkerchiefs, but he always said that they were remnant stock, and he was enabled to purchase them cheaply.'

'I am in a position to state positively that he has never purchased anything of the kind from his employers.'

This statement, of course, deeply affected both mother and daughter, and I was glad to get away, having first ascertained from Mrs. Walker the address of George Barrington's parents in London.

I went straight back to the firm, and when I showed the brooch to the manager he at once recognised it as having formed part of the jeweller's stock, and said that Barrington had not bought it, but stolen it. The retail value of it was seven pounds ten. I requested that he would say nothing to Barrington in the meantime, and I lost no time in going to the telegraph office and wiring to London, to ask that inquiries might immediately be made as to the position of the Barringtons.

In the course of a few hours I received the information that the address I had given was in a mews in Chelsea, that old Mr. Barrington was a coachman in the service of a livery stable-keeper, that his wage was a pound a week, and his wife earned a few shillings a week by charing.

This was a very painful revelation to have to make to Mrs. Walker and her daughter, but I felt it was my duty to make it, however painful it might be.

The poor girl, while being much cut up, was also highly indignant at being so shamefully and cruelly deceived, and she produced a great many things he had given her, and which I took charge of. I ascertained that Mrs. Walker and her daughter were highly respectable—the husband and father having held a responsible position in the Customs for nearly thirty years. At his death he was enabled to leave his widow two hundred a year, and his daughter a hundred a year in her own right.

The next day dawned as a bitter and terrible one for George Barrington, who was arrested and lodged in gaol. The blow seemed to fall upon him with an effect that appeared to stun him. It was as if he had not really realised that he had been guilty of crime. He had been held in thrall and fascinated by Annie Walker's beauty; and being a weak-minded man, he had tried to pose before her as a person of some consequence. He had not looked ahead to the time that must inevitably come when his imposture must be discovered, for, even if he had escaped detection of his thefts, Annie, if he had married her, would have found out that he had deceived her. But it is a singular fact that this class of criminals never do look ahead. His delinquencies were to serve the purpose of the moment, and he, in common with his kind, thought, no doubt, that when he had gained that for which he sinned he would blot out the sin with living the rest of his life honest and upright. He acted on the principle, in fact, that the end justifies the means.

There could be no doubt as to the force of the blow, now that his sin had found him out. He seemed to be perfectly crushed, and for several days it was with the utmost difficulty he could be prevailed upon to take food. He had been living in a dream, and had awakened now to find that the dream had been a hideous mockery. He felt that the shame the dream had led him into could never be faced, and that it was better to hide himself for ever in that darkness which no light from this world can ever pierce; and so one morning, when the warder went into his cell to take him his breakfast, and before he had been brought to trial, he was found quite dead. He had committed suicide during the night in a novel way. He had broken his tin plate in halves, and with the jagged end of one half he had sawn into the veins of his left arm, and so had bled to death. And he was found lying on his back in a pool of blood, and pinned to his breast was a scrap of paper on which be had written with blood this pathetic line—'All for Love's Sake.'

The Haunted House

⊕

In one of the suburbs of Glasgow there used to stand a very old
house known as the 'Braes'. It had originally been part of a
farm, but various circumstances had changed its character, and,
having undergone considerable alteration, it became the residence
of a lady from the south named Walker—Miss Helen Walker, as she
was called. When she first came to live at the Braes she was a well-
preserved, buxom woman of about thirty-five years of age. Nothing
was known of her antecedents, as she was particularly reticent about
herself and her affairs; so that those curses of every community—
the prying gossips—who pay attention to everyone's business but
their own, felt deeply aggrieved because they could not learn anything about her. One thing, however, was manifest—she had means,
for she had given a good round sum for the Braes, and she paid cash
for everything. Her household consisted of a woman about sixty, who
acted as cook and housekeeper, and a young girl, who filled the position of general servant. In addition, there was an old gardener, the
husband of the housekeeper, and he devoted much attention to the
garden, for Miss Walker had a passion for flowers. Miss Walker did
not by any means exclude herself from society, such as it was, and
she occasionally visited in the neighbourhood, but she preferred to
have visitors at her own house. Of course, much speculation was rife
as to the causes which had induced the lady to lead such a retired
life, and one thing that led to a good deal of wonderment was the fact
that she never seemed to have any relatives to see her.

However, the lady was by no means an anchorite nor a miser,
and she certainly appeared to enjoy existence. She was pleasant

and affable to all who came in contact with her. She was fond of animals, and kept a number of birds, two cats, three or four dogs, and a pet goat.

For some time Miss Helen Walker seemed to live her life in a very smooth and uninterrupted way, until she became acquainted with Mr. John Cameron. This gentleman was about forty, and followed the occupation of a farmer, his farm being about five miles from the Braes. Mr. Cameron had succeeded his father, who had been a careful, frugal, and saving man; but the son seemed to have been cast in a different mould, for he got into difficulties with his property, and cultivated a taste for whisky, and this taste sometimes placed him in very undignified positions.

A year or two after Miss Walker came to live in the neighbourhood Mr. Cameron 'pulled himself together', as the saying is, and the rumour ran that he had an eye on the lady. At any rate, he managed to get an introduction to her, or perhaps he was his own introducer; but, whichever way it was, it is a testimony to his abilities to make himself agreeable that he became a very frequent visitor at the Braes, and, of course, this caused an endless subject for gossip and even a little scandal—though Heaven knows why there should have been a scandal. But there are some people so vilely constituted that they seem to find their only happiness in thinking evil of others. Every community is cursed with such people. They make it their first care to pick holes in other folk's coats. Such people are the meanest specimens of depraved humanity which an all-wise Providence permits to exist on this earth. Of course, even in the days of Horace, human nature was much the same as it is now. People delighted in scandal even then, and they roll the savoury morsel under their tongues with no less gusto in this nineteenth century. They take a morbid delight in finding out something bad about their neighbours. Then they tell it to their friends in the strictest confidence, and the friends do the same with somebody else. Of course, the story gathers as it goes, for each scandalmonger adds to it or alters it according to his whims and fancies. As we all know, Horace said ages ago—

There is a lust in man no charm can tame
Of loudly publishing our neighbour's shame,
On eagles' wings immortal scandals fly,
While virtuous actions are but born, and die.

Miss Walker and Mr. Cameron appeared to get on very well together, and the scandal, if they heard of it, certainly did not affect
them. It was whispered that John was going to marry Miss Walker,
and that it would be a real good thing for him 'if only he would keep
himself steady'.

It would seem that about this time, however, some cowardly vaga-
bond, either male or female, wrote an anonymous letter to the lady,
cautioning her against John, and saying that he was a spendthrift,
was unsteady, and bore but an indifferent character. These charges
were in a large measure justified, no doubt, but it is probable that
had John won the lady for his wife it might have altered his character entirely for the better. The letter influenced her, and the result
was she terminated the relationship. This course seemed to affect
Cameron very severely, and for a time he abandoned himself to
recklessness, and drank heavily. Then he appeared to suddenly
alter, and become, morose and sullen, and on one occasion was
heard to utter threats against the lady who had 'thrown him over',
as he put it.

About six months after the rupture it began to be rumoured that
there were 'strange goings-on' at the Braes, and these goings-on
were due to ghosts. The reader will smile at this, of course, but, as
will presently be seen, the ghosts became such a serious matter
that I was called in to exorcise them.

The ghostly manifestations began by the ringing of bells at all
times, and in a way that defied detection.

This went on for some little time, and then, to vary the mo-
notony of the proceedings, the ghostly visitor began to promenade
the house in the dead of night, rattling chains and sighing and groaning in a very moving way. Possibly these ghosts were meant to represent the restless spirits of criminals who, ages before, had been
hung in chains.

So long as the ghostly visitants had confined their manifestations to the ringing of bells, clanking of chains, and sighing and groaning, they might have remained undisturbed, although it would appear that Miss Walker was much distressed. But by-and-by the spirits became mischievous, and took to breaking the windows. It was averred by the servants that panes of glass were smashed in full daylight without any visible cause. Then one night some coals that had that day been put into the coal-house were removed and piled up in the dining-room, to the ruin of an excellent carpet. But a still more serious piece of wanton mischief was the total destruction one night of a stout oak fence surrounding two sides of the garden. The fence was forcibly torn up; and the posts scattered far and wide, while the growing crops in the garden were trampled down or rooted up.

Miss Walker had by this time become thoroughly alarmed and very much distressed, for she was foolish enough to believe that all the mischief was being wrought by supernatural agency.

One evening she was standing in her dining-room talking to the housekeeper. The table had been set for supper, when suddenly, before the very eyes of the lady, the cloth was whipped off the table, and glass, plates, and silver were sent flying, the glass and plates being shivered to atoms. This extraordinary occurrence had such an effect on the nerves of Miss Walker that the poor lady fainted. Another day she was sitting reading in the drawing-room when there was a great crash, and a valuable mirror over the mantelpiece was shivered to atoms, some spiteful ghost having hurled the heavy coal hammer at it.

This sort of thing continued for months, until the persecution became intolerable, and it began to tell seriously on Miss Walker's health. Moreover, she was now subject to another annoyance, for 'the doings at the haunted house' had become notorious, and attracted crowds of idle and curious people, and some of these, taking advantage of the confusion that reigned, snapped up anything they could conveniently and without risk lay their hands on. But nothing seemed to disconcert the unruly spirits, who were utterly without commiseration for the poor lady, who had become thoroughly broken down with nervous anxiety, for one stormy night during a deluge of rain they pulled a lot of slates off the roof, thus letting the water into the house, and causing a great deal of damage; and a few nights later, this was followed by what was almost a more fiendish trick. It was the day after the washing day, and a great quantity of linen was spread out in the kitchen to air preparatory to being stowed away in the presses. In the morning when the family came down there was not a piece of linen that had not a number of holes burnt through it. Valuable sheets, pillow cases, bolster covers, table cloths, and other articles were thus rendered worthless.

By this time Miss Walker had become quite prostrated, and it was absolutely necessary to call in a medical man. This gentleman, being less superstitious than the simple-minded body, suggested that an attempt should be made to capture the ghosts, and in order to effect this the services of a detective might be advantageously employed. At first Miss Walker opposed the suggestion, for, as she stated, she witnessed things herself of so extraordinary a character that she was perfectly sure human agency could never have effected them. The doctor, however, was too hard-headed to be convinced on such evidence, and he urged his suggestion with more force till at last the poor lady gave a faint-hearted consent; and as the doctor happened to know me, he dropped me a note asking inn to call upon him without loss of time.

On my going down to his place, he at once told me the whole story of the haunted house, and he informed me that not only had his patient suffered serious pecuniary loss, but her health had been undermined.

'Now, you know, Donovan,' he added jocularly, 'you've laid a good many rogues and rascals by the heels in your time; see if you can't lay these mischievous ghosts.'

'I'll try,' said I, 'and if they are made of bones and flesh I think I'll have them.'

In setting about my task my first step was to ascertain the constitution of Miss Walker's household, that is, the number of people in her employment, and then I paid a visit to the lady herself. I found her very ill, and she had all the appearance of a person whose nerves had been subjected to repeated shocks. She had a look of premature age in her face, and she was irritable, easily excited, and nervous.

When I asked her if she had reason to think anybody was playing tricks on her, she not only expressed profound astonishment at the question, but displayed decided anger, saying—

'What do you take me for, sir? I have seen things done in this house that human hands have never done.'

'Then you are firmly of the opinion that all the mischief has been the work of supernatural agency?'

'Undoubtedly I am.'

I could hardly repress a smile at this, but I asked her to kindly give me some particulars of what she had seen, and she at once related to me most of the things I have already mentioned. But, in addition; she vowed she had seen a heavy table dragged across the room without being touched, and massive chairs tossed up as if they had been feather pillows.

I listened with great patience to all she had to tell, and when she finished she exclaimed—

'I hope you are convinced, for you won't imagine that I could state what is not true?'

'Oh, dear, no, madam,' I answered; 'I assure you I do not imagine anything of the sort. But I confess to a strong desire to be a witness to some of these manifestations, and to that end perhaps you will permit me to spend a night or two in your house?'

At first she objected to this arrangement, but on my urging my request she yielded, and she gave me the use of a bedroom.

The first night of my stay nothing occurred, but on the second night I was startled by a great crash downstairs. It was about twelve o'clock, and I had previously ascertained that the servants had retired. I had provided myself with a dark lantern, which was already lighted, and seizing this I sallied forth and hurried down to the corridor, where I found lying on the floor a valuable marble clock, or rather what remained of it, for it was smashed to pieces. This clock had stood on a carved bracket nailed to the wall in the passage. The bracket was all right, but the clock had been forcibly pulled off.

While I was trying to solve the problem how it had been done, the various bells in the house commenced to ring. I went into the kitchen where the bells were hung, and found them clashing and banging about like mad, but in the course of a few minutes they ceased their pranks, and I went upstairs. On a landing I was met by Miss Walker, who had a scared, horrified look on her white face.

'Are you convinced now?' she gasped. 'What was it that made the noise?'

I told her about the clock, and she wrung her hands in grief, saying that she set great value on that clock, as it had been given to her by her mother.

I went back to my room, and soon all was quiet again. While feeling a little puzzled, I was resolved to track the malicious ghost down. In order to be ready to spring out should any more 'manifestations' occur, I left my door ajar, and placing a chair near it, sat down to wait.

In about half an hour I was sure I heard footsteps on the stairs, and going down on my hands and knees I peered through the space made by the open door, and presently I saw the figure of a man coming up the stairs, creeping cautiously along the passage, passing my door in so doing, and then ascending the second flight of stairs, which led to the upper storey. I could not distinguish the man, it was too dark for that, but I could understand that he had no boots on, and trod with great caution.

I did not seize him, as that would have been premature, and I wanted more proof; but I felt sure that the ghost of Miss Walker's house was a very substantial one. The following morning, when the servants were all busy downstairs, I went up to the top of the house between the slates and the beams over which all the bell wires passed. I found that to each wire a piece of thin, strong wire was fastened, this piece being about half a yard in length. The free ends of all these pieces were gathered together and fastened round a steel ring, and from the ring a string led through a hole in the ceiling to a room below, and this room was the one occupied by the gardener. Now the meanest intelligence would at once perceive that by this simple but ingenious arrangement a tug at the string would set all the bells clanging at once, and in order as far as possible to prevent detection, the industrious ghost had brought the string into a cupboard or wardrobe, where it was quite concealed by clothes hanging up.

In the course of the forenoon I had an interview with Miss Walker, and asked her if she did not think it possible that one of her servants had been playing tricks upon her, but she was so excited by the previous night's proceedings that she was scarcely rational, and all I could get out of her was that my suggestion was preposterous.

Fortunately the doctor came in just then, and I managed to whisper to him that I had discovered the ghost. I left him with his patient, then I went downstairs. The cook and housekeeper was busy in the kitchen, and I got into conversation with her. I may mention that the servants did not know who I was—that is, they did not know what my mission was there, but they had been given to understand I was a relative.

I led the old woman on to the subject of the manifestation that had been carried on so long and had had such a cruel effect upon the owner of the house. She waxed enthusiastic on the subject, and talked with such volubility that I could not get a word in edgeways for some time. Nor did I try, for I had an object in letting her talk, But at last, when her tongue had tired a little, I said—'Of course, you quite believe that all these things have been the work of genuine ghosts.'

She at once broke out in another flood of words, and the inference she wished me to draw was that if I did not believe that they were disembodied spirits who had played the pranks, then, indeed, I was a fool beyond all hope.

'Well,' I answered, 'I intend to get these ghosts under lock and key, and let them see what the inside of a Scotch prison is like. That will be a new experience for them, won't it? And they will be able to take back strange news to the other world.'

She turned very pale at these words, and became very confused in her manner; and, leaving her to her reflections, I went out into the garden, where the gardener was at work. Without a word of preliminary warning, I laid my hand heavily on his shoulder, and said sternly—

'I am going to arrest you for playing the ghost.'

The man almost fell to the ground in a fright, and while his teeth chattered and his knees knocked together, he stuttered out this answer—

'Oh, Lord; dinna dae that, man. I'm only a puir instrument in the maiter.'

'What do you mean?' I demanded.

'It's Master Cameron wha's responsible,' stammered the old wretch, and thereupon he made a clean breast of the whole affair. By his confession I learned that Cameron had bribed him and his wife and the other servant to annoy Miss Walker and trade upon her fears, and to do as much damage to her property as they possibly could.

The hammer that had been hurled through the mirror had been thrown by the gardener, and the reason of the clock falling from the bracket the second night I slept in the house was that he had pushed it off with a long stick, and had then hidden himself in a closet under the stairs. The clothes had been burnt by his wife, and all the other manifestations had been managed between them; and, owing to Miss Walker's fears and belief in the supernatural, the wretches had found it an easy matter to impose upon her. I lost no time in informing Miss Walker that I had found out the ghosts. At first she could not credit what I told her, and when she did her indignation knew no bounds. Of course, the servants were at once discharged, and I lost no time in getting a warrant for Cameron's arrest on a charge of conspiracy. The gardener and the two female servants were witnesses against him, and the case was so clear that he was sentenced to two months' imprisonment and to pay the damage done, which was appraised at a hundred pounds.

Miss Walker soon recovered her health, and, in thanking me for my services, she assured me that it would take a great deal indeed to make her believe in ghosts again.

A Wolf in Sheep's Clothing

L ate one wet and dismal Saturday night a girl, about twelve years of age, was brought into a Glasgow police station charged with pilfering from a shop door. This kind of petty theft is, as is well known, one of the greatest nuisances that shopkeepers who expose their wares outside have to contend against. Of course it has been said, and not without some show of reason, that if tradespeople will place their goods so as to tempt those who have little knowledge of, and less respect for, the laws that govern *meum* and *tuum*, they themselves are to blame, and they should have no redress. But it must not be forgotten that the law in effect says, 'He who surreptitiously carries off property to which he has no legal claim or right is a thief, and for the crime of theft there is a graduated code of punishment'. Now the loser of property by theft may be contributory to his own loss by carelessness or stupidity; but while justice might be disposed to deal more leniently with a thief who had had temptation prominently placed in his way, the principle would have to be recognised that carrying off anything without the owner's consent and to his loss and injury is theft.

The foregoing remarks are somewhat digressive, although they have a very direct bearing on what I am about to relate. These robberies from shop doors had of late been on the increase, and as a matter of course there had been the usual outcry against the unfortunate police, that they were not doing their duty. The girl spoken of above as having been brought into the station was caught *flagrante delicto*—that is, in the very act of pilfering some cheap pocket handkerchiefs that, together with a miscellaneous collection of goods, were exposed for sale on a tray outside the shop of a little draper's in a low quarter of the town. As the owner of the shop had been victimised several times, he insisted on giving the girl into custody, and so, notwithstanding her weeping and wailing and protestations of innocence, she was marched off to the station. On arrival there she had, with remarkable determination, refused to answer any questions as to her name, age, or where she came from, and as no amount of threatening had the slightest effect on her obdurate nature, there was no help for it but to lock her up as a 'nameless prisoner'.

On Sunday morning duty led me to the station, and my attention was called to this girl. Consequently I went to the cell in which she was confined. She was a dirty, draggle-tailed, rusty-haired looking child. Well, that is, she was a child in years, but her face was old with vice and preternatural cunning. Had it only worn the innocence and sweetness of childhood it would have been an interesting and even a pretty face, for the features were regular, but the skin was rusty with foul air, bad living, and dirt. The only clothing this miserable waif had on was a chemise that must have been a stranger to the wash-tub for many long months, and a cotton gown which only reached to just below the knees. She had no shoes or stockings on, and her legs and feet were tanned with dirt and exposure to the weather. The moment I looked at her I felt quite sure that, though a mere child as far as years were concerned, she was well versed in the ways of vice. There was a singular expression of precocious duplicity in her dark blue eyes, and her manner was that of a grown woman; she was saucy, pert, and utterly without the timidity which is characteristic of childhood, especially of the female child.

'Well, young lady,' I exclaimed, 'where do you come from?'

'What the devil has that to do with you?' she answered.

I confess that this rather staggered me, for I hardly expected such an expressive and defiant response.

'Oh, well,' I returned with a laugh, 'I am rather interested in you, and should like to know where your home is.'

'You are a nice sort of fellow to be interested in me, ain't you?'

she snarled, as she turned up her nose and curled her lip with lofty scorn.

'At any rate, I might be of some use to you,' I suggested, 'if you will give me some particulars of yourself.'

'I ain't going to give you any particulars,' she snapped.

'Won't you tell me your name?'

'No,' she answered with great decision.

After a few more questions, and finding I could make nothing of her, I left, remarking—

'Well, perhaps the bailie tomorrow will be able to bring you to a sense of your position.'

At this she broke into a laugh that was as rusty as her skin and reddish hair, and more like the laugh of some old whisky-drinking harridan than a young girl.

As it was not a case in which I could interfere, or had anything to do with, I troubled myself no further about it, although, having an excellent memory for faces, I felt sure I should not forget hers, as I had photographed it well on my mind.

I may mention here that when she was brought before the magistrate she was just as resolute not to give any information about herself. And as they could not force her to say what she was determined not to say, there was no help for it. As she was not known, and had not actually stolen the goods, the magistrate dealt very leniently, and sentenced her to seven days for vagabondage. On being released at the end of the week a man was instructed to watch her and see where she went to, but the precocious child was too 'cute, and evidently having some suspicion that she was being followed, she doubled backwards and forwards, led her follower a fine dance, and ultimately gave him the slip altogether.

When I heard this I couldn't help laughing, but, nevertheless, I felt sure that this girl was a dangerous young vixen, and had come out of a den of thieves; so I determined to keep my eyes open, and if I came across her again track her to her lair.

Six months passed, and I saw nothing more of this interesting young lady, and, in fact, more important and pressing matters had for the time being. put her out of my mind, when one day I was present in an official capacity at a grand flower show in the West End. In moving about amongst the crowds of ladies and gentlemen who thronged the spacious marquee in which the show was held, I suddenly started as I saw the face of a girl that instantly brought to my mind the face of the half-naked waif I had questioned in the police station six months before. My memory rarely or never played me false in regard to faces, and I felt convinced I could not be mistaken in this one. There was the same precocious cunning, watchful expression, the same rusty complexion and reddish hair, the same thin, hard lips, and blue eyes, which were as restless as a wild animal's. But I saw the face under different aspects now. It was well washed and clean, and her hair had been pomatumed, combed, and brushed. It was only a wisp after all, but it was tied in a hunch with a bit of red ribbon. She was dressed well, of course, wore boots and stockings, and had on a grey hat, somewhat rakish in its cut, and rendered brilliant with a gaudy scarlet feather. She was in company with a woman who was elegantly dressed in an embossed velvet mantle that reached to her heels. She was somewhere about fifty, with a genial and apparently kindly-looking face; her hair, which was iron grey, was neatly arranged over her forehead; and for head-dress she had a bonnet of tulle and gauze, adorned with flowers. There was one thing that seemed out of place and made her conspicuous, that was, she wore dark blue folding eye-glasses. Probably anyone less experienced in criminal life than I was would at once have come to the conclusion that this woman was undoubtedly a lady, and that he was mistaken with regard to the girl. But I should have been prepared to have staked my existence on the statement that that girl was the ragged, dirty, impudent waif of six months ago, and that being so, what was she now doing in her altered character, and in company with this well-dressed lady?

It was an interesting situation, and I felt convinced I was now on the eve of a revelation. I followed the girl and the woman about, never losing sight of them with the exception of about five minutes.

This was due to some commotion caused by a lady fainting. She had fallen and obstructed the flow of the human stream, so that there was a good deal of jostling and crowding together. However, I caught sight of my party again. They were hurrying away from the crowd; I followed them. They went outside of the marquee into the open grounds, and sat down on a seat.

A quarter of an hour later a policeman who knew me said—

'I hear that a lady has been robbed of her purse containing a large sum of money.'

'Have you got any particulars?' I asked.

'No,' he said, 'I have only just heard it from one of our men.'

I did not wait to ask or hear anything more, for at this moment the girl and the woman rose and hurried away, and giving them a little start I followed in their wake. They passed out of the grounds and engaged a cab at the gates. I got into another cab, told the driver who I was, and promised him treble fare if he did not lose sight of the other cab. We drove for three-quarters of an hour, then my man stopped at the top of a street far over on the south side, and, told me that the other cab had stopped near the bottom of the street, and I saw the woman and girl alight; saw the woman take out her purse, pay the cabman, and then enter a tenement building.

I hurried along as fast as my legs would carry me, and as I reached the tenement a woman was just coming out. I stopped her and said—

'A lady and young girl have just come in here, I think?'

'Yes; I passed them on the stair.'

'Can you tell me the lady's name?'

'Yes; she's Mistress Robertson.'

'What flat does she live on?'

'The third.'

Thanking the woman for her information, I waited until she had gone away; then I slipped off myself, as I wanted something more definite to go upon before I tackled the mysterious Mrs. Robertson.

A little later I began cautiously to make inquiries in the neighbourhood as to what reputation the lady bore, and there was a unanimity of opinion that she was 'a dear, kind, excellent woman,' and so good to the poor about her. She was a widow, so I was told, with one daughter living with her. She had a good many visitors, and numerous 'nephews and nieces' constantly calling upon her.

This information set me pondering. Was I mistaken? Was I doing an injustice to a charitable and honest lady? I might have been more disposed to think so had that girl not been with her. Then came another thought — Had that girl been rescued by the lady from the gutter, and altogether reformed since I last saw her?

I must say in common honesty that I was puzzled and could not quite make up my opinion; and while in this state of quandary, I stepped into a tobacconist's shop to buy some cigars, thinking a smoke might be of assistance. While in the shop some special chance sent in the very girl in whom I felt so much interest. She had changed her fine clothes, and was now clad in a cotton gown, and had a shawl over her head.

'If you please, Mr. M'Taggart,' she began, and instantly I recognised the rusty voice, and my doubts rolled away, 'my mother will be much obliged if you'll give her Scotch pound notes for this.'

The *this* was a ten-pound Bank of England note which she laid on the counter.

'I'm awfully sorry,' replied Mr. M'Taggart, 'but I haven't so much now; I'll get it for you though.'

'Oh, I think I can do it,' I exclaimed. Fortunately I happened to have a considerable sum with me, as that afternoon I had cashed a bank draft. I produced a five-pound note, and five notes for one pound, and, handing these to the girl, she took them in exchange for her ten-pound note. As she did so I fancied she looked at me rather curiously, as though she thought she had seen me before. But she didn't say anything beyond a 'Thank you,' and she went off.

As I took my departure a few moments later, I felt intuitively that that ten-pound note was destined to play an important part in this little drama. And I thought so because ten-pound English bank notes were exceedingly scarce in Scotland, and it was rather strange that anyone living in that particular neighbourhood should have been possessed of one.

The following morning when I went down to the Central on business, I heard that the lady who had her pocket picked the previous day at the flower show had lost an elegant sealskin purse, which contained, besides some papers and memoranda, six Scotch pound notes, a ten-pound Bank of England note, number A.B. I00,000. 7.C; a small gold ring set with turquoise, and a morsel of tissue paper containing a tress of hair.

On looking at the number of the ten-pound note which had so strangely come into my possession, my feelings may be imagined when I found it was the number of the stolen note. With a smile of self-satisfaction that I could not restrain, I said to my chief—

'I can put my hand on the thief who stole that purse.'

'Don't make too sure,' he responded incredulously. 'I don't think it was an ordinary thief but some accomplished rogue, who won't be fool enough to circulate that tenner in this part of the country.'

I smiled again as I replied—

'Well, we'll see.'

A little later in the day I took a good man in plain clothes with me, and proceeded to Mrs. Robertson's. My ring at her door bell was answered by a neat-looking servant, who showed me into a comfortably-furnished room. In a few minutes Mrs. Robertson—the 'lady' I had shadowed on the previous day—appeared. She was dressed in black, with white cuffs and collars, and on her head she had a lace cap trimmed with pink ribbon, which contrasted well with her silvery hair. She bowed gracefully and smiled benignly as she said—

'Whom have I the honour of addressing?'

'I have called upon you in the interests of my profession,' I answered prevaricatingly.

'You are a lawyer, I presume?' she said sweetly.

'No, not exactly,' I replied, 'but permit me to ask if you have a daughter?'

'Yes, I have one dear child,' she replied in the same soft, silky way, which was suggestive of a purring pussy.

'Could I see her?'

'I am sorry to say she is out. But permit me to inquire your business.'

'All in good time, my dear madam. I think you and your daughter were at the flower show yesterday?'

'Oh yes,' she answered quickly, and still smiling and purring; and I could not help thinking that if she was the swindler I deemed her to be, then she was the most self-possessed female thief I had ever come across. 'The dear child is so fond of flowers, and she bothered me so much to go, that though I wasn't very well I yielded. It's so hard to refuse children anything, you know.'

'It is,' I responded; 'but now, Mrs. Robertson, I am going to ask you a question that possibly you may be able to answer satisfactorily.'

'Well, sir, what is it?' she asked sweetly and rubbing her soft white hands together.

'Your so-called daughter changed a ten-pound Bank of England note last evening in the shop of Mr. M'Taggart, at the foot of the stair?'

'Oh yes,' she said in the same sweet way, and still smiling, 'but there was nothing unusual in that, was there?'

'Very unusual, Mrs. Robertson, since you ask the question. But tell me, please, how did you get the note?'

'I have a brother in London, and, being in my debt, he sent that note in part payment.'

'When did he send it?

'Let me see now. It will be a week ago.'

'Most remarkable!' I answered ironically. 'Now it happens that only as recently as yesterday that very note was in the possession of a lady at the flower show, who had her pocket picked.'

I watched her narrowly as I said this, and for the first time the expression of her face changed, and I saw a look of alarm come into it.

'Impossible!' she exclaimed, now betraying anxiety in her tone.

'Not impossible, Mrs. Robertson,' I said, 'but it is absolutely true. Now, that being so, how do you explain the discrepancy between that fact and your statement?'

She had recovered her self-possession and said—

'You are simply mistaken, sir.'

'Very well, we'll test that by-and-by. But now tell me this: how was it that your daughter, as you term her, was arrested, in rags and tatters, six months ago, for attempting to steal handkerchiefs from a shop door?'

She turned pale now, and became agitated as she cried— 'My daughter arrested! Impossible! It's false! It's a base calumny!'

'Well, of course, it is within the bounds of possibility that I am mistaken,' I returned as I rose, 'but we'll see.'

I went to the outer door and called in my man, who was waiting. Then returning to the room I said—

'My name is Donovan, madam. You have heard of me?'

'Yes; you are Donovan the detective,' she gasped.

'I am, and I arrest you on a charge of theft.'

She uttered a sigh as if it were a sigh of relief, and smiling benignly again she answered in a quiet, self-possessed manner—

'I suppose Fate has played me false at last. So be it.'

'Fate, no doubt, has played you false,' I said, 'since Fate placed that identical ten-pound note in my possession last night.'

'You detectives are wonderful people,' she answered, 'and you seem to be the most wonderful of the lot. I should like to kill you, I should.'

This was the first time she had shown anything like passion, though it was not passion so much—it was rather an indication of the treacherous calm she was so well able to maintain, and which spoke too surely of her dangerous nature.

Leaving my man in charge of this extraordinary old woman I proceeded to search her rooms, and I was rewarded by finding her 'daughter' in the kitchen, and a few words addressed to her convinced me at once that she was the ragged young thief who had served seven days in prison six months ago. In a box in the old woman's bedroom I also found a miscellaneous collection of purses, dozens of them, which showed that the young lady was an expert pocket-picker. Amongst these purses was the identical one that had been stolen the day previous.

The only other person in the house was the servant, and she seemed utterly stunned as the revelation came upon her, and when she could speak she exclaimed—

'Only to think of that kind, gentle, quiet old woman being a thief!'

'Ah,' I said, 'there is many a wolf in sheep's clothing.'

I sent the girl for a cab, and then I took the old woman and the 'daughter' to the station, leaving my man in charge of the house: and as I was not sure about the young vixen, for she seemed to me capable of anything, I handcuffed her by one wrist to her 'mother'.

Further investigations enabled us to accumulate a mass of evidence against our chief prisoner, and we were enabled to make some startling revelations. Her quiet, subdued, and lady-like manner had enabled her for years to carry on an extraordinary system of theft. She exercised a remarkable power over the minds of children, and she had a perfect school of boys and girls, and she trained them to become most expert pickpockets. The girl who lived with her was not her daughter, but a child she had procured from its parents, both of whom had been convicts. The father had died in prison, and the mother a year later of small-pox. Mrs. Robertson had known the parents, and had taken the child when it was only four years of age. She was in the habit sometimes of lending this child to a friend, when she was then sent out as a ragged waif, and so well trained was the child in all the arts of vice that she could play with equal skill the characters of a starveling or a well-dressed young lady; but nevertheless, her nature was defiant, artful, vicious, and fierce.

Gradually we spun a web around this dangerous old woman from which there was no escaping, although she got a very able man to defend her. She was put away for a long term of years, while the girl was sentenced to a year, to be followed by six years in a reformatory.

We thus cleared the city of two very dangerous characters, and for a time at least had stopped the wolf in sheep's clothing from preying on the flocks of human baa-lambs.

The Pearl Button

※

Late one autumn afternoon a noisy crowd of men were assembled in a wayside public-house situated on the South Road, about twenty miles from Glasgow. There had been a horse fair held in the neighbourhood, and, business being over, a large number of those who had been attracted by the fair had betaken themselves to the inn to wash the dust out of their throats. A good many of these men were known to each other, being farmers and small dealers from round about. But a number were strangers entirely to the neighbourhood, and of course there was the usual sprinkling of sharps and sharks, knaves and rogues.

Amongst the strangers was a pedlar—a little, fussy, bletherin', and yet withal good-tempered fellow who had been attending the fair with a view to the disposal of a stock of cheap jewellery, ribbons, laces and a various assortment of nick-nacks beloved by women, including cottons, threads, buttons, tapes, &c.

It appears that he had been unusually fortunate in disposing of his wares, and as a result his pack had been lightened, while his purse had grown heavier in a proportionate ratio. As the man was of a bibulous disposition, he had adjourned to the public-house after his business had closed; and, having imbibed freely, his tongue had grown loose, and he boasted of the amount of money he had taken that day. He proved to be an entertaining fellow, and in possession of a fund of anecdote, and as he had a somewhat racy way of telling his stories he became the centre of a group of admirers, and between him and them a liberal exchange of drinks took place.

Amongst those who seemed particularly attracted towards the little pedlar were two men who were strangers to the district. They said they were brothers, that they belonged to Coatbridge, and had come to the fair to try and pick up cheap three or four good, useful, working horses, but had not succeeded in getting what they wanted. One of these men was a big, powerful fellow about five feet ten and a half. The other was a smaller man, though a powerful and determined-looking fellow. He was deeply marked with the small-pox, while his brother had a starred scar on the left temple, as if he had received a tremendous blow at some time with a bludgeon. These two men seemed to be particularly gracious to the pedlar, who took drink from them, and stood drink in return. They did not impress the rest of the company, however, favourably; and some of those present thought they were getting a little too familiar with the pedlar, who was silly enough to boast of the amount of money he had that day taken, and several times during the afternoon he drew out his old leather wallet and displayed a number of bank notes, as well as a small quantity of gold. On one of these occasions, the landlord, who was present, noted the greedy looks of the brothers, and he heard one of them ask the pedlar how much he had alto-gether, to which the pedlar replied—

'I hae mair than forty pounds, for I drew twenty frae the savings-bank afore I left hame, because I'm going on to Glasgow tae pur-chase stock for my bit shop that my old woman looks after when I'm awa'.'

As soon as the landlord got the chance he warned the pedlar against the folly and danger of telling his affairs to strangers, and he urged him, for safety's sake, to deposit his money in his keep-ing. But the little man waxed wrath, and said he had been able to take care of himself for fifty years, and that he had carried hun-dreds of pounds about with him without ever losing it, and he had no fear now. Of course the landlord could do nothing more, but, being suspicious of the brothers, he took good note of them, so that he might be able to describe them if necessary.

For some time after this the three men occupied a table to them-selves in the large room used by the customers, and a quantity of drink was consumed, until about seven o'clock the brothers rose to go. The pedlar announced his intention of remaining a little longer, and the brothers departed alone. It was a dark rainy night, with a cold wind blowing, so that the light and warmth of the public-house were certainly more conducive to comfort than the external gloom and damp.

Soon after eight the pedlar prepared to take his departure. He was then very much befogged with the alcoholic beverages he had consumed, and the landlord tried to induce him to spend the night in the house, telling him he could have a good bed, and would be made comfortable. The little man, however, was stubborn, and again expressed indignation at the imputation of his inability to take care of himself.

He announced his intention of going to Kilmarnock, which was between four and five miles distant and where, as he stated, he had a brother, who kept a small general shop in the town, and his intention was to pass the night with this brother. To all entreaties be turned a deaf ear, and having partaken of a final 'nip,' he gathered up his things, and with a husky 'good nicht,' he went out, his gait being anything but steady, although he was far from being absolutely intoxicated.

Early the following morning a farmer driving in his cart from Kilmarnock called at the public-house in a state of fright, and reported that he had seen the body of a man lying by the side of a ditch on the road. At first he thought the man might be asleep or ill, and he got down to examine him, when he was horrified to find that he was dead. He described the dead man as being short in stature, and evidently a pedlar, as his pack was lying near him, although it had been opened and rifled.

From these particulars the landlord at once came to the conclusion that the dead man was the pedlar who had been at his house the night before; so he lost no time in reporting the circumstances at the rural police station a mile away, and that done, he and a constable and two other men set off for the spot described by the farmer. There, sure enough, they found the unfortunate pedlar as dead as a door nail. He was lying on his back, with his left arm bent back under his head. His face depicted horror, the eyes starting from their sockets, while the tongue protruded from the mouth, and in the death agony had been bitten through.

So far as could be seen then there were no marks about the body, so that the man might have died in a fit. His pedlar's box and pack were lying near. The latter had been opened and rifled, while the box was quite empty. Some odds and ends were scattered about, though they were of small value. Not a penny piece was found on the body, so that the man had evidently been robbed: but still that did not prove that he had not died a natural death; and all things at that moment seemed to favour the theory that he had died in a fit, and some unprincipled person discovering the body had taken the opportunity to possess himself of all the dead man's property. For a moment it was thought that this might have been done by the farmer who gave the information; but the thought was dismissed as soon as formed, for he was known to be a highly respectable man, who had farmed land in the neighbourhood of Kilmarnock for upwards of forty years.

The scene of the robbery, if not murder, was wild and lonely. A pine wood bounded one side of the road, and a broad ditch intervened. On the opposite side of the road was a steep embankment that was topped with a row of trees. It was at the foot of this embankment the body was lying.

The dead man was at once conveyed to the station, and as soon as possible a medical examination was made, and this examination at once disproved the theory of natural death; for on the right side one rib, and on the left two ribs were broken, and the chest was deeply bruised, showing that the unfortunate man had been knelt upon, and so much strength and violence had been used that the ribs had been crushed in, a portion of one of the fractured bones penetrating the lung. The doctor pronounced an emphatic opinion that these injuries could not have resulted from a fall; but, beyond all doubt, had been caused by someone kneeling upon him. Moreover, there were other evidences of a struggle. The dead man's clothes were disarranged; his waistcoat had been torn open so forcibly that the buttons had been dragged off.

Within a few hours of the body being found I was on the scene of the crime, and I learned all the foregoing particulars. I, of course, had an interview with the old farmer who had discovered the body, but he knew nothing beyond what had already been stated.

From the landlord I ascertained that the pedlar had carried his money in an old yellow leather pocket-book, and this pocket-book he kept in a pocket inside the breast of his shirt. That circumstance at once explained why the waistcoat and shirt had been torn open. It was to get at the pocket-book. It was probable the unfortunate pedlar had lain down on the road and gone to sleep, and while in that condition had been attacked. A struggle had ensued, during which the attacker knelt on his victim in order to keep him quiet. There were marks on the dead man's wrists, too, showing that they had been tightly grasped during the struggle.

In searching about the spot I found the old yellow pocket-book in the mud of the ditch a few yards from where the body was lying. Of course there was no money in it. The thief had been shrewd enough to see that to retain such a thing would be to run consider-able risk of detection, and so had got rid of it after transferring its contents to his own pocket. Round about the spot where the body had been discovered were the imprints of three distinct pairs of boots. Some of these imprints had been made by the dead man's boots, as proved by testing them; but the others were larger alto-gether, and one pair had nails in the soles; the other, no nails, but an iron rim on the heels. Now the pedlar's boots had neither nails nor iron rim. The inference to be drawn, therefore, was that two men had been engaged in the robbery, and these details and cir-cumstances pointed the finger of suspicion at the two brothers who had been drinking with the pedlar the night before.

Amongst the things in the pack was a card of pearl buttons. Now these buttons were not ordinary ones, but extraordinary, inasmuch as they were of the colours of the rainbow, and of peculiar bril-liancy; and these colours seemed to vary with every movement of the eye. The iridescence, in fact, was as unusual as it was attractive. In size, the buttons were about that of a shilling. The remarkable colours and lustre of these buttons were what attracted me, and having casually examined them I put them amongst the other things, never dreaming for a moment that they were destined to ultimately help me to solve the mystery of the pedlar's death.

There being no room to doubt that robbery and murder had been committed, my next step was to try and find the two brothers; and the landlord of the inn described them with such circumstantiality that I thought it would be an easy matter to trace them, and I lost no time in putting a printed description of them into circulation; but nevertheless, at the end of a week, a fortnight, three weeks, they were still at large, and no trace of them had been found. I need scarcely say I was exceedingly annoyed at this, for I had counted on their capture as an easy matter. That they had not been captured proved to me one thing at least—they were strangers to that part of the country. They were in fact loafers and adventurers, who had attended the horse fair with an eye to plunder.

Six months slipped away, and yet these men who were so very much wanted were still at large. That fact to me was a source of irritating annoyance, and yet somehow or another I could not abandon the idea altogether that I should ultimately bring them to book. I had faith in my star, and I had succeeded in so many cases that I could not bring myself to believe I should fail in this. Of course, during those six months I had not been idle. I had had many other things to occupy my attention; but still, as the saying is, I kept one eye ever on the look-out for the ruffians who had done the poor old pedlar to death.

At the end of the six months it chanced that a show of Clydesdale stallions and other horses was being held not far from Glasgow; and as horse shows, more than any other kind, attract rascaldom, I took my way to this one to have a look at the rascals and rogues who, I knew, would congregate there in great strength. I saw more than one fellow there who had, much against his will, been lodged at her Majesty's expense, and mingling with the crowd were many low-browed villains who, judging by their physiognomies, would have cut the throat of their nearest relative for a pound note. In the course of the afternoon I went into the tent where the refreshments were sold. The place was thronged with a noisy and excited crowd of men, whose sole topic of conversation was money and horses. Elbowing my way gradually amongst them, I suddenly started as I saw, gleaming on the waist-coat of a powerful-looking man, a pearl button identical with those I had found on the card in the murdered pedlar's pack. The waistcoat was a double-breasted brown cord, such as is frequently affected by a certain class of farm labourers. The iridescence of this particular button was as remarkable as the ones on the card. This in itself would scarcely have seemed to me peculiar, save for one thing—the button was the only one of the kind on the waistcoat. The others were pearl buttons, but of quite a different pattern, and without the lustre which made the other so conspicuous.

From the button my eyes naturally wandered to the man's face, but it did not answer the description of either of the two men I had been so long looking for. That description stated that both men had full beards and moustaches and 'longish' hair, and one was described as being marked with the small-pox, while his companion had a starred scar on the left temple. Now this man had no small-pox marks or no scar. His hair was cut short, and he had a red moustache, but no beard, while his face seemed to indicate a simple-minded, good-humoured sort of man. But still that button seemed to me to be too remarkable to ignore it, and I was resolved to learn something about it. I therefore got into conversation with the man about horses—a subject that he waxed warm about—and it led to our taking a nip together.

'That's a peculiar button,' I said, when the opportunity occurred, and putting my finger on the button as I spoke.

'Yes. I never saw a button that had so many colours in it.'

'Where did you get it from?'

'Well, I think my old woman bought some of them from a neighbour of ours.'

'How long ago do you think it is since she bought them?' I asked carelessly.

'Oh, well, as near as I recollect about five or six months ago. When I was putting my clothes on yesterday morning to come down here for the show I found a button off my waistcoat, Of course I kicked up a row; and as I was in a hurry, the old gal sewed this brilliant thing on. But, as I told her, it looks like a carbuncle.'

'Then you don't live in this neighbourhood?'

'No. I come from Newcastle.'

'What was the name of the neighbour from whom you got the buttons?'

'Jack Sinclair.'

'Is he marked with the small-pox?'

'No, but his brother Bill was.'

I felt the blood quickening in my veins as I heard this, and I asked quickly—

'Has Jack got a scar on his forehead?'

'Yes.'

'Then where is Bill?'

'Oh, Bill is dead. He died about three months ago. He took ill of typhoid, I think they call it, and died in the infirmary.'

I got 'Jack's' address from my informant, and in answer to his pointed question as to why I had asked so many questions, I replied that I had reason to believe 'Jack' and 'Bill' had been concerned in a robbery, whereupon my informant slapped his thigh, and exclaimed—

'Well, hang me if I haven't always thought there was something queer about those fellows.'

A few minutes later I had telegraphed to Newcastle asking the authorities to arrest Jack Sinclair, and saying I would be there in the morning to identify him.

Armed with a warrant, I set off that evening for Newcastle, and found my man already in custody. He had been living for a long time in a quarter of the town where the population was of a very nondescript character, and it would have been difficult for anyone to have told exactly how his neighbours got their living. Some 'did something about the docks and wharves,' others 'attended race meetings,' others again were hawkers, and some got their living 'the Lord alone knew how'.

The moment I looked upon Jack's face I felt sure of my man, although he was clean shaved; and when I said to him—'You will be tried in all probability for the murder and robbery of a pedlar on the Kilmarnock road,' he became deadly pale and greatly agitated, and condemned himself by exclaiming— 'It wasn't me who murdered him'.

In due course Jack was brought to trial, and when it was proved beyond all doubt that on the night of the murder he had been drinking with the pedlar, and had been heard to ask him questions about his money, he felt that the game was up, and he confessed that he and his brother had planned to rob the old man, and had laid in wait for him, and he had told them he was going to Kilmarnock, but he vowed that they had no intention of killing him. That was an accident. He had struggled and fought very much, and to keep him quiet Bill got hold of his wrists and knelt on his chest, while Jack tore open his shirt to get at the much-coveted money.

Bill, in his excitement, had used too much violence, and they were alarmed to find the old man becoming insensible, but they thought he was only fainting, and having taken some things from his pack, including a card of pearl buttons, they made off, and they had no idea that they had killed the pedlar until they read of his death in the papers. With that fatuity which seems peculiar to criminals, however clever they may be in other respects, they sold amongst their neighbours the things they had stolen from the murdered man's pack, and amongst the things so disposed of was that card of buttons, one of which was destined to bring this man to justice.

As there was no direct evidence to prove that he really killed the pedlar, he was given the benefit of the doubt, and escaped with fifteen years' penal servitude; but the possibilities are he would have got off altogether, and have cheated justice, had it not been for that fatal pearl button.

The Mysterious Disappearance of Helen Atkinson

I t is now ten years since the country was stirred to its very heart by the remarkable case of Helen Atkinson. In fact, nothing for a long time had created so much widespread interest, not only on account of the elements of tragic mystery in connection with the case, but because it proved to be one of those social problems which set thousands of busy brains to work trying to find its solution. It almost seems incredible, but it is nevertheless perfectly in accordance with the truth, that I myself received upwards of two thousand letters on the subject, all of them apparently emanating from perfectly sane people, and yet the majority of them were as wild in their conjectures and theories as they could possibly be; while not a few were violently abusive of the authorities for what the writers were pleased to term 'the supineness' of the police. It is almost unnecessary to say that this accusation of supineness was perfectly unjustifiable. But there are a class of thoughtless but amiable people who are infinitely more ready with blame than praise if the world does not happen to jog along precisely in accordance with their own views.

The Atkinsons were a humble but very respectable family, who kept a small grocer's shop in the west-end of Argyle Street, Glasgow. The household consisted of Mr. Atkinson, a man well advanced in years, his wife, considerably his junior, their son, a youth of fifteen, and their daughter, Helen, aged twenty-two. They kept one female servant, and a young man as an assistant in the shop. Helen was an unusually good-looking girl, and though she bore the reputation in the neighbourhood of being 'vain and flighty', her respectability no one ventured to impugn. Her parents were very serious and church-going people, and they had to the best of their ability exercised a strict supervision over their daughter. She had been well educated for her class, was a strict church-goer, and for many years had been a teacher in a Congregational Sunday school. With the exception of a certain waywardness, she had never, according to the statements of her father and mother, given a moment's uneasiness to her relatives. For four years before she so strangely disappeared she had been courted by a young man named Robert Stevenson, a bookbinder by trade, in the employ of Messrs. Farran and Oakendale, the well-known printers and bookbinders. Stevenson was said to be a steady and industrious workman, and was capable of earning good wages. The only charge against him was that he was a little too fond of gaiety and company, and when not with his sweetheart he was in the habit of spending his evenings with a class of young men who were calculated to somewhat lower the tone of those who associated with them; though possibly the worst charge that could be brought against them was that they were wild and thoughtless. For some time Helen met her lover in secret, as her parents objected to him, for no other reason, I believe, than that they thought their daughter might make a better match. He attended the same church and Sunday school as his sweetheart, and so the two had frequent opportunities of meeting. Helen succeeded at last in reconciling her parents to Stevenson, and after that the young man was a visitor at the house, and invariably on a Sunday evening accompanied the girl to her home. Her father, who was in a bad state of health, was anxious that the young couple should be married, as he wished to see them comfortably settled before he should be called from earthly scenes, and he promised not only to furnish a house for them, but on the marriage morning to present them with the sum of two hundred pounds. This offer ought to have tempted most young men of Stevenson's social standing, but he was proof against it, giving as his reason that he preferred to lay by a little himself, and by postponing the marriage for another year he would be in a better position.

About six months later Helen returned from church one Sunday evening alone, and when her parents asked what had become of Stevenson, she said she had left him at the church door, but indicated no reason for his not accompanying her to her home as usual. And as she seemed to be somewhat irritable, the conclusion arrived at was that there had been a lovers' tiff, which would duly right itself, so no further questions were asked. Helen retired to her room to take off her things, and when a little later she appeared at the supper table she had quite recovered her usual serenity, and seemed, if anything, more than usually cheerful. When Mr. Atkinson had said grace, and was helping his family to the supper, Helen suddenly jumped up to go to her room, saying that she had forgotten her pocket-handkerchief. When a quarter of an hour had elapsed and the girl had not returned Mrs. Atkinson sent the servant to see why she had not come. In a few minutes the domestic came back, and said Helen was not in the room, and in fact did not seem to be in the house at all. This somewhat startling announcement caused Mrs. Atkinson to jump up and go in search of Helen herself, but with the result only of proving the servant right. In Helen's room her jacket and bonnet, as she had taken them off when she came in, were lying on the bed, and her Bible, Prayer-book, and a small scent bottle, which she invariably carried, were on the dressing-table. The mother therefore felt no uneasiness, and yet was a little puzzled to understand why her daughter had gone out again. Access to the street could only be gained by a side door, which opened into a court at right angles with Argyle Street, as on a Sunday the shop door was never used, and was always secured with an iron bar and a padlock. Anyone going out or coming in by the side door must pass the kitchen, but the servant said she had not observed Miss Atkinson pass after coming in from church.

Mrs. Atkinson, in the course of some minutes, went into the court to look for her daughter. It was a November night, and a thick fog was hanging like a pall over the city. As Mrs. Atkinson opened the door the Tron Church was chiming a quarter-past nine. After peering up and down the court, and calling 'Helen' several times, she walked to the bottom of the court, where it opened into the main street, along which a great number of people were moving to and fro, but Helen was nowhere to be seen. Although naturally much surprised, the poor mother did not feel any uneasiness, notwithstanding that Helen had never done such a thing before, and she expected every minute to see the girl walk in.

The supper was finished in silence. Half-past nine chimed, then a quarter to ten, but Helen did not return, and for the first time the parents began to feel some alarm. Mr. Atkinson and his son then went in search of the girl, but without any result. They returned soon after ten, and kept going out and returning up to eleven o'clock, but failed to get a trace of Helen.

The distress of the unhappy parents may now be imagined, and at half-past eleven the father went down to the police station, and at once the telegraph was put into operation, and every station in Glasgow was apprised of the girl's disappearance. There was very little sleep for anyone that night in the Atkinson household, and when the morning came the parents were almost beside themselves with grief.

As soon as it was fully daylight Mr. Atkinson went over to Robert Stevenson's residence on the south side of the water. Mr. Stevenson, senior, said that his son was still in bed, an altogether unusual circumstance, as he was due at his work at eight o'clock. But he had not come home the previous night till after midnight. He was immediately informed of the circumstance which had brought Mr. Atkinson to the house, and quickly appearing on the scene, he exhibited the most poignant distress, and at once volunteered to join in the search, sending word to his employers that he would not be able to attend to his duties that day.

When Wednesday night came, and no trace of the missing girl had been found, the worst fears were entertained. It was then that I was requested to take the matter in hand, and from the first I suspected foul play. Handbills were issued and extensively circulated, while every newspaper, big and little, commented on the disappearance. By the end of the week there could no longer be any doubt that the girl had vanished completely, for not only did we exhaust all the usual channels of information open to the police, but there was not a hospital, infirmary, or lunatic asylum at which inquiries were not made, as well as at the steamboat piers and the railway stations, but it was all of no avail. By this time the papers had taken the case up as a subject for good 'copy', and long articles were written about it, so that public attention was attracted to the humble and hitherto obscure Atkinsons. As day after day went by without bringing any revelation of the mystery, the interest and excitement increased, and the newspapers from John O'Groat's to the Land's End made capital out of this 'mysterious disappearance'. Yet in spite of the wide-spread publicity, and the offer by the unhappy father of a reward of a hundred pounds, not a scrap of information could be obtained. Helen Atkinson had as effectually disappeared as if the earth had opened and swallowed her a thousand fathoms deep.

The prevailing theory, in Glasgow at least, was that the girl had been drowned in the river and her body carried out to sea. For my own part, although I did not say so, I had no faith in this theory, and for a very substantial reason. At the time the girl left her home the tide had just commenced to run up, and it continued to flow for five hours and forty-two minutes. Therefore, had she fallen in the water she would have been carried so far up that the ebbing tide would scarcely have done more than bring the body down again to the Broomielaw. But even supposing it had been swept down as far as Dumbarton, the ebb by that time would have ceased and the flood set in. The result of this would be that in a very few days the corpse must have been stranded on one of the vast stretches of mud and slime which are left exposed between the upper reaches of the river and Dumbarton every time the tide ebbs. And had it been so exposed the many hundreds of eyes which were on the watch, rendered doubly vigilant by the offer of the hundred pounds reward for the girl dead or alive, would have been sure to discover it. No, she was not drowned, at least not in the river. Of that I was perfectly convinced, but so confident was public opinion that she was that I kept my own opinion to myself.

When I first began to interest myself in this strange case I had several interviews with young Stevenson, and I confess that at first I had some suspicion that he knew of the girl's whereabouts. But this suspicion soon passed away. He told me that on leaving the church they had quarrelled, as she most unjustifiably accused him of being unfaithful to her. In fact, as he put it, she seemed determined to pick a quarrel. She left him in a temper, and as he was much annoyed and excited he joined some companions, and with them adjourned to a notorious shebeen, where he stayed till nearly midnight. This story I was enabled to confirm to the very letter, and I therefore had to turn my attention to other quarters in my attempts to unravel the mystery.

With some reluctance the parents gave me permission to search the girl's room, my hope being that I might get a clue from some letter or papers that had been in her possession. I found a bundle of letters from her lover, but they were all of the usual kind. There were a few other letters from relatives and girl companions, but all very commonplace, and I put them aside with an exclamation of disappointment. At last, however, I found in a small drawer of her dressing-table a half-sheet of note-paper without envelope, on which was written in a clerkly hand the following line:

Do you intend to adopt my advice? Say yes or no.

There was something about this that I thought worth investigating, though I should not have attached any special importance to it had I not discovered in the fire-place some morsels of another note that had evidently been torn in pieces, and partly burnt. The only morsel I could make anything out of was a scrap about the size of a five-shilling piece, on which in the same handwriting as the above were these detached words:

... are a fool
... adopt my advice

> mother and father will never know
> ... all will be well.
> —ately yours,   Sandpiper.

Incoherent as this was I felt that at last I had got a clue to the mystery, for it was not difficult to fill in the breaks, which I did, and in its expanded form the fragment read thus:—'You are a fool if you do not adopt my advice, for your mother and father will never know, and all will be well.— Affectionately yours'.

It needed no very great amount of astuteness to determine that 'Sandpiper' was a fictitious name, and by it I hoped to unravel the riddle. My first course was to inquire of Mr. and Mrs. Atkinson if they knew the handwriting, but they both said they did not. Subsequently, however, Mrs. Atkinson remembered having received two or three letters for Helen, and she felt confident now that they were addressed in the same handwriting. The conclusion that I now came to was that Helen had had a second lover, and following out this idea, I sought an interview at once with Stevenson, and by dint of cautious questioning, learned from him that he had occasionally had suspicions that Helen was not true to him; and that for some time before their final parting he had observed that she seemed to be suffering from great distress of mind. Assuming that what he said was true, and I had no reason to doubt it, my theory was strengthened, and I proceeded to steadily act upon it. In a few days I received another piece of evidence from a member of the police force, who stated that on the Sunday night when Helen so suddenly disappeared he was on duty in Argyle Street, and while passing near the Atkinsons' house he saw a man and a young woman talking together in a doorway. The woman was without hat or jacket, and thinking they were merely a pair of lovers wishing each other goodnight, he took no notice of them, and when he returned ten minutes later they had gone.

Of course this did not prove much, because it was no uncommon thing on a Sunday night for servant lassies to pop out of their masters' houses for a stolen interview with their sweethearts. But taken in connection with the other links I had gained, I felt it was corroborative of the theory I had formed.

It was now a month since the girl had disappeared; and, as already stated, not only did letters pour in from all parts of the country, but scarcely a day passed but one or other of the great journals referred to the case, and insinuated that it ought not to have been possible for a girl to so suddenly disappear without traces of her whereabouts being discovered. That it is possible, however, for people to disappear for good and all is proved every day, especially in a great city like Glasgow. My next step was to insert an advertisement in the agony columns of the papers, worded as follows:

Sandpiper.—You are in danger. Your movements are watched. Be careful. If you see this answer it, so that I may know you have seen it.—A True Friend.

This advertisement appeared for a fortnight in the Glasgow, Edinburgh, and London dailies, and day after day I eagerly scanned the various journals in the hope that my ruse might produce something. At last, when I almost despaired, the following appeared in the London *Telegraph* and *Standard*:

A True Friend.—Thanks. I am all right. I have nothing to fear, however.—Sandpiper.

In a very few days I was in possession of the original copy of this advertisement, and found that it was in the same handwriting as that on the scraps of paper I had discovered in Helen's room. The next course was to get hold of the writer, whoever he was, for he held the key of the mystery, and without him the mystery, I was sure, would never be solved. I knew enough of human nature to feel sure that a man who would thus be tempted into answering an advertisement of that kind might be easily trapped; and so I inserted another advertisement in the two dailies named. It was worded thus:

Sandpiper.—Give me a clue to your address, for I have something of the highest importance to communicate.—A True Friend.

I had arranged that a confederate in plain clothes was to be in attendance at each of the offices for the next few days, and the clerks at the advertisement counters were instructed to take note of anyone presenting an answer, and give information immediately to the plain clothes man. On the third day a slatternly girl, about fourteen years of age, entered the *Standard* office, and handed in the following:

A True Friend.—Write first of all to J. Johnstone, Poste Restante, London.— Sandpiper.

The girl, who was overwhelmed with fright, was at once conveyed in a cab to Scotland Yard, where I had an opportunity of interrogating her, and I learned that she was a servant in a house at Kennington, and the gentleman who had sent the advertisement was a lodger in the house. In less than two hours this lodger was under arrest. He proved to be a young man, who for obvious reasons shall be called John Blank. He was very well connected indeed, his family being Edinburgh people. He had been a clerk in an Edinburgh bank, but had been dismissed for inattention to his business. As he had given his parents a great deal of trouble, his father presented him with a sum of money, and refused to have anything further to do with him. It appears that he then went to Glasgow, where he made the acquaintance of Helen Atkinson, and owing to a peculiar habit he had of whistling, he was nicknamed the Sandpiper. To Helen he represented that he was a person of consequence, with the prospects of a fortune, and he had induced her to go through a Scotch form of marriage under an assumed name, but until he could take her to live with him she was to keep up her connection with Stevenson. As she saw the prospects of maternity staring her in the face, she tried to prevail upon her supposed husband to declare the marriage, but on the plea that it would utterly ruin him with his friends if he did, he refused, and threatened to commit suicide if she made it known. Yielding at last to the persistent pressure he put upon her, she consented to go to a house in a low part of Glasgow, which was kept by a notorious woman and her husband, named Macdonald. It was arranged that the unfortunate girl was to leave her home as she did, and, when the affair was over, return and inform her parents that she had been persuaded to visit London with a companion on an escapade. A fortnight later the poor girl gave birth to a dead child, and owing to neglect in her case, puerperal fever set in, and three days later she herself was dead.

The wretches in whose house she had died were terribly alarmed, and, being exceedingly ignorant and illiterate, they shrank from giving information, fearing that they would be hanged. They therefore dug a large hole in their cellar, into which they thrust the bodies.

All these facts were easily verified, and as there was no charge that could be substantiated against John Blank, he was discharged, and left to the lashings of his own conscience.

The Macdonalds, in whose house Helen died, were duly brought up for trial, and as there were previous convictions against them, they were each sentenced to twenty years' penal servitude.

The sad fate of poor Helen Atkinson caused universal grief, and the execrations of all honest men and women went out against the scoundrel who had so ruthlessly betrayed her, but whom the law could not touch. It was a terrible blow to his family, and his mother took it so much to heart that she lost her reason. He went out to India, and two years later I heard that he had been thrown from a horse in the jungle, near Bombay, and was killed on the spot. It seemed a fitting retribution for a man who could so heartlessly betray a confiding girl.

A Terrible Deed

One morning in the early summer a farm labourer employed on a farm not far from Strathaven was crossing a field belonging to his employer, in which were a number of stacks of hay, when he was horrified to observe the dead body of a woman lying behind one of the stacks. He knew at the first glance that she was dead, because her eyes were fixed and glassy; her face was like marble, and puckered up into an expression of agony; the lips were parted, revealing the teeth and the tip of the tongue, which had been bitten through. The front part of her dress was also covered with clotted blood. She was lying on her back, one leg drawn up, her arms outstretched, and the hand clenched.

The man immediately ran back to the farm and stated what he had seen. Then some of the men said that they thought they had heard a woman's scream two or three times in the dead of night, but not feeling sure that the sounds were really the screams of woman, they had gone to sleep again without making any attempt to find out if anything was wrong. The farmer, Mr. George Duncan, who was an exceedingly intelligent man, at once noted down all the details about the body which I have mentioned. Then he had the dead woman covered over with a tarpaulin without disturbing her position in the least, and information was despatched post-haste to Glasgow. I was at once requested to proceed to the spot, and make every investigation necessary, and within half-an-hour of getting my orders I was driving to Strathaven in company with our police surgeon. On arriving at Mr. Duncan's farm, another medical man was summoned from Strathaven, and as soon as he came we proceeded to make an official examination. That made by the doctors was at first only cursory, and was more to enable them to ascertain the cause of the woman's death. They were then in a position to say that the poor creature's throat bore marks of strangulation; but there was one or more punctured wounds in the breast, and it was impossible to state then whether death had actually resulted from strangulation or stabbing. But one thing they were positive about, the woman had not met her death by her own hands, but at the hands of someone else. I thereupon proceeded to make a drawing of the position of the body and its surroundings. That done, my next step was to critically examine the ground near where the body was lying. First, let me say that Duncan's farm was situated in a lonely position. It stood back from the main road about a quarter of a mile, and was reached by a private lane. The field where the body was found was a narrow strip, running from the house to some ploughed land. It was used principally for stacking hay and straw. There were twelve stacks altogether, and they stood in two parallel rows. In one corner of the field nearest the house was a drinking pond for cattle. The bothy used by the farm hands abutted on the field, and screams proceeding from any part of the field could have been heard in the bothy. Therefore, the men were no doubt right when they said they heard screams. The field was parallel with the lane, from which it was separated by a thickset hedge. Access to the field was gained by means of a gateway leading out of the farmyard, so that anyone wanting to get in must either force a way through the hedge or go through the farmyard and enter by the gateway. All these particulars I noted, and, of course, set my value upon them. The ground about the body was soft—that is, without being absolutely muddy, it was soft enough to retain the impressions of footsteps, and my examination led me to determine that the ground had been tramped upon by two persons, and there was unmistakable evidence that there had been a struggle. There was one patch where the footsteps were jumbled together upon the ground; that patch was sloppy owing to the tramping, which had squeezed the water out of the spongy ground. Then there was another point my examination enabled me to determine. After the victim had fallen on her back the criminal had knelt over her, not on her but straddle-legged across her, and in this position probably had rendered her partially insensible, and had then stabbed her. I arrived at this conclusion by, to my mind, irrefutable evidence, and that evidence was that on each side of the body were knee prints. Having established this point, my next care was to critically examine the footmarks, and I settled that there had only been two persons present, the victim and the slayer. One set of foot-marks were clearly those of the dead woman, as proved by her boots. The others were smaller, and were made not by a man's boots but a woman's. Here then was a startling problem to solve. Was the murderer a woman, or a man wearing woman's boots? If the latter, he must have been a very small man, or at any rate have had extraordinarily small feet. But the more I pursued my investigation the more I inclined to the belief that the murderer was a woman, and at last I got a piece of evidence which convinced me that I was right. I found tramped into the mud close by the head of the body part of an earring of a somewhat novel pattern. It was a tiny ball of hollow gold. On each side of the ball a very small garnet was set. The hook that held the ball in the ear had been broken. 'This ring,' I thought to myself, 'belonged to the person who did the murder, and that person was a woman.' The dead woman's ears were not bored for earrings. The portion I had found had probably been wrenched out during the struggle. I next directed my attention to determining how the murderer had left the field; and here the footsteps helped me. They were clearly traceable towards the hedge and the bottom of the field. They were, however, lost after four or five yards, owing to the ground hardening. But they directed me to a gap in the hedge farthest from the house. It was not a big gap, but large enough for a medium size person to squeeze through, and when I came to examine it I found a morsel of grey woollen cloth adhering to the thorny hedge. 'A woman has passed through here,' I said, 'and in doing so has left a piece of her dress behind.' That piece of dress and the broken earring I jealously secured, for I knew how valuable they might prove as clues. My investigation being completed so far, the victim's body was conveyed to Strathaven, where the doctors began their part of the business. The dead woman was good looking—decidedly so. She had fair, wavy hair; blue eyes and good teeth, with a plump, well-rounded figure; her clothes indicated a person in a humble position in life, not the humblest, but she might have belonged to any class from a tradesman's wife to a pedlar. She had on a good dress, but it did not correspond with the piece of cloth I had got from the hedge. She also wore good boots and stockings, but her underclothing was coarse, and some of it much mended and patched. Robbery had not been the motive of the crime, because in her pocket was an old leather purse containing a sovereign, a one pound note, three shillings, and half a crown, with a few copper pieces. On her wedding finger she wore a wedding ring, and another ring of some value, being set with pearls and rubies. There was not a scrap of written paper on her person that would have tended to establish her identity, nor was her linen marked with any name or initials. But round her shoulders, under the dress, she wore a cream-coloured handkerchief, made partly of silk and partly of cotton. I believe the manufacture of this sort of handkerchiefs is or was peculiar to Lancashire and Yorkshire. They are usually sold for gentlemen's mufflers. The one round the woman's neck bore in one corner the initials R. A. I need scarcely say I took possession of that handkerchief as being calculated to afford me another clue. These letters, of course, would have stood for the initials of scores of names; but, nevertheless, I knew what value to attach to this small link, and I was hopeful that it might help, at any rate, to put me on the track of the criminal.

And now I come to the medical aspects of the case; and they have such an important bearing that I must detail them. I have already mentioned that there were marks on the neck, which showed the victim had been partially strangled; and the deducement to be drawn from this was that there had been a struggle between the criminal and the intended victim, who had been overcome by the throat being compressed, but, as was subsequently proved, that was not the immediate cause of death. The victim was a somewhat small woman, and from the smallness of her bones and the softness of the muscles, she could not have been possessed of any great deal of strength, and so would have been easily overcome by the pressure on the throat. But she had also been stabbed twice in the breast—once to the right of the sternum, not a very deep puncture, though it would have proved a dangerous one had she not been killed outright. The second blow had been delivered with great force over the heart. In putting his finger into this wound, one of the doctors gave a start and exclaimed, 'Good heavens, there is part of the knife still in the woman's body'.

This remarkable circumstance naturally surprised us all, for the weapon had obviously broken, and the blade was left in the wound.

The following day a *post-mortem* examination was made as soon as the sheriff's order had been obtained, and this examination led to the extraordinary discovery that part of the blade of a knife was, as the doctor had stated the day previous, still in the body. This portion measured no less than five-and-a-half inches. It was very sharp pointed, and bore on the blade the name of a Sheffield cutler. It had the appearance of being what is known as a dagger knife. That is, a pocket knife with a long blade that shuts up like the ordinary knife, but can be jerked out, and is held back by a spring, and thus forms a most formidable dagger.

I have often wondered how it is that such dangerous weapons as these knives are allowed to be sold in the indiscriminate manner they are sold now. The sale of these and cheap revolvers ought to be prohibited except under stringent restrictions. The possession of such weapons is often the incentive for criminally inclined persons to take the lives of their fellows.

In the case of the poor woman I am dealing with great force had been used. The knife had entered between the fourth and fifth ribs, passing through the left lung and grazing the heart. This wound was of course mortal, but the medical testimony was to the effect that it did not necessarily produce instantaneous death, and the victim might have lived from a minute up to half an hour after receiving the wound. This would no doubt account for the agonised expression of the face.

The breaking of the knife was obviously an accident and one point to try and determine was where was the handle. The autopsy revealed the fact that while the woman's heart was weak, she was in all other respects perfectly healthy, and might have lived for many years. Her apparent age then was not more than thirty.

It was now clear that a brutal and cowardly murder had been committed, and it was surrounded with all the elements of mystery. I had by this time formed certain opinions, and I put this question to the doctors, and asked them to give me an unqualified answer.

'Could that knife have been driven into the victim's body by a woman?'

'Yes,' was the answer, 'if she was a moderately strong woman.'

'It would not require an extraordinarily strong woman to produce such an effect, would it?' I asked.

'Oh, no, for the knife, as you see, is long, sharp, and narrow bladed, and a woman possessed of fair muscular power, and by means of a good swinging blow, could have driven the weapon in as we have found it.'

My next step now was to institute a minute search for the remaining portion of the knife, but though I searched over at least half a square mile of ground from where the body was found, the handle of the knife was not discovered. The search was so thorough that had the object we sought for been within the radius named it could hardly have escaped detection. The criminal, therefore, had carried it off.

It was an easy matter to establish the fact that the victim was a stranger in the district, and presumably the criminal was also; but though the dead woman's description was circulated far and wide, her identification could not be proved.

I saw at once that to unravel the threads of this mystery would not be an easy task, unless some blundering on the part of the criminal should put me on the right track. Naturally, I asked myself, 'Why had the criminal and the victim come to this lonely farm?' Its out-of-the-way position seemed to indicate that the murderer

had been acquainted with that fact, and so selected it for the per-
petration of the crime. But then how was it that the victim had been
lured there? I confessed that that puzzled me, for I had come to the
conclusion that the murder had been committed by a woman—
firstly, on account of the footprints, which were hardly those of a
man's foot; secondly, the broken earring; thirdly, the piece of cloth
sticking to the hedge, and which had been torn from a woman's
dress. And, in addition, the doctor's statement showed that there
was nothing improbable in my theory that it was a woman's hand
that had driven the knife into the victim's body.

It will be seen from the foregoing that if my theory had any
soundness in it, we were at once confronted by circumstances which
were no less mysterious than novel. Inquiries were immediately set
on foot to try and find out if the victim had been seen at all in the
neighbourhood. But on this point there were conflicting opinions.
Some people said a woman answering the description had been
observed in Strathaven the day previous, but when these people
were allowed to see the body, they could not state decisively that
they had seen her before. Death, however, especially death by violence, so changes a person as to make recognition very difficult by
those who were not well acquainted with the deceased before death.
I therefore came to the conclusion that she had probably been in
Strathaven on the previous day as suggested, though, even if this
was so, it advanced us no nearer to the solution of what was a most
difficult problem. What was necessary in the first instance was to
get the dead woman recognised, so that we might know who she
was, and that done it would be a good step on the way towards
discovering who it was who had so foully slain her. Strangely enough,
however, no one identified her. The crime, of course, caused great
sensation in the quiet neighbourhood, where murder was almost a
thing unknown; and equally, of course, the country people from
round about flocked in to Strathaven, and were allowed without 'let
or hindrance' to see the body. But unless the dead woman had belonged to the neighbourhood, it was not likely that these people
would know her, and that they failed to recognise her was proof that

she was a stranger. Four days passed, and then we were necessitated to bury the remains, having first of all photographed them from various points of view. And so ended the first act of this strange tragedy. As is usual in such cases, there were all sorts of wild theories, and the police came in for the stereotyped abuse; while any number of well-meaning but silly people wrote letters to the papers and to the detective department of the police, pointing out what ought to be done, and what ought not to be done, in order to bring the criminal to justice. It is needless to say that these effusions had no effect, neither did they provoke comment. We whose duty it was to vindicate the majesty of the law knew our own business best, and were not likely to be influenced by the chattering of irresponsible people, as the late Lord Beaconsfield would have dubbed them. One thing was very clear to us—we had got an exceedingly difficult case to deal with, and no trace of the criminal having been got within a week of the crime, his or her chances of escape were greatly increased. The failure to get any trace satisfied me that the parties had come from a distance. By that I mean they did not belong to the immediate neighbourhood, but I thought it very probable that they did belong to Glasgow, unless they were mere tramps in the vagrant sense, and roamed the country without fixed habitation. From the very first, however, the tramp theory did not find favour with me, and I will give my reasons for this. There was nothing in the murdered woman's appearance to indicate the tramp, and tramps, as a rule, do not have such a sum of money on their person as was found on her. Then again, the piece of earring I had picked up was not such as would have been worn by a woman of the genus tramp. The boots that she was wearing were also another point against the idea of her being a tramp; they were almost new; and her underclothing was too good and too clean for a woman of the vagrant class. I therefore dismissed the idea of her being a vagrant from my mind, and I assigned to her a somewhat higher position— either that of a better class of servant—probably a house or chambermaid—in a genteel family, or a tradesman's wife, in a humble way of business. Why I say 'a better class of servant' is that her hands did not indicate that she had been in the habit of doing any hard or very dirty work. While they were not the hands of a lady, there was a softness and whiteness about them which would not have been had she occupied the position of a mere scullery wench.

Although I felt that the case was a very difficult one, I did not like to think that it would entirely baffle us. To despair would have been entirely contrary to my disposition, and when, one morning about a fortnight after the murder, my chief said to me—

'Well, Donovan, I am afraid the Strathaven affair will have to be relegated to the long list of undiscovered crimes,'

I answered—

'It is far too early to say that yet, sir. I confess it's a puzzler, hut the most intricate puzzles are capable of solution.'

'Oh, yes,' he returned, 'every puzzle must have its answer, but some are so difficult that even a genius may fail to find the solution.'

This remark put me on my metal. I could not bear the idea of failure. I never did like to think that the ruffians of society had more brain power and keener intelligence than the organised forces of law and order. I have frequently advanced as an axiom that criminals, even the most hardened and practised of them, betray themselves ultimately by some act or acts of stupidity that a child could not overlook. And in this case I was strongly of opinion that sooner or later something would come to light that would enable me to run the criminal down; and, as I pondered over the matter, it began to dawn upon me that already a thread was lying to my hand that I might be able to follow up, until it changed to a rope encircling the culprit's neck. This thread, I frankly confess, I had at first overlooked, for, however practised and painstaking a man may be, some small detail may at first escape his observation.

And this was my case. I had overlooked a detail, or rather it had not struck me until I began to ponder over the matter. It was this. Whoever had committed the crime could not be an entire stranger to the place. My reason for coming to this conclusion is easily given. A person wholly unacquainted with the farm and its neighbourhood would have found no small difficulty in getting to the spot in the dark, for the farm was, as I have already remarked, a considerable distance from the main road. Then, again, why should an utter stranger have selected such an out of the way spot when a field much nearer would have answered the purpose? The more I took this view the more I inclined to a belief that the murderer was acquainted with the farm. I therefore began to question Mr. Duncan, the farmer, about the people he had in his employ.

'Surely,' he exclaimed with some indignation, 'you don't think that any of my people have been guilty of this butchery?'

'Never mind, sir, what I think,' I replied, 'my business and my duty are to hunt down the criminal. A crime has been committed, that is certain, and my experience of criminals suggests certain possibilities. It is, therefore, clearly my place to test these possibilities, hence the reason for my inquiries.'

A little reflection soon showed him that I was right, and he at once gave me a list of all his servants. I asked many searching questions about the females, for it grew upon me that the murder had been committed by a woman, and naturally this idea prompted the query, Why should a woman have done it? And logic at once responded—'She did it out of jealousy.' Assuming, therefore, that I was right, it followed as an inevitable sequence that the murdered woman had had a lover and a rival, and in a fit of madness begotten by the jealousy the rival had resorted to this dreadful method to get rid of one who, probably, was more successful than herself in winning the man's affections.

In Mr. Duncan's employ there were at least a dozen females of very varying ages, and I managed with, as I think, some adroitness to have a word with each of these females without arousing her suspicions, and after that I felt positively certain that not one of them, either directly or indirectly, had had anything to do with the crime. I was, in consequence, baffled, but still with doggedness, pigheadedness if you like, I stuck to my text that the crime had been committed by a woman. But then you see my pigheadedness, if that is the term to be used, was the result of many years' experience in unravelling very knotty points in connection with criminals. This experience had taught me to view things from a very different standpoint to that taken up by the general public. And little matter of details that escaped the public eyes were to me items of grave importance.

My failure to detect amongst Mr. Duncan's female servants any sign that would have acted as a guide baffled me, as I have said, but it did not daunt me, and I stuck to my theory about the murderer being acquainted with the neighbourhood. So I was led by this to inquire about servants who had left the employ within a comparatively recent period.

'Oh!' exclaimed Mr. Duncan, 'you see at every hiring term we are always shifting our hands. With some exceptions, farm servants, as a rule, don't stick long in a place. They have always got a notion that they can better themselves by getting a place where they won't have so much work. It is therefore not easy for a farmer with a large holding to keep much count of all the folk he may have had in his employ in the course of half a dozen years.'

'I can well understand that,' I answered, 'and yet, perhaps, you can tell me if you have had a woman in your service who might, under given circumstances, have been guilty of such a deed as this?'

He scratched his bald pate in a very puzzled way, for my question had confused him, and he had to rattle his brains a good deal before he could arrive at a definite opinion.

'Well, you see,' he remarked thoughtfully, 'that's a gey difficult question to answer, because anything I might say would tend probably to throw suspicion on a person who was innocent.'

'Probably it might have that tendency,' I answered, 'but I should know what value to set upon your information. If it seemed to me to contain no element of suspicion I should have no suspicion. If, on the other hand, it should strike me as being worth acting upon with a view to further investigation, you may rest assured I should proceed with the utmost caution. It is never my habit to do things rashly, and I should be very sure of my position before taking any steps that would be calculated to jeopardise the honour and liberty of any one.'

This argument satisfied him, and he replied, 'I am sure you would, I am sure you would, for it's a dreadful thing you see for an innocent person to fall under suspicion of having been concerned in such a foul deed as this. Now, there is one person I mind of who was with me for a year, and left two years ago. Her name was Jessie Macfarlane, and she had charge of the dairy.'

'Oh, indeed, and do you remember anything peculiar about her?'

'Well, I mind she was a braw-like lassie, but, man, she had an awfu' temper.'

'She was passionate, was she?'

'Ay, she used to flare up like a powder mill.'

'And what did she leave you for?'

'Well, she wasna very steady, and I put her awa.'

This bit of information, meagre as it was, caused me to feel considerable interest in Jessie Macfarlane, and to want to know more about her.

'Why did you put her away?' I asked.

'Oh, I couldn't do with her here, for she was gey light-headed, and her face was that pretty that all the lads on the farm were just raving about her.'

'What do you mean when you say she was light-headed?'

'She was no' serious enough for me. She was just aye giggling and laughing, and flirting with the lads so that they couldna mind their wark.'

'Humph,' I muttered, as my interest in this young woman deepened, and I felt that it was my duty to know more about her. Of course it was not altogether an uncommon thing for a good-looking female in an establishment where many men were kept to be a source of worry. For men, no matter what their station in life, are attracted by a pretty face, and will vie with each other in paying it homage. And a woman who is conscious of her power in this respect needs to have a strong will and evenly-balanced mind if she is to avoid getting 'light-headed,' as farmer Duncan termed it. On the first blush, therefore, it may appear as if I was not justified in harbouring even a shadow of suspicion against the pretty Jessie

Macfarlane. But the detective eye sees things that the untrained eye cannot see. And if the reader will bear in mind that, firstly, I had brought myself to regard as almost certain that the murder had been committed by a woman; and, secondly, that the murderer was acquainted with the farm, it will be better understood why I should come to feel some suspicion that Jessie Macfarlane might know something about it. At any rate, she fitted in with my theory of the crime. She was a missing link in the chain I had been making up, and I was not the person to pass by this link without testing it and examining it in every possible way. I must prove myself either wrong or right beyond all question of doubt before I should feel satisfied,

'Tell me, Mr. Duncan,' I said, 'do you think now that this Jessie Macfarlane might have become capable of committing such a dreadful crime as this?'

The point blank question staggered him a little, and I saw that as a conscientious man he was troubled. Naturally, he was reluctant to say anything that might tend to cast a slur on an innocent person. But, on the other hand, he so fully recognised the heinousness of the tragedy that he felt everything possible should be done to bring the criminal to justice.

'Upon my word,' he said, 'I scarcely know how to answer you. I always thought that there was a bit of the devil in Jessie, and I've often said I pity the man who gets her.'

'What was your reason for coming to that conclusion?'

'Well, I couldn't avoid it, seeing the temper she had.'

'She was passionate, then?'

'Indeed, ay. She would just fairly rave when she was crossed.'

'Was she partial to any particular servant of yours?'

'Yes, I think she was smitten with a lad named Ralph Saunderson.'

'Was he smitten with her?'

'I've heard say as he was.'

'Where is he now?'

'He left me the term before last. He got about two hundred pounds through the death of an uncle, and he told me he was going to start a grocer's shop in Glasgow.'

'And what became of Jessie'?'

'I don't know where she went to.'

After this information I needed no second thought as to the course I should pursue. My way was clear before me. Jessie Macfarlane and Ralph Saunderson either knew something about the murder or they did not, and it was obviously my duty to prove one thing or the other. I therefore set about trying to find Saunderson. This was not a very difficult task, and I discovered him installed in a humble shop near Stobscross, Glasgow.

He was a man, as far as figure and face went, who would be attractive to some women, for he was by no means a bad-looking fellow, although somewhat dull-witted and heavy of intellect. He was rather in a despondent mood, and had been drinking, for his business had not prospered, and he had not only lost his money but was in debt.

I learned these particulars not from himself, but in the neighbourhood. He was of a reticent disposition, an uncommunicative and cunning sort of man. By cunning, I mean that he would do things slyly and secretly, and keep his counsel about them. But though I came to this conclusion in regard to him I could not believe him capable of committing so cold-blooded a tragedy as that which had taken place at Duncan's farm.

I found that he knew nothing about the murder, and I did not question him about it. But I asked him if he was acquainted with one Jessie Macfarlane, and I watched him narrowly as I put the question, though his somewhat stolid countenance betrayed no emotion or surprise.

'Oh, ay,' he answered, with apparent unconcern. 'I knew Jessie.'

'Were you courting her?'

'Not exactly.'

'But you were sweethearting her?'

'Yes. I was spoony on her at one time.'

'And she was spoony on you?'

'She was.'

'You say she was. Does that mean that you have given her up?'

'Well, you see we didn't get on very well together.'

'Why?'

'Her tongue and her temper did not suit me.'

'She has a violent tongue, has she?'

'Yes. She was always nagging at me, and I couldn't stand it.'

'Was she jealous of you?'

'She was.'

'She had cause to be, perhaps?'

This question aroused him from his lethargy. He had hitherto answered my questions in an uninterested and mechanical sort of way. Now I saw his eyes light up and the colour in his face deepen as he said quickly—

'Look here, mister, what is your little game? and what are you catechising me like this for?'

'I have a reason.'

'Maybe you have. But you'll get no more out of me till I know what you are driving at.'

'Well, just answer me one more question,' I said. 'Where does Jessie live, and when did you see her last?'

'Tell me what you want to know for?' said he.

'No, I won't tell you now. But take my word for it, if you don't answer my question, you may get yourself into serious trouble.'

For the first time something like an expression of fear swept over his face, and with a sort of growl he said—

'She stops at Paisley.'

'Whereabouts?'

He gave me her address, and said that he had seen her within a fortnight, but had had a violent quarrel, and had not seen her since.

'Did you quarrel about a woman?' I asked.

'Yes,' he answered, reluctantly.

I was now determined to make a bold shot, and searching his face keenly said—

'Would you be surprised to hear that the woman is dead?'

He fairly staggered and gasped out—'Good God! you don't say so.'

'Well, I have reason to think so. But tell me her name and describe her to me.'

'Her name is Annie Muirhead, and she's parlour maid to Mr. —— at Partick.

'You've been courting her?'

'Yes.'

'And did Jessie Macfarlane know of that?'

'Yes, she did.'

'And that was the cause of quarrel between you?'

'It was.'

I could no longer doubt now that I was on the right track, and that my theory was correct. A madly jealous and passionate woman had killed her more successful rival, and I was confirmed in this when by further questioning I elicited from Saunderson that he had told Annie that he intended to give up his shop and go back to work on Duncan's farm. For Mr. Duncan, so he said, had always promised to take him back any time he would go. His description of Annie Muirhead tallied exactly with that of the murdered woman, and when I told him that Annie had been killed he became deeply affected, and cried like a child. Half-an-hour later I was driving to Partick, and soon ascertained that Annie Muirhead had been missing from her place for nearly a fortnight. She had asked for a week off to go and see a sick sister, as she said, who lived at Berwick, and she had not been heard of since.

So far, then, my idea about the tragedy was fully confirmed, but it still remained to be seen whether Jessie Macfarlane was the criminal. It was reasonable to suppose that she was, but still there was no actual proof, and before proceeding to extremity I resolved to learn something more about Jessie, and so went down to Paisley.

I found that she was living in a very poor quarter of the town with her mother, but I was told that I could not see her as she was exceedingly ill and in bed. On my urging that it was absolutely necessary to her welfare that I should be allowed to see her, the mother consented at last to let me go into her bedroom.

I found her utterly prostrated, and evidently suffering from hysterical nervousness. She was a really pretty woman, as far as the mere features went, but there was something in her face that was not agreeable. It is really difficult to say what this something was. Yet there was a something. I noticed that my entrance caused an expression of alarm in her eyes, and in a feeble voice she asked—

'What do you want with me, sir?'

My position was an extremely painful one, for there could be no mistake about the woman's illness. But men in my profession have to think of duty before everything else. If this unfortunate creature had really been guilty of that awful crime she must pay the penalty, and pity could not be allowed to interfere with the stern demands of Justice. I therefore said, as I took my seat by the bedside—

'I've come to ask you some questions about one Annie Muirhead.'

I saw the woman's face contort with a look of horror and fear as I said this, and I was certain now that she was the murderess.

'What about her?' she asked fiercely.

'She's been murdered,' I answered bluntly.

'I know it,' she exclaimed, and then she broke into wild hysterical screams, and I left her to obtain a warrant for her arrest. I returned in about two hours, and was met by the mother, who was wild with grief, and as soon as she saw me she exclaimed—

'Oh, sir, my poor lassie's dead. She's taken something that's done for her.'

This proved to be too true. A little while after I had left Jessie Macfarlane had ended her existence by swallowing a large dose of oxalic acid which had been used for cleaning some brass things.

Further investigation led to the discovery in Annie Muirhead's box of a letter which had evidently been forged by Jessie Macfarlane. It was written as if it had come from Saunderson, and he was made to say that he had gone back to Duncan's farm, and it begged of her to meet him and he would get a lodging for her for a few days in Strathaven.

This forged letter led her to her doom, and the light it threw upon the matter made the rest clear. There is no doubt that

Saunderson had shamefully trifled with the feelings of Jessie, and she being of a passionate, fiery, and revengeful temperament, resolved to murder her more successful rival, and the cunning of her nature was displayed in the way she lured her victim to that lonely farm, thinking probably that it would render the detection of the crime impossible. The fierceness and determination with which she slew her victim suggested uncontrollable passion that fell little short of actual madness. Further confirmation that the guilt was hers was furnished by the fellow earring to the one I had picked up being found amongst her things, and the morsel of cloth I had taken from the hedge was the same as one of her dresses, which was rent, and a piece was missing. It was also much stained with blood. Thus what promised at first to be a profound mystery was fully cleared up, and the deed, terrible as it was, was marked by the usual vulgar elements which distinguish this class of crime.

The Story of a Diamond Ring

One morning about eleven o'clock a very stout, red-faced, bald-headed, well-dressed, gentlemanly-looking man bounced into the central Police Station in Glasgow, and with much puffing and blowing, for he was greatly excited, he said he had been robbed of a diamond ring valued at £200. I say that he 'bounced in', and there is no other way to express it, for he was one of those fussy individuals who make themselves heard, felt, and seen, and who force themselves upon you with an obtrusiveness that is often ludicrous and wholly objectionable.

The Superintendent on duty, who was a cool, deliberate man, eyed the stranger, whose portly form was clothed in expensive garments. Across his expansive abdomen stretched a massive gold chain of the ship's cable pattern. In his cravat a handsome pin sparkled, and he had two or three rings on his fat fingers. Although a little loudly dressed, there was nothing flash about him. That is, his clothes and jewellery were good. It needed only half an eye to see that, and from his appearance and style there was no reason to suppose that he might not have been in possession of a ring of the value stated.

'Pray be seated, sir,' said the Superintendent politely. 'You are a little excited now.'

'Excited?' bawled the individual, and striking the desk with his ponderous fist, 'excited, what do you mean? I am not excited. I'm as cool as you are. But if I am excited, is there any wonder? Don't YOU think you would be excited if you had lost a ring worth two hundred pounds?'

The Superintendent smiled as he answered—

'Well, sir, I don't know how I might feel, for I have never had the good luck to possess so valuable a piece of property. But be kind enough to give us some particulars of your loss. What is your name, sir?'

'My name is Samuel Featherstone.'

'You are a stranger to Glasgow, I venture to think?'

'Well, I don't live here if that's what you mean, but I come here often enough. I'm a partner in the firm of Blank, Blank, and Co., of Wood Street, London, and I travel for the firm.'

'Oh, yes. Then where are you staying now?'

'At the —— Hotel.'

'Were you robbed of the ring in the hotel or outside?'

'In the hotel. There's no doubt about it. I've been in the house for two days, and I had the ring all right last night.'

'Then do you suspect any one?'

'Yes, of course I do. I suspect the chambermaid.'

'What are your reasons for suspecting her?'

'Well, I'm sure it was her,' said the gentleman, fuming and puffing again.

'But have you any proof?'

'I've got no actual proof, but I'm going to give her in charge anyway. She expressed admiration for the ring last night, and she's the only person who has had anything to do with my room. I'm as sure that she has taken it as I am that I have got a head on my shoulders.'

At this stage of the proceedings a message was sent to me, as I happened to be on the premises, and in a few minutes I was in the lower office, taking stock of this fat and fussy individual. The foregoing particulars were related to me, and, having listened to them, I said—

'Now, Mr. Featherstone, I would remind you that it is a very serious business to make such a charge against a person unless you have very good evidence to go upon, and you run some risk of an action for false imprisonment.'

'And pray, sir, who the deuce are you?' he demanded in a vulgar and blustering way.

'Oh, I am only a very humble person,' I replied, 'but I've had some little experience of cases of this kind, and it's taught me caution.'

The Superintendent mentioned my name, and Mr. Featherstone, with haughty demeanour, said that he had never heard of me, whereat I expressed deep regret that I was so unfortunate as not to be known to him.

'Well, that doesn't matter,' he answered, patronisingly. 'You know me, no doubt. Anyway, you know my firm.'

I was compelled to confess that up to that moment it had not been my privilege to have heard of either him or his firm. Whereat he waxed wroth again, and cried out—

'Well, I wouldn't give much for your commercial knowledge. Why, my firm has been doing business with Glasgow for fifty years.'

'Possibly; and while deploring my supreme ignorance, I would venture to remark that I am not a commercial man but a detective, and have spent my life in hunting down criminals.'

'Oh, you are a detective. Well, look here, Mr. Donovan, just you take and get this ring back for me, and I'll give you a tenner.'

'I must decline your offer of reward,' I said. 'I am paid for doing my duty, and my best efforts will be directed towards recovering your property.'

'Well, a tenner is not to be sneezed at,' he observed. 'Anyway, you've got yourself to please. I want my ring back, and if you get it I shan't forget you. I've got plenty of money, and can be liberal with it, but, darn it, I don't like to be robbed of a halfpenny.'

'Quite so. Most men take the same view.'

'You see,' he went on, 'it's not so much the value of the ring I care about. But it was given to me by our employés.'

'That apart, two hundred pounds' worth of property is a serious loss, and cannot be viewed with indifference,' I said. 'But now coming to business, Mr. Featherstone, what are your reasons for suspecting the chambermaid?'

'I've already told you she is the only one who has had anything to do with my room. She was admiring the ring yesterday, and when I spoke to her about it this morning she went as red as a turkey cock.'

'But that is hardly proof of guilt.'

'Look here, sir,' he cried irascibly, 'I'm open to bet a thousand pounds that girl is the thief. Anyway I charge her with the theft, and am going to give her in charge. I'll take all the responsibility.'

'Very well,' I replied, with a shrug of the shoulders. 'But I had better go with you to the hotel.'

In a few minutes we were on our way there, and *en route* I ventured to ask my gentleman if he had been anywhere the night previous.

'Yes; I dined with some friends,' he answered.

Fixing my eyes on his rubicund countenance, I ventured to suggest the possibility of his having dined not wisely, but too well. Whereat he blustered up again, and vowed that all he had taken had been a few glasses of champagne, a little hock, some dry sherry, and a couple of whisky toddies after dinner.

'Well,' I remarked sententiously, 'after all, things are judged relatively, and what is a mere toothful to one man might send half-a-dozen others into the gutter.'

'God bless my life!' he exclaimed, 'I'm one of the most temperate of men.'

'Yes, so it seems—judged by some standards,' I answered, but my point was lost upon him.

On arriving at the hotel I found that Mr. Featherstone was very well known there, having used the hotel for some years. The landlord was greatly troubled about the loss of the ring, for Mr. Featherstone was an exceedingly good customer; and, though an excitable and fussy man, he was not at all a bad fellow.

This information, of course, was given to me privately, and I ventured to ask the landlord if there was any reason to doubt that his customer had really been the possessor of so valuable a piece of jewellery.

'Doubt, not a bit of it,' replied the landlord a little hotly. 'I know the ring well, and he's a fellow with any amount of money, and fond of jewellery.'

'Just so. Tell now about this girl he suspects.'

'That's Mary Matthews,' and the landlord scratched his head, and there was a puzzled expression in his face. 'I don't know what to think,' he added musingly.

'Do you suspect her?'

'I won't express any opinion,' he said decisively.

'Has she been with you long?'

'No, not very long, and she's under notice to leave.'

'Why?'

'Because she's too good-looking.'

'Umph! I understand.'

'Well, you see she is rather a silly-headed kind of lass, and you know you can't keep gentlemen in a house like this from talking to a pretty lass, and Mary Matthews is just one of the kind that are always giggling and carrying on, and I won't put up with it.'

'Ah, poor lass,' I remarked, sympathetically. 'And now will you be good enough to send for her?'

Mary was duly sent for, and in the meantime Mr Featherstone had gone up to his room to have another look round. But with no result. He could not find his ring.

When Mary came into the room she looked frightened and nervous. She was about twenty-two years of age and remarkably pretty, and the sympathy I had felt for her before seeing her was increased now as she stood before me, for I knew that such a pretty girl in her station of life would need a good deal of mental balance to enable her to resist the many temptations that would come in her way.

'Good day, Mary,' I said gently in order to set her at her ease, as well as from a habit I had cultivated of always treating women, no matter how degraded, with a certain deference. For I liked to think that chivalry was not quite dead, and that some small vestige of it was to be found in my composition. This is by the way, however, and I hope the reader will pardon the digression. 'You are aware, Mary,' I continued, 'that there has been a diamond ring lost in the house.'

'Yes, sir,' she answered, as she burst into tears, 'and Mr. Featherstone accuses me of stealing it. But I am as innocent as the baby unborn.'

'I think it was your duty to attend to his bedroom?'

'Yes.'

'Have you seen the ring?'

'Yes. He showed it to me, and asked me if I would like to have a ring like it. He said it was worth two hundred pounds, and I said if I had so much as that I should think I had a fortune.'

Although I should not have said so then, for I was always careful not to express an opinion to an accused person at such a time, I may state now that, after this brief conversation with Mary, I felt perfectly convinced of her innocence. Her manner was unmistakably that of an innocent person.

At this stage Mr. Featherstone burst into the room, and seeing Mary standing there like Niobe, all tears, he exclaimed—

'Well, young woman, what have you got to say for yourself now? Come, you had better make a clean breast of it.'

'Oh, you villain,' she sobbed out with passionate energy. 'How dare you say that I have got your ring?'

'I dare say it, because I know you took it.'

'Excuse me,' I interposed, 'but you had better leave this matter in my hands.'

'Well, look here, Donovan,' he said with vulgar familiarity, 'just ask her if she did not say she would like to have the ring.'

Mary spoke up for herself before I could reply, and she exclaimed with fiery indignation—

'He was talking a lot of nonsense to me yesterday, and asking me if I would like to be his wife, and two or three times he struggled with me, and tried to kiss me, but I would not let him.'

'I just larked a bit with you; that was all,' put in Mr. Featherstone somewhat sheepishly.

'When he came in last night,' Mary went on, 'he was muddled with drink, and when I went to his room to light his gas he tried to kiss me again, but I just fought him, and wouldn't let him.'

'When did he complain of losing his ring?' I asked.

'This forenoon, after he came up from breakfast, he had left some rings and other things on the table, and I was in the room making the bed when he came in. He couldn't find his diamond ring, and he turned round and said—"Look here, where's that diamond ring?" '

' "What do I know about your ring?" I answered.'

'When I told you you had taken the ring didn't you go red in the face?' asked Mr. Featherstone in. his excitable way.

'I daresay I did,' she answered indignantly. 'And so would you if anyone suddenly accused you of stealing.'

'Well, my lass,' he remarked with objectionable self-assurance, 'you can't get over me whatever you may do with Donovan here. You've taken that ring, I'll bet a thousand on it.'

'Oh, you beast,' she hissed, as her indignation got the better of her.

'Hush,' I said. 'You had better not use harsh names.' Then, turning to Mr. Featherstone, I asked—

'Do you still persist in your charge, sir?'

'Undoubtedly I do.'

'I would caution you that this is a serious matter, and if the girl is proved not to have stolen your ring you may get into trouble.'

'I know what I'm about,' he answered. 'You do your duty, that's all you've got to do.'

'Very well,' I replied. 'I know my duty, and will do it. But I understand you to say that you are willing to bet a thousand pounds on the girl's guilt?'

'Yes, I am.'

'Suppose she turns out to be innocent, would you give her the thousand pounds?'

'Yes, I'm hanged if I wouldn't,' he answered with, as I thought, a good deal of bounce.

I turned to Mary, and, addressing her quietly, said—

'Well, Mary, my lass, you will have to go to the station with me.'

She burst into hysterical sobs at this announcement, and protested that she was an honourable and honest girl, and that it would break her father and mother's heart if they knew she had gone to prison.

I soothed her as well as I could, and promised that I would sift the matter to the very bottom; and I told her that if it was proved that she had not taken the ring I would see that she was well compensated for the wrong done to her.

Mr. Featherstone sneered at this, and said I had no business to say such a thing. I remarked that I was master of my own speech, and if he was of opinion that I had exceeded my duty in any way he could report me at headquarters, With this parting shot I told Mary to put on her things and come with me, and that I would take her to the station in a cab, and nobody in the street would be any the wiser. The poor girl seemed very grateful, and though sobbing bitterly she did as I told her, and I drove her down to the Central, Mr. Featherstone following in another cab in order that he might prefer the charge.

The formalities having been gone through, the girl was told that if she could find any one who would be caution for her, or as they say in the south, give bail, she would be let out, but with brokenhearted sobs she replied that she knew nobody who could do that, and so she was locked up.

My interest in Mary Matthews had been thoroughly aroused, no less my disgust for the obtrusive and vulgar Featherstone, and I was resolved to leave no stone unturned to get at the truth. My first step was to ascertain something about her antecedents, and I found that her parents, though humble and poor, were highly respectable people, and when they heard of their daughter's disgrace they were overwhelmed with sorrow. I could find no one who had a single ill word to say against Mary, unless it was that she had been somewhat of a flirt. But I was not surprised at that. A pretty girl such as she was, and in her station of life, would be sure to have plenty of admirers, and it was only human nature—at any rate, woman's nature—to feel flattered at this homage to beauty, and she could hardly resist flirting, as it is called. But though Mary had been guilty of this weakness, I learned that there was a serious engagement between her and a young man named Horace Mollison, by trade a joiner. This young fellow bore a most excellent character as a steady, persevering fellow, and a good workman. He had been trying for a long time to get sufficient money to furnish a house, and then he was going to marry Mary.

When he was told that his sweetheart had been arrested on a charge of theft he seemed terribly cut up, and much exercised in his mind as to whether to believe her guilty or not.

I next turned my attention to Mr. Featherstone. I ascertained that he bore the character of being an impulsive man, and a strictly honourable one. He was a married man, with a family of four children, and was exceedingly well off. He was a worshipper of the flesh pots of Egypt, and ministered in every way to his carnal pleasures. He was a free liver and fond of dining well; and though sometimes he got merry, as the saying is, he was considered on the whole a sober man, and never took anything during business hours.

On the night that he lost his ring he had dined with some friends, and I was careful to inquire of them if they had noticed his diamond ring on his finger, and they were positive that they had. I then traced his movements after he had left his friends, which he did about eleven o'clock, and I found that he went straight to his hotel and had a glass of toddy with the landlord in the latter's private room.

'Had he his ring on his finger then?' I asked the landlord.

'I cannot express a positive opinion, but I am almost sure he had. I had seen the ring so often that of course it did not attract my attention as otherwise it might have done. Particularly as he had other rings on his fingers.'

This narrowed the inquiry down to a small margin, because, if the landlord's supposition was right, Mr. Featherstone must have lost the ring in the house. He himself was perfectly positive he had the ring when he came in. He would not even qualify this by saying it was within the bounds of possibility that he might not have had it. He was *positive* that he had.

'Now, tell me, Mr. Featherstone,' I asked, 'do you go to bed with your rings on your fingers?'

'No. I always take them off, because my hands swell a little at nighttime.'

'The hands of stout people generally do,' I said. 'But as you are so positive about having the ring on when you came in, perhaps you can as positively state that you remember taking it off?'

'I be hanged if I can,' he exclaimed frankly, which impressed me more in his favour, 'but I think I took all my rings off and put them on the dressing-table.'

'Did you notice them in the morning when you got up?'

'No. I went downstairs to the breakfast-room leaving my things on the table.'

'You were absent-minded, perhaps?'

'Yes, a little.'

'Ah! You had dined well the night previously,' I remarked ironically.

'Oh, well, if you like to put it that way,' he answered snappishly. 'I daresay it had something to do with it.'

'Then it was when you came up from the breakfast room that you missed your ring?'

'It was.'

'Did the ring fit tightly on your finger?'

'No; not very.'

'Would it slip off easily?'

'Well, no; not unless my hands were soapy?'

'Just so; do you wash your hands with your rings on?'

'Not as a rule.'

'Perhaps you do when you've dined well?' I suggested.

'Look here, what the deuce are you driving at?' he asked gruffly.

'I want to find out whether you washed your hands last night with your rings on?'

I saw that this question caused a changed expression in his face, as though a new idea had struck him, and an idea too that caused him some trouble.

'Now that you mention it,' he answered, 'I believe that I did.'

'Where?'

'In the lavatory.'

'Then it will be my duty to have the drains of the lavatory searched,' I observed.

'By all means,' he said; 'but I think you will have your trouble for nothing.'

The lavatory, which was only a small place, was fitted with the tilting basins—then a comparatively new invention. There were only two of these basins in the room, and I lost no time in obtaining the services of a plumber. I need scarcely tell the readers that drains of this kind are trapped by a syphon, or more properly speaking a bend like the letter U in the pipe. Anything heavy, like a ring for instance, would be apt to stick in this bend, and my hope was that if Mr. Featherstone had lost his ring when washing his hands it would be found. The first pipe we opened to search was fruitless, but in the second my hopes were realised, and the missing ring was found. I was overjoyed at this for Mary's sake, and I felt also it would teach Mr. Featherstone a much-needed lesson.

He was not in at the time the ring was found, as he had some business appointments to attend to, and I did not see him until the afternoon. He received the announcement in blank amazement, and bit his lips in vexatiousness of spirit at his own stupidity.

'For God's sake,' he cried, 'go and get the girl out of prison.'

'Oh, yes,' I answered, 'she'll come out of prison, but you know you bet a thousand pounds on her guilt, and although nobody took your bet you've morally lost it.'

I lost no time in securing Mary's release. She had then been locked up for three days. Mr. Featherstone came to me in great distress of mind; his bumptiousness had left him, and he was ready to eat humble pie.

'Look here,' he said, 'this matter must be hushed up. I wouldn't for the world it got to my people's ears. Now tell me what ought I to give the girl?'

'Nothing less than the thousand,' I answered, 'that you were ready to stake on her guilt.'

'By heaven, I'll do it,' he exclaimed, much to my surprise, and he kept his word.

He made me her trustee, and placed a thousand pounds in a bank, empowering me to hand it to her when she was married.

Mr. Featherstone thus proved that, although in some respects a fool, he was at least an honourable man.

Two months later I had the satisfaction of attending Mary's wedding with Horace Mollison, and of handing her as a dowry a cheque for a thousand pounds. The young couple flourished and prospered, and the last I heard of them was that they were considered to be well off, for the husband was steady and saving.

The Mystery of a Tin Box

I happened one morning to be leaving the central station in Glasgow when I was accosted by a starved, wretched-looking, draggle-tailed little lassie, with a shawl over her head, who said in a voice rusty with want and exposure to all weathers—'Please, Mister Donovan, I want to speak to you.'

I was naturally surprised to hear myself addressed so familiarly apparently by a gutter waif, and I was struck also by her air of easy self-assurance, which was that rather of an experienced woman instead of a child. For though I could not see her face very well, her appearance generally was suggestive of a girl of about ten or twelve years of age.

'Who are you?' I asked, suddenly confronting her.

'I'm called Maggie M'Gee,' she answered.

'M'Gee, M'Gee,' I mused, wondering where I had heard the name, as it seemed familiar to me.

'How do you know me, Maggie?' I asked, trying to peer into her face. But the daylight had faded, and her face was screened by a shawl.

'I mind you when I was in Court when my grandad was being tried,' she answered.

'Oh, now I remember;' I exclaimed. 'Your grandad is known as Jamie the Miser. Eh?'

'Yes, sir. That's what folk ca' him.'

This man, whose name was James Dougal, but who was generally known as 'Jamie the Miser', was one of the most cunning old rascals in Glasgow. He was frequently being brought up for begging and obstruction, and when a small fine was imposed he used to whine about his absolute poverty, and vow by everything sacred he could think of that he 'hadna a saxpence to save his soul'. The result was, he was always locked up; for rumour had it that Jamie was a miser, and had a nice little hoard stored away somewhere. Socially he was one of those human pariahs who seem to be utterly beyond the reach of teaching, preaching, philanthropy, or example. They are born pariahs, live pariahs, and die as pariahs, and nothing will change their nature, no more than the rain will wash the spots off a leopard. That is, nothing has been able to change them up to the present. What that costly organisation, the School Board, may do in the future remains to be seen.

I had had occasion six months or so before this to become rather intimately acquainted with Jamie, as I had arrested him on suspicion of being concerned in a robbery. A baker's shop had been entered by thieves one Sunday morning, and a considerable sum of money stolen, including thirty-five £1 notes. For this robbery we arrested three men and a woman. The men were Old Jamie, a nephew of his, and the nephew's son. The woman was the nephew's wife, or at any rate passed as such, which is much the same thing with these sort of people. The nephew and son were convicted; the woman was discharged, for though there was not a shadow of a doubt that she had aided and abetted the male prisoner, no legal evidence could be got against her, and so she escaped by the skin of her teeth, as the saying is. This woman was known as Sarah Henderson, and she, her husband, the son, which was not her son, and the old man had all been living together in two rooms in a wynd off the Briggate. Jamie had got off for the same reason as she had—that is, there was no evidence forthcoming against him. We could not prove that he knew of the robbery. Had his own statements been worth anything he must have been one of the greatest martyrs who ever suffered persecution at the hands of the barbarous laws of civilisation, which will not allow poor thieves and murderers to do as they like, notwithstanding they live in a free country.

With groans, sighs, lamentations, and forcible appeals to the powers above, Jamie the Miser vowed his innocence, and declared that it

was a burning shame that such a poor, weak, harmless old man as he
was should be treated in such a harsh way. These protestations of innocence, of course, availed him nothing, but as the law cannot convict
without evidence sufficient to establish guilt, the cunning old rascal
went free. But the strangest part of the affair was this—the bank notes
were never discovered. It was intimated to the two younger male prisoners that if they would aid in restoring the money to the rightful owner,
who was a poor man, and in danger of becoming insolvent through his
loss, it might weigh in their favour when sentence was being passed.
The elder of the two gave up the greater part of the loose cash that had
been stolen, amounting to a few pounds, but he swore that he had lost
the notes. He said that he had the notes in his pocket soon after the
robbery, but he became insensible through drink, and when he recovered he found he had lost the notes, and he had not the remotest idea
what had become of them. Little incidents that came to light served to
corroborate this statement, and the question to determine was what
had become of the notes? As I have already intimated, the question
could not be answered; the money was not forthcoming, and the poor
baker had to grin and bear his loss, though part of it was made up to
him through the kindness of his neighbours.

Through this affair I had become acquainted with Maggie McGee,
who was in the Court at the time her relatives were being tried, and
I learned that she was the child of the old man's daughter, who had
died in the hospital some time previous owing to an accident.

Such, then, was my knowledge of the interesting family, of which a
representative in the person of this forlorn slattern now accosted me.

'Well, what do you want with me, Maggie?' I demanded.

'It isna me that's wantin' you. It's my grandad.'

'Oh, and what does your grandad want?'

'I dinna ken, He just telt me to see you and say you must come
to him at once.'

This was a rather peremptory order, but it immediately occurred to
me that the old villain, either from motives of revenge or remorse, wanted
to make a revelation about the robbery at the baker's.

'And where is your grandad?' I asked.

'He's lying in his bed. He is very ill, and canna get up.'

This strengthened my idea about the remorse, and so telling the girl I would go with her at once, we started off. I followed her to one of the noisome wynds off the Briggate, and then up a dark and greasy stair to an apartment that was unutterably filthy and ill smelling. Here in a room, the floor of which was black and slippery with the grime and dirt of ages, Jamie the Miser was lying on a wretched bed, and was covered up with a heap of rags that were the colour of the floor from dirt. There was no fire, although the weather was very cold, and no light. But Maggie struck a match as we entered, and lighted about an inch of candle that was stuck in an old blacking bottle. Jamie raised himself up on his elbow and groaned. His face was exactly like an ancient chimpanzee. It was withered, puckered, and dried up. The nose and chin almost met. He had small, restless, cunning eyes, with red eyelids, and no eyelashes. A short, thin fringe of yellowish grey hair fell over his retreating forehead, and added to the repulsiveness of his appearance.

'Who is that?' he cried. Then, as he recognised me, he whined, 'Oh, it's you, Mr. Donovan! The Lord bless you for coming.'

'And what's the matter with you, Jamie?' I asked, as I went to a small window, the glass of which was opaque with dirt, my intention being to open it, and let in some of the purer air from the outside. But the old wretch screamed out—'For the love of heaven, Mr. Donovan, don't open the winder. I've got the cold in all me jints now, and you'll kill me. It's the warmth I want, but the Lord pity me, I'm too poor even to get a wee bit fire.'

'Well, what is it you want with me?' I said. 'Be quick and tell me, and let me away out of this, or I shall be poisoned.'

'Gae awa doon the stair, Maggie,' the old fellow said to the girl, and she in obedience to the order left the room. Then he invited me to sit on the bed in the absence of a chair, but I preferred to give that dirt heap as wide a berth as possible, and I requested him to state his business quickly.

'Weel, Mr. Donovan,' he began, 'I ken you are the cleverest man in all Glasgow for finding oot thieves—'

'Well, look here, that's enough of that,' I exclaimed, cutting him short. 'What have you sent for me for?'

'Weel, I'm coming tae it,' he whined. 'I've been robbed, and I want you tae fin' oot the thief and get my property back.'

'Robbed,' I echoed, with a laugh. 'And pray what did you possess that was worth stealing?'

'Naething tae the likes o' you, sir, but muckle tae a puir auld fellow like me.'

'Come now, let me know what it is you've lost,' I said, beginning to have suspicions.

'Weel, sir, it's just a sma' tin box wi a wee bit padlock. I kept it here, doon under the bed-claes, and its gane, and the Lord kens it will be the death of me.'

'And what was in the box?' I asked growing more interested.

'Nothing o' muckle consequence to anybody save a piur man like mysel. There was just twa or three pounds I've been scraping taegither these dizen years or more tae keep me frae starving in me auld age, and an auld, auld watch that wouldna sell for sax shillings.'

'Anything else?' I asked, as I watched the workings of the ugly and cunning face, and noted that his bead-like eyes were fixed on me as if he was trying to read my thoughts.

'Yes, that was all, forby a few bit things that are no worth mentioning.'

'What are they?'

'They are no worth mentioning,' he repeated. Then, as if in supplication; he put his withered hands together and moaned out— 'Man, if ye can only get the box back before it's opened the Lord will bless you. Get it, man; get it, will ye, and I'll gie ye the twa or three pounds that's in it, though it's all I've got for my auld age.'

I was disgusted with the revolting old hypocrite, and began to suspect that the box contained something of much greater value than what he had enumerated. He was a cunning old wretch, but he had over-reached himself in his cunning this time. And I resolved to know his secret by hook or by crook. I pressed him to tell me what the 'few bit things' were that were not worth mentioning, but I could get nothing out of him. He whined, and whimpered, and groaned, and vowed that he would die of starvation if his box was not recovered with its contents untouched. He described the box to me as a tin one, something in the shape of a cash-box, with a lid on hinges, and fastened in front with a small brass padlock.

'Did the thief take the key?' I asked.

'Na, na, na,' he cried exultingly, and as though he thought no power on earth could open the box without the key; and undoing his ragged shirt in front, he produced a small key that was attached to a piece of string round his neck. 'Na, na, they didna get the key.'

'But you don't suppose that not having the key will prevent the thief from opening the box?' I remarked.

I saw his small wicked eyes open to their fullest extent as I said this, and the brown of his parchment-like face gave place to a certain ashen greyness, the result of fear. And in a sudden burst of excitement he almost sprang off the bed as he screamed out—'Man, I never thoucht of that. For the love of heaven get the box back, Mr. Donovan, get it back before the cursed thief opens it, or if you don't it will be the death of me.'

I told him that I did not think his death would be any great loss to the community at large, but nevertheless I would try and get his box back. I resolved to do this, not so much on his own account as on my own, for I was exceedingly anxious to know what the box contained. There was a mystery about it that I felt it to be my duty to solve.

'Now answer me,' I said. 'Do you suspect any one?'

'Yes.'

'Who? Yon lassie?'

'Na, na, she wouldna dae't. It's Sal Henderson, wife tae ma nephew, wha's daeing his time for robbing Wullie Thomson, the baker.'

'Oh, oh, so Sal's at the bottom of this, is she?'

The old man ground what few stumps he had remaining in his mouth, and hissed out the one word—

'Yes.'

'How do you know?' I queried.

'Because she's the only body wha's been in the room save the lassie, and she didna ken of the box.'

'Did Sal?'

'Yes.'

'And when was your box stolen?'

'It must have been taen since the morning, for I had it there at eight o'clock. Then I fell asleep, and it was after I woke that I found it gone.'

'And have you any idea where Sal is?'

'Na, but may be she's just drinking in some of the public hooses wi' a lad they ca' Wullie Bauchle.'

As there was no other information to be got from the old fellow, I prepared to go. Then he set up his whining again, and with various appeals once more to heaven, he swore that if he didn't get his box back he would die.

I didn't think that, under any circumstances, his days in the land would be many, for the lamp of life was flickering then. But he evidently did not imagine he was going to die, and even in that supreme hour the miser's greed was depicted in every lineament of his face.

Knowing what I did of Sal and her habits, I did not deem it probable that she would go far out of the neighbourhood. If she had stolen the box, and the circumstances pointed to her conclusively, she had done so because she must have had a pretty good idea that the old miser had a considerable sum hoarded up in it. And having possessed herself of that sum, her one aim would be to drink it away as fast as possible with a chosen few companions. I therefore looked in at most of the publichouses in the Briggate and the Saltmarket, and at last my search was rewarded by finding her in a helpless state of intoxication in company with the fellow known as Willie Bauchle, who was as helpless as she was. They were both sleeping in one of the small rooms in a notorious public house in the centre of the Saltmarket.

'How long has she been here?' I asked of the landlord.

'Well, she was in two or three times in the forenoon; then she went away, and I didn't see her again till about an hour ago, when she came back the waur of drink, as you see. She went in there with her lad, and I couldna get them away.'

I need scarcely say I did not believe this, for I knew the fellow to be a great rascal.

'Has she spent any money here?' I asked.

'She changed a pound note in the forenoon, and she and Willie had two half ones.'

This changing of a pound note, assuming it was true, and there was no reason to doubt it, meant that Sal was in funds, and I felt sure the money had come out of the old man's box.

'Now,' I said sternly to the landlord, 'get two or three of your men, and put that man and woman on the street.'

He seemed disappointed and annoyed that I was thus depriving him of what he considered, no doubt, a profitable customer. But he had no alternative but to comply with my command, and so in a few minutes Sal and Willie were lugged out of the box and deposited on the pavement in the street. Then I summoned two constables, and ordered them to convey the precious pair to the station as drunks and incapables. I followed, and had them searched. Willie's worldly possessions consisted of a shilling, an old iron tobacco box, and a very dirty pipe. In Sal's pocket there was nothing worth speaking of, but in an artfully-contrived pouch in her stays ten one pound notes were found concealed. This was an important discovery, and I no longer had any doubt that in the old man's tin box there must have been a considerable sum. That Sal was the thief did not admit, in my mind, of any questioning.

About nine o'clock the following morning I went round to the station, and visited Willie first of all. He was a small-brained rascal, without two ideas in his head. He seemed to be suffering much from his spree. He told me that he had met Sal the previous morning, that she had invited him to take a dram, and she changed a pound note to pay for it. She gave him a shilling, and then they had other drams, going from place to place until he lost his senses, and remembered nothing more. As I had every reason to believe this story, he was turned out with a caution. Then I went to see my lady Sal. She still seemed a little dazed from the effects of her debauch, and when she saw me she was evidently struck with fear, for she guessed something had gone wrong.

'Well, Sal, how do you find yourself this morning?'

'I have a sore heid, and the sight of you doesna mak' me any better,' she growled, as she nursed her head in her hands. Then fiercely she exclaimed—'Who brought me here?'

'I had you brought here, Sal, my dear,' I answered with a smile.

'Then may the deil twist you, and you can let me awa' again as soon as you like.'

'No, Sal, I'm not going to let you away until I find out what you've done with Jamie the Miser's box.'

'Me!' she roared, springing to her feet. 'Me! What dae I ken aboot his box?'

'You stole it, Sal,' I replied calmly.

'You lie,' she hissed, 'I'll defy ye tae prove it.'

'Oh, I think I shall be able to prove it. But tell me now, where did you get the pound note you changed yesterday?'

'I didna steal it any way. I've had money of my ain saved up syne lang syne.'

'Ah, just so,' I remarked sententiously. 'You are a likely sort of young woman, you are, to have money saved up. I suppose you had also saved the ten pounds we took from your stays?'

Her face blanched at this, and she seemed staggered for a moment; but, quickly recovering herself, she said with a giggle—

'Of course I did. I had twelve pounds saved, and I spent twa of them.'

I was for the moment checkmated by the creature's audacity, and I saw that it would be difficult, if not impossible, to get evidence against her. Besides, I had my own reasons now for wanting to know more about the tin box, and so I quickly worked out a little scheme in my mind, and said to her—

'Well, you'll be allowed to go, but you'll not get the ten pounds in the meantime until you've given proof that the money is legally yours.'

She flirted her fingers in my face as she made answer—

'Man, Donovan, you can keep the ten pounds if you like, and much good may it dae you.'

This indifference to the money strengthened my opinion that she knew where to put her hand upon more, namely, in the tin box, and my scheme was to find out where the box was. In the course of half-an-hour she was set free, and as she hadn't a bawbee upon her I was sure that her first move would be to get some money in order to slake her thirst. As soon as she was clear of the station, therefore, I followed her.

Like a rat that unexpectedly escapes from a trap, and makes direct for its hole, so she went direct, and at a rapid rate, to the wynd where Old Jamie lived. But she did not go up the stairs to his lodging. Giving a hasty glance round, she suddenly disappeared in an ashpit at the bottom of the wynd. I hurried up in time to see her take from a hole in the wall the tin box which Jamie had described to me. In a moment I sprang upon her and seized her with the box in her hand. She fought and struggled with me like a wild cat, but I managed to handcuff her and drag her out of the filthy place, and blowing my whistle, I soon had the assistance of some constables. None too soon, for some of the human tigers of the wynd had gathered up, and there is no doubt they would have attempted to rescue her, and perhaps have knocked me on the head. As it was, they were cowed, and we conveyed the sweet Sal to the station, where the contents of the box were examined, and were found to consist of forty-one pound notes, two five pound notes, two or three gold bracelets, a gold watch, a gold pencil case, and a very handsome brooch.

This, then, was old Jamie's hoard, and I had not a doubt that the most of it was stolen property; doubly stolen, in fact, for Sal had stolen it from him.

A little later I went round with two assistants to see the old rascal. It was evident he was very near his end, and Maggie, who was attending him, said that he had been delirious. However, he was not so at that moment, but sprang up with great eagerness as soon as I entered, and cried out in a sort of raspy whisper—

'Weel, weel, have you found the box?'

'Yes,' I answered.

He gave vent to a prolonged chuckle of delight, and fell back on the pillow with his hands clasped.

'Yes. I've got the box, Jamie, and know what's in it'—he groaned here—'and unless you can account satisfactorily for its contents, not only will it not be restored to you, but I'll have you taken off to the station.'

He groaned again and again, and rolled about as if in agony. Then, presently, he held forth his trembling, scraggy hands pleadingly towards me and faltered—

'I'll tell you, I'll tell you, but dinna tak me awa. Some of the money is what was stolen from the baker. I took it awa frae my nephew when he was drunk, because I kent he would waste it all in a day or twa.'

This was a revelation, but it was what I had suspected.

'Very well; now as to the jewellery,' I said.

'I bought it, I bought it, I bought it,' he muttered three times. Then he seemed to sink into a dazed, half-comatosed state, and appeared so exhausted that I deemed it advisable to let him alone and go for the police doctor. That gentleman was not able to attend for two hours, and when he did go he found that the wretched old man was a corpse.

I was enabled to get Sal convicted of dealing with stolen property, knowing it to be stolen, and I had the satisfaction of being instrumental in restoring the thirty pounds to the poor baker.

We could get no clue to the ownership of the other things, and so they went to swell the long list of unclaimed property in charge of the police authorities.

Appendix

The tales are presented in the order in which they originally saw light in the *Dundee Weekly News* (*DWN*), not in the collections. Below is the order of publication in periodical form with dates, and their chapter order in *The Man-Hunter*, 1888 (*MH*), *Caught At Last!*, 1889 (*CAL*) and *Tracked & Taken*, 1890 (*T&T*).

The Saltmarket Murder Case: *DWN* Jan 28 & Feb 4 1888 (*MH*1)

The Lady in the Sealskin Cloak: *DWN* Feb 11 & 18 1888 (*MH*2)

The Tuft of Red Hair: *DWN* Feb 25 & Mar 3 1888 (*MH*4)

The Pearl Necklace: *DWN* Mar 10 & 17 1888 (*MH*5)

A River Mystery: *DWN* Apr 7 & 14 1888 (*MH*9)

The Skeleton in the Cupboard: *DWN* Apr 28 1888 (*MH*11)

The Gentleman Smasher, A Strange Story: *DWN* May 5 1888 (*MH*7)

How I Snared the Coiners: *DWN* May 12 1888 (*MH*12)

The Record of a Strange Adventure: *DWN* May 19 1888 (*MH*13)

The Robbery of the London Mail: *DWN* May 26 &Jun 2 1888 (*CAL*7)

All for Love's Sake: *DWN* Jun 23 1888 (*CAL*11)

The Haunted House: *DWN* Jul 7 1888 (*CAL*4)

A Wolf in Sheep's Clothing: *DWN* Jul 14 1888 (*CAL*10)

The Pearl Button: *DWN* Aug 4 1888 (*MH*5)

The Mysterious Disappearance of Helen Atkinson: *DWN* Sep 8 & 15 1888 (*MH*10)

A Terrible Deed: *DWN* (*T&T*2)

The Story of a Diamond Ring: *DWN* (*T&T*5)

The Mystery of a Tin Box: *DWN* (*T&T*7)